"What could another woman give me that you cannot?" Lancelot whispered. It was more like a groan.

She sat back on her heels, looking down at him from under slitted lids. "Safety. She would bind your life around with the garlands of comfort and surety. She would keep your hearth and home and fill it with kindness. Your future would be known and beloved, a tale well told and filled with love and laughter. I foresaw this future for you in my gazing crystal, long before you went into the stone sleep. I had hoped you would have found her instead. Perhaps you still can."

"She sounds marvelous. A paragon. Undoubtedly a good wife and mother."

"Many long for a crumb of such happiness as she could give."

"Well," said Lancelot, "when we find her we should introduce her to Beaumains. She sounds like his type."

Nimueh let out an exasperated breath. "Why not you?"

"I have you."

ENCHANTED GUARDIAN

SHARON ASHWOOD

MILLS & BOON

First Published in Great Britain 2016
By Mills & Boon, an imprint of HarperCollins*Publishers*
1 London Bridge Street, London, SE1 9GF

© 2016 by Naomi Lester

ISBN: 978-0-263-92180-9

89-0816

Our policy is to use papers that are natural, renewable and recyclable products and made from wood grown in sustainable forests. The logging and manufacturing processes conform to the legal environmental regulations of the country of origin.

Printed and bound in Spain
by CPI, Barcelona

Sharon Ashwood is a novelist, desk jockey and enthusiast for the weird and spooky. She has an English literature degree but works as a finance geek. Interests include growing her to-be-read pile and playing with the toy graveyard on her desk. Sharon is the winner of the 2011 RITA® Award for Best Paranormal Romance. She lives in the Pacific Northwest and is owned by the Demon Lord of Kitty Badness.

For the Demon Lord of Kitty Badness, conqueror of fuzzy slippers and bane of the computer mouse. Long may your reign of terror continue.

Prologue

In case you're wondering, heroes and villains are real. So is magic, and so are monsters. They're not just children's tales or relics of a long-ago past.

Take Camelot, for example. It belongs to the present just as much as it did to once upon a time, and its story goes like this:

Long ago, King Arthur won a mighty battle against the demons, but what should have been victory quickly turned to Camelot's doom. Some say it was evil luck and others say it was the enchanter Merlin's arrogance for, in his desperation to defeat the enemy, Merlin tried magic no one had seen before. The result was disaster. The final spell of the war ripped out the souls of Camelot's fae allies and reduced them to emotionless shells.

The Queen of Faery swore vengeance against Merlin, the king and all the mortal realms. In defiance, the warriors of Camelot sacrificed everything they had, or loved, or ever hoped to be in order to keep us safe. Merlin cast an enchantment, turning the mighty Knights of the Round Table to stone statues upon their empty tombs. There they lie ageless and undying, ready to rise when humanity's hour of need is greatest.

Yes, heroes are real, and so are the villains. The pitiless Morgan LaFaye is ruler of the beautiful and deadly fae. Once allies, now they feed on mortal souls because they've lost their own.

Now the Queen of Faery is poised to invade. If she has her way, our world is about to end.

It's time for Camelot to rise.

Chapter 1

*R*un.

Her feet flew over the pavement, swift and all but silent. She ran like a deer, leaping over obstacles and dodging from path to lane, road to filthy alley. She ran like the wind because her death was behind her. She ran like prey.

Hide.

She found cover at last, though it was barely enough. There were two stairs down to a basement door, just enough of a dent in the narrow road for concealment. Crouching low, she made herself as small as she could. When that wasn't enough, she huddled on the ground, her knees and palms on the dirty concrete.

Words came out of the dark, soft and cruel. "Where are you? I want to see your beautiful face."

She held her breath, clamping both hands over her mouth to keep from gasping. Her lungs burned with exhaustion, crying out for a soothing gulp of air she dared not take.

"Nimueh, where are you? Nim—oo—ay." Her pursuer's voice lilted upward in mockery. "Oh, resplendent Lady of the Lake, hear my call. The queen wants a word."

A word? Queen Morgan LaFaye wanted her dead. At least she'd paid Nimueh the compliment of sending one of her private assassins instead of any old thug. Nim squeezed her eyes shut. There was no traffic after midnight in the commercial district and no one she could run to for help. Not that the fae ran for help from humans.

"You took the enemy's side," he added. "Nobody liked the prince, but he was her son. You participated in the murder of the heir to the throne of Faery."

As if Nim needed an explanation for the Queen of Faery's wrath. Before this, she'd been one of LaFaye's advisors, and she knew defying Morgan LaFaye was seriously stupid. But dread of Prince Mordred had overtaken Nim's fear of his mother. After a tour of the prince's dungeon, she'd decided *someone* had to put an end to the maniac. Better that than end up one of his broken toys.

"Come, my lady. Let's finish this." A note of boredom crept into the assassin's voice even as he spun his long knife in the air, making the fine steel sing. "Your magic won't help you now. Weave a spell and I'll scent it like blood in the water."

If that was true, he had one of the queen's tracking amulets. No doubt that's how he'd found her tonight, though for months she'd barely used her powers in her effort to hide among the humans. To complicate things still more, the amulet protected the wearer from magical attack, so Nim couldn't blast her way to freedom.

She silently cursed. The assassin had her. Fae were immune to age and disease, but a blade to the heart could still end her life. For all her natural advantages, right now she was as vulnerable as a human.

Think.

Without lifting her head, Nim scanned her surroundings, counting on her dark clothes and a knit cap to blend into the night. Like much of the neighborhood, the brewery where she hid was a derelict nest of trash and cobwebs, half the windows boarded up and the other half gaping mouths with teeth of jagged glass. Something crawled over her hand and she flicked it off before she could stop herself. Nim silently cursed, afraid her pursuer's sharp eyes would detect the sudden movement.

The next few seconds were an agony of suspense as she waited to feel that blade kiss her spine, but instead, his unhurried footfalls echoed in the empty street. The skin between her shoulder blades twitched. Then stopped. A hesitant scuff of shoes on pavement told her the assassin was looking around, his gaze slithering over the street to find her. She waited, silently willing her nerves under control.

Unexpectedly, he gave an impatient sigh and moved to the left, his footfalls leading away from her refuge. Luck? No. What little luck she'd known had slipped through her fingers long ago.

Nim counted out long minutes before emerging from her hole, silent as a shade gliding against shadow. She glanced around, finding a street number on the gate across the road. Ironically, she'd been on her way to this neighborhood when the enemy had picked up her trail. He'd all but chased her to her intended destination, a run-down warehouse three blocks away. If she could hide there, she would be reasonably safe until daylight filled the streets with humans again. The rules of lore and magic were clear about hiding the shadow world from mundane eyes. Not even the Queen of Faery's assassin would parade their world's existence before humans. At least, not yet.

Nim crept forward, calculating the safest route. If she kept close to the building, she could avoid the few pools of light from the windows above. She made it as far as the corner before the assassin sprang, knife flashing. Instinct saved her as she spun away and flung up an arm. Pain seared as fae-forged steel sliced her leather sleeve. Her breath whooshed out in shock, every nerve screaming. For an instant, she teetered on the edge of panic but, even with her magic sidelined, the Lady of the Lake fought for her life.

Nim used the momentum of her spin and slammed a booted heel into her attacker's shoulder. She was half his weight, but the force of the blow made him drop his weapon and stagger back a step. She scooped up the knife, driving the point into his hip until it ground against bone. The assassin's mouth stretched in a silent scream. Even now, the brutal training of LaFaye's private guards held fast. No one ever heard their cries.

Nim quit while she was ahead. She wrenched the blade free and fled, every step making her arm throb. The warehouse she wanted, a century-old hulk of brick, was straight ahead. She had to get in without telltale magic, but that worked to her advantage. Her opponent wouldn't expect a fae noblewoman to use plain, old-fashioned burglary skills.

When Nim reached the foot of the wall, she slid the knife through her belt and climbed. Her injured arm was almost useless, but she was a fae raised in the ancient woods of the Forest Sauvage and climbing was second nature. Nim used the knife to jimmy open the window, slipped inside and dropped lightly to the floor. Dust flew up in a choking cloud.

There was just enough light from the grimy upper windows for Nim to make out the shapes around her. Boxes and crates were stacked in haphazard rows and, according to her research, they housed part of a private art collection that was strewn across the country in hidden treasuries like this. The owner was dead, the heirs locked in a legal battle that had already lasted decades. No one was absolutely sure where all the loot was stored.

Nim had investigated quite a few warehouses before her hunt had led to Carlyle, Washington—right back to where her search had begun. Who'd have thought even a rich eccentric would stash priceless treasures in a town where the most notable industry was a medieval theme park? But then, if she'd thought about it, the collector had been born in Carlyle. An elementary mistake, forgetting humans were sentimental that way.

But the hunt was behind her. Now she just had to find the one item that mattered.

She walked slowly up and down the rows, her feet silent on the carpet of dust. She was still wound tight, all too aware the assassin was outside, but this place was better than any cloaking spell. Low-level magic hummed among the artifacts, covering any trace of her presence. The collection came from Babylon, the Egypt of the pharaohs, Greece, Rome and the cold Viking fjords. And there were pieces from medieval Britain.

She stopped before a large, steel-strapped crate and dusted off the label. It was torn, but there was enough text left to tell her she'd found what she was looking for. The crate was too tall to reach properly, so she dragged another box close to use as a step stool. She used the assassin's long knife to pry up the lid until she could force the fingers of her good hand into the crack. Fae strength did the rest. The top came off with a squeak of wood and nails. She set it aside gently, making as little noise as she could just in case someone—like her assassin—was within earshot.

It was a primitive packing job, nothing like the customized containers used to ship art from proper museums. There was a waterproof lining, but then loose packing material filled the empty spaces. The rats had been inside, chewing the fibrous fill to dust. She brushed it away in long sweeps of her bare hand.

Her fingers slowed, meeting the kiss of cold stone inside the crate. It was here, literally in her hands. For a human, the moment would have brought triumph, hope or even anger, but Nim was fae. All she could manage was a muted shadow of feeling, for her people felt no love, no desire, none of the wild passions that had made the immortal fae what they were. Their vital fire was in ashes—unless they turned to utter and complete monsters, willing to commit any atrocity to regain what they had lost.

Still, Nim had curiosity enough to quicken her movements, clearing the features she'd known so very well once upon a time. She leaned deeper into the crate, finding stone hands, a sword hilt that in life had been studded with rubies, and the curve of an arm. Bit by bit she uncovered a knight—her knight—frozen by Merlin into a stone effigy. Finally, she looked into the face of Lancelot du Lac.

"Oh!" Her soft exclamation hung in the dark space, strangely forceful against the dusty silence. She hadn't seen him since before the demon wars. Whatever she had expected, it hadn't been this sudden compression of time, where the heartbroken woman she had been collided with the ruin she was now. And all these centuries, Lancelot had remained unchanged.

His features had never been meant to be so still, so robbed of color. His hair had lingered between autumn brown and gold, changing with the seasons and the sun. A beautiful youth, he had matured into a sternly handsome man. The lean angles of his face were the same as she remembered, all aristocratic cheekbones and a long, straight nose. Lancelot was King Ban of Benoic's son, from a bloodline as old and noble as it had been impoverished. What they had lacked in coin they had made up for in pride. She could see it in the cut of his lips and the clean angle of his jaw. The one thing that had softened his expression were his deep-set eyes. The darkest brown, they had shone with every impulse he'd ever had. It took a measure of innocence to be as noble as Lancelot had been when she'd first met him. She wondered if any shred of that boy had been left when he'd finally been turned to stone upon his empty grave.

Despite herself, Nim traced Lancelot's face, relearning the contours with her fingertips. His lids, the planes of his cheeks, the dip beneath the bow of his lower lip. In repose, his cheeks were smooth, but there were creases when he smiled. Once, he had smiled often.

He'd been called Lancelot du Lac for her sake, for she was the Lady of the Lake. He had been her protégé, her lover and her champion before ambition had drawn him to Arthur's side—and before the young queen, Guinevere, had stolen away his love. Before he betrayed... Nim's breath hitched, snagged by memory, but the strange sensation didn't last. It was only the echo of remembered jealousy—once fierce as a ravening tiger, now cold as grave dirt.

And yet bitterness had a way of leaving its taste behind even now. How ironic that the man she'd loved so fiercely was before her and utterly at her mercy. Guinevere was long dead. Nim was at long last fully in control. She could shape their future together, remake everything exactly as she'd wanted—if only she wasn't cold inside.

If only he hadn't stopped smiling long before he'd been turned to stone.

Nim leaned down, balancing carefully so that only her lips brushed his. She exhaled, her warm breath bouncing back almost as if he'd sighed against her. But she was not fooled. The shape of his mouth was right, but there was none of the yielding pleasure of its soft touch. There was no demand, no promise. Nothing. He was as cold and stiff as a fae.

Nim frowned. Like all her kind, she knew exactly what she'd lost. Without souls to leash their powerful natures, the fae could easily turn into nightmares. Of course, the queen was counting on that very quality to conquer the mortal realms. She'd honed the fae's loss into a weapon.

A few at a time, Nim's people had returned from their home in the magical realm called the Hollow Hills. They infiltrated human cities in positions of influence where their grace and charisma—and lack of compassion—could do the most damage. When the queen was finally ready, the takeover of the mortal realms would be unstoppable. Brutal. Absolute.

Nim was no warrior, but she could not watch her people transform into monsters for LaFaye's pleasure. Nim still remembered who they'd been before confusion, fear and addiction had made them slaves to the queen.

Blood dripped from her wound onto Lancelot's cheek. She wiped it away, suddenly conscious the stone effigy was in truth a living man. Without taking her eyes from Lancelot's face, she fished in her coat pocket for her phone, scrolled through her contacts and selected a number.

Morgan LaFaye's only real foe was her kinsman, Arthur Pendragon, who had become the king. The family tree was complicated, human, witch and fae families intermarrying until few could make sense of the bloodlines. LaFaye had always believed Arthur had stolen the crown of Camelot, but had never been able to seize it for herself—especially not after Nim had given Arthur the sword Excalibur, the one weapon that could kill the fae queen. If Nim wanted to fight LaFaye, her best bet was to help Camelot.

That was why she was here in this warehouse. The one hundred and fifty tombs housing the Knights of the Round Table had been scattered. So far only a handful of knights had been awakened from the stone sleep—but now she'd located one more.

Lancelot had always been Arthur's champion, and that was, Nim told herself, the reason she'd worked so hard to find him. It had to be more than the need to see his face one more time, and to know that her heart was truly dead. Being a fae didn't guarantee a fairy-tale ending.

But now she was done, and it was time to seek help to disappear so completely that not even LaFaye's assassins could find her.

The phone rang twice before someone picked up.

"Medievaland Theme Park," said a deep male voice. "Come for the fantasy, stay for the feast."

Nim cleared her throat, her gaze inexorably returning to Lancelot's face. With the merest whisper of magic, she disguised her voice and caller ID. "I have an anonymous tip for your king."

Chapter 2

"Ugh," said Gawain in disgust. "You're barely two months out of your stone pajamas and you think you know how the modern world works."

"They hadn't invented pajamas when Merlin turned us," replied Lancelot du Lac to his fellow knight, "and all I'm saying is that I find it hard to believe we are breaking the law by patrolling the streets for murderous fae."

"The human authorities are particular about executions. They like to do it all themselves."

Dulac—he was Dulac among the men, never Lancelot—shook his head. He'd awakened to a drastically reduced Camelot in a new and strange world. "Then what are we supposed to do? Pat the fae on the head and tell him to run along back to his homicidal queen?"

They were walking the night-dark streets of Carlyle. According to Gawain, it was unusually warm for this part of the world, and Dulac took his word for it. The heat had developed a second life as the sun sank like an exhausted balloon, leaving skin sticky and tempers short. The taverns promised iced drinks and easy laughter, but that would come later. Dulac and Gawain had work to do.

"We do all our work in secret. The rules of lore and magic are…well, let's just say people think everything we stand for belongs in books for wee kiddies." Gawain's Scottish accent deepened to a burr. "It's demoralizing. Explaining that enchanted knights are waking up because Queen Morgan has mobilized revenge-happy faeries to attack and destroy the mortal realms—well, my lad, that's a speedy trip to the madhouse."

"I'd already be there if it wasn't for you and Arthur," Dulac said honestly. "I don't know how you managed when you were the first to wake up."

"It got better once I found Tamsin," Gawain said, referring to the witch who was his lover—the same witch who had revived Dulac from the stone sleep. "Before her, I only had the spell to fall back on."

Merlin's spell had provided a wealth of basic information, bridging centuries of change in language and a thousand mundane details, such as how to work an elevator or what a stoplight was for. There were still gaps, but Dulac was quickly figuring them out.

It was the larger changes that bothered him. "Nothing here is friendly. There are barely any armorers. Very few horse markets. I'm not certain this time requires a knight like me."

"Of course it does," Gawain said gruffly. "And you have to admit there are advantages to this day and age. I do like indoor plumbing."

"I'll give you that one," Dulac agreed. "And coffee."

Dulac had shed his sword and armor for smaller blades, a battered leather jacket and jeans. He stopped at a corner, waiting for a low black car to drive by before he crossed. The rumble of its engine called to something inside Dulac.

He'd owned powerful chargers, reveled in their speed and power. These vehicles were the warhorses of the modern age. He wanted one badly enough that his palms itched. It was hard to save the world when your only option was public transit. He stepped off the curb, swearing when a cyclist nearly clipped his toe.

"I'm going north from here. There's plenty of problems up around the White Hart," said Gawain once they were across. "South is yours to patrol."

Dulac nodded, paying close attention to what Gawain had to say. This was his first time out on his own since awakening, and he would take nothing for granted.

"Listen, there's been an increase in fae sightings in Carlyle and we don't know why," said Gawain. "Don't assume a lone fae is actually alone. Keep your fights out of sight of humans, and come back in one piece."

With that, they gripped one another's forearms in salute and parted.

Once Dulac went south, the road grew darker and his mood along with it. He'd seen little of the fae after the demon wars, but he'd got an education since awakening in Carlyle. There was no question that Camelot's one-time allies were now a fearsome enemy and, as Gawain had said, getting far too common on Carlyle's streets.

Hugging the shadows, he closed the distance between himself and a fae male walking ahead. Ordinarily, they were easy to spot. Most were tall and slender, with skin ranging from olive to the rich brown of ancient oak. Their eyes were brilliant green, their hair as pale as moonlight. All were inhumanly beautiful. This one, however, wore a sweatshirt with the hood drawn up and his body bent forward. Obviously, he didn't want to be recognized.

Dulac didn't need to ask why. The male was following a dark-haired woman who walked briskly through the puddles of streetlight, handbag swinging in time with her steps. There was an air of impatience about her as if she was late and rushing to an appointment. At that distance, Dulac couldn't see her well, but caught the impression of a willowy beauty. Moving swiftly, the fae kept back just enough to remain unnoticed, but moved imperceptibly closer with each block. He was hunting her just as Dulac was hunting him.

Abruptly, the woman turned and trotted up the steps of a community hall brimming with noise and lights. Dulac relaxed, slackening his steps now that she was safely inside—until the fae turned and followed her through the doors. She was more than a random victim; she was a target.

On full alert again, Dulac jogged to catch up. The signboard outside the hall announced the event was a wedding celebration. Was the woman a guest?

He took the stairs two at a time and shouldered his way inside. The doors were propped open to let in fresh air, although the breeze wasn't putting a dent in the sweltering atmosphere. The place was dim and echoing, the walls and floor plain wood. The ceiling, crisscrossed with crepe paper streamers, was open to the rafters. The milling press of bodies set Dulac's nerves on edge, confirming the reason he was there. Events like these—where people were crowded together, unguarded and a little drunk—were a predator's favorite hunting ground.

Dulac straightened his spine, feeling steadier now that he had a job to do. As long as there were villains, there *was* a purpose for knights like him.

He strode into the center of the room, searching the crowd. Blasts of amplified sound blared from the small stage where a band was setting up. Finding no sign of the fae, Dulac pushed through the crush at the back of the hall to discover a bar.

He was rewarded almost instantly when he saw the woman from the street perched on one of the stools. Her hair was dark and cropped at the shoulders, her bangs cut in a severe line across her brow. Her dark blue dress was crisp and businesslike, the only feminine touch a pair of extravagantly high heels that made her legs seem endless. But there was something that caught his eye besides her elegant figure. The way her long, slender limbs moved, or the curve of her spine, or the tilt of her head—something about her was extraordinary. Instantly, his body tensed in pleasure and warning.

The woman was fae. Then she turned her face in his direction, and he was looking at his Nimueh.

"It would take a soulless monster to hate a wedding like this," said the young human in a daring yellow dress. "Don't you think?"

The Lady of the Lake had barely sat down after hurrying through the streets to get there. She sipped her drink and manufactured a smile. "Have you taken a poll?"

The woman—barely more than a girl, really—leaned against the bar, her eyes shining in a way that went beyond the champagne. She was on a romance-induced high. "A poll?" She had to speak up to be heard above the happy crowd.

"Of soulless monsters. I'd be interested where they fell on the bell curve of wedding-haters."

The girl gave a surprised laugh. "Right beside the father who had to pay for it all."

She held out a hand and smiled, showing tiny white teeth. "I'm Susan, Antonia's cousin."

Nim saw it at once—the girl had the bride's red hair and milky skin. "Nim Whitelaw. Antonia's boss."

"Enjoy the party." Susan picked up her ginger ale and fluttered off toward the stage, a violin case in one hand. Obviously, she was one of the musicians.

Nim watched her go with faint interest. Speaking for soulless monsters everywhere, it was hard to hate weddings—or like them, either. Once upon a time, fae weddings had been swathed in starlight and garlands of living butterflies. The bride and groom would have slept in the woods on a bed made from the down of griffins to give their love the strength of lions. But that was all in a past that Nim was slowly forgetting.

"Top you up?" asked the bartender, holding the bottle above her glass. His look was filled with an invitation that had nothing to do with chardonnay.

"Thank you," Nim said to be polite, even though she'd barely had time to touch her wine.

"Don't you own that bookstore?" the bartender asked as he poured a generous measure. He was staring at Nim's neckline and would have missed the glass if she hadn't given it a magical nudge to the left. She'd gone nearly six weeks without using her powers, and the tiny push felt good.

"I do. Antonia is my employee." Nim had always been careful to honor those who served her well. By coming here, Nim kept at least that much of herself alive.

It was also one of the last things Nim would do in Carlyle. After months of searching—and hiding from any potential assassins—she'd finally located the contact who'd promised to help her disappear for good.

"Tony's my sister-in-law. She said you've been away on vacation."

"I just got back last night."

Bored with the man, Nim glanced toward the dance floor. The music hadn't started but Antonia, with a white lace veil over her curling red hair, was the magnetic center of the crowd, laughing and hugging everyone who came to greet her. The groom stood at her side, shaking hands and grinning as if he'd won the richest lottery in all the mortal realms.

Nim had never felt as alien as she did in that moment, witnessing that bond. She didn't belong at a wedding, with her empty, silent heart. She set down her glass and slid off the bar stool, suddenly sure she had to escape. All that happiness was just too much to witness.

It was then she saw him. She did a double take, sure it was a perverse trick of memory that summoned the face of Lancelot du Lac, that the wedding atmosphere had stirred the dying embers of old dreams. But then she realized Arthur must have acted on her information. Lancelot had risen from the stone sleep, and was before her in warm, living flesh.

Even for this modern age Lancelot was tall, his broad shoulders filling out a worn leather jacket as easily as they had a warrior's garb. Her first thought was to slip away but, with the uncanny intuition of an expert swordsman, he looked straight at her. As she watched, he went rigid, a flicker of shock widening his eyes. Clearly, he'd just recognized his old lover beneath the hair dye and contact lenses.

It had been one thing to see his statue, his features frozen in stone. Lancelot alive and breathing was completely another story. His dark, liquid gaze skewered Nim, looking deep into places she'd forgotten.

Shock took her, and Nim took a step toward him before she knew what she was doing. A sudden, irrational urge to throw her wine—or perhaps a fist—overtook her. She wasn't capable of anger, but she owed that vengeance to her younger self. He hadn't just broken her heart when he'd left her for Camelot. He'd pulped it. The ghost of those emotions ached like a limb lost in battle, reminding her how she'd wept in lonely grief.

He pushed away from the bar and prowled her way. The summer sun had bleached streaks into his dark gold hair, and he swept it from his eyes in a gesture she remembered well. But familiarity ended there. There was a hardness around his mouth she didn't remember. When his gaze held hers, assessing every line of her face, his expression was too guarded to read.

"Nimueh." He shook his head as if willing himself to wake from a dream. His deep voice brought the past rushing into the present. She remembered hearing that voice in the dark, when it had gone soft and lazy after the intimacies of love.

"Nimueh," he said again, this time with more strength. She hadn't heard that accent for centuries—it was French, but not the French she heard now. It was something older and rougher that went straight to her core. Once she had adored the way he said her name, caressing each syllable as if she was something good to eat. Then he'd set about proving it with his generous mouth on every inch of her flesh.

"Nimueh," he said one more time, as if her name was a prayer. Emotions chased across his face—shock, grief, happiness, guilt.

She held his gaze, willing his feelings to stop. She couldn't return any of them and she didn't want to answer his questions. "These are modern times. Just call me Nim. Nim Whitelaw, bookstore owner."

He tensed at her words as if the flat statement had surprised him. "That doesn't sound like you. It's too plain."

"That's the point." Instinctively, she looked around at the crowded room, wondering who might see them together. But no one seemed to take the slightest notice of their conversation.

He was looking her over. "You look almost human with brown eyes and dark hair. Why change your appearance?"

It was a good question, but it was none of his business. She leaned closer, lowering her voice in case fae ears could eavesdrop over the din. "Walk away. Leave. It would be far better if you never mentioned our meeting. Understand that, if you ever cared for me."

"What do you mean? Of course I cared for you. I still do."

"Oh." Words deserted Nim, making her feel like an awkward child. It was a most unpleasant sensation—her insides felt oddly fizzy, as if she'd swallowed an entire case of champagne. A dim memory said the sensation was panic or perhaps excitement. Such feelings couldn't be, but Lancelot had a way of making the impossible happen. After all, once upon a time she'd fallen in love with him—a penniless mortal with nothing more than good looks and a steady lance, pun completely intended.

She waited a moment, hoping she would think of something to say, but her mind remained blank. Or crowded. She couldn't decide which, but the sensation was overwhelming. The need to run and hide ballooned inside her, threatening to stop her lungs.

"Goodbye." She spun on her heel to leave.

Chapter 3

He caught her arm, pulling her up short. Nim scowled down at the long, strong fingers. Fine scars ran along his tanned knuckles, evidence of a life around blades. Heaviness filled her, a primitive reaction to the strong, aggressive male taking control of her in the most basic way. Once it might have grown into anger or lust, but now it confused her.

"Take your hand off me," she said, letting her voice fill with frost.

"No." He pulled her closer, turning her to face him. "You will answer my questions."

Nim jerked her arm free. They were so close, she could feel his warm breath against her skin. "About what?"

His nostrils flared as if scenting her. Still, Nim studied his tense jaw and the blood flushing his high cheekbones. The heat of his emotions made her feel utterly hollow. His hand closed around her wrist again, almost crushing her bones.

"There are too many people here," he growled.

"There are enough people here for safety. Perhaps I don't want to answer you."

His eyes held hers a moment, dark fire against the ice of her spirit. That seemed to decide him, for he pulled her close and took a better grip on her arm. "Come with me."

"Where?"

He didn't reply, but steered her toward the door, moving so fast she skittered on her heels. She thought about calling out—she knew people there, even if they weren't actual friends—but it went against her instincts for secrecy. When he pushed her down the stairs and back into the night, the velvet dark seemed to muffle the sounds around them. He paused at the bottom of the steps, seeming to consider where to go next.

She took the opportunity to pull against him, but this time he held her fast. "Don't."

The threat was real. Her fighting skills were nothing compared to a knight's. Lancelot could crush or even kill her with a single blow. Still, that didn't make her helpless, and she would not let him forget that fact. Rising up on her toes, she put her mouth a mere whisper from his ear. "You forget what I can do. My magic is nothing less than what it was when I was the first among the fae noblewomen. I can defend myself against your brute strength."

Just not against what he'd done to her heart. She closed her eyes a moment, feeling his breath against her cheek and remembering the past for a long moment before she denied herself that luxury. "Let me go," she repeated.

In response, he pulled her to the side of the building, refusing to stop until he was deep into the shadows. The ground was little more than cracked concrete there, tufts of grass straggling between the stones. He pushed her against the siding, her back pressed to the rough wood. "Not until I've had my say."

He had both of her arms now, prisoning Nim with the hard, muscled wall of his chest. Anyone walking by might glimpse two lovers in a private tête-à-tête, but Nim drew back as far as she could, something close to anger rising to strike. No one handled her this way, especially not him.

"Then talk," she said through gritted teeth.

"Aren't you even surprised to see me?" he demanded.

"Why should I be? Your friends are awakening, why not you?" She wouldn't tell him it was she who had traced his tomb and called his king. She needed to squash any personal connection between them. Even if she was whole and their people were not at war, he had betrayed her.

He put a hand against her cheek, his fingers rough. She jerked her chin away, burning where his touch had grazed her.

His expression was bitter. "You know why we wake."

The threat of her queen. She dropped her voice so low he had to bend to hear her. "I'm not your enemy. Not that way."

"Aren't you?" The skin around his eyes and mouth grew tight. "I was told you work for Morgan LaFaye now."

"I did," she confessed. "Not anymore. She does not have the interests of the fae at heart."

But he was relentless. "I'm told you were caught by Merlin's spell along with the rest. I know what the fae have become."

Soulless. As good as dead inside. Lancelot didn't say the words, but she heard them all the same. "It's true," she replied. "It's all true."

His expression was stricken as if hearing it from her lips was poison. Good, she thought. Better to be honest. Better that he believe her to be the monster she was.

"Maybe that's true for some. I don't believe that about you. You still have too much fire."

With that, he claimed her mouth in an angry kiss.

Nim caught her breath, stifling a cry of true surprise. The Lancelot she'd known had been gentle and eager to please. Nothing like this. And yet the clean taste of him was everything she remembered.

His mouth slanted, breaking past the barrier of her lips to plunder her mouth. The hunger in him was bruising, going far beyond the physical to pull at something deep in her belly. Desire, perhaps, or heartbreak. She wasn't sure any longer, but she couldn't stop herself from nipping at his lip, yearning to feel what she had lost. A sigh caught in her throat before she swallowed it down. Surely she was operating on reflex, the memory of kisses. Not desire she might feel now. The warmth and weight of him spoke to something older than true emotion. Even a reptile could feel comfort in the sun. Even she…

Still, that little encouragement was all the permission he needed to slide his hand up her hip to her waist and she could feel the pressure of his fingers. Lancelot was as strong as any fae male, strong enough certainly to over-power her. That had thrilled her once, a guilty admission she'd never dared to make. She'd been so wise, so schol-arly, so magical, but an earthy male had found the liquid center of heat buried under all that logic and light. They had always sparked like that, flint against steel.

But then his hand found her breast and every muscle in her stiffened. This was too much. Memory was one thing, but she wasn't the same now and she refused to have a physical encounter that was nothing more than a ghost of what it should be.

Nim pushed him away. "I don't want this."

Something in her look finally made him stop, but his eyes glittered with arousal. "Are you certain about that?"

Nim went very still and cold inside. Whether it was anger or the absence of it was irrelevant. It was all she could do not to touch her powers and simply *make* him leave. "Be careful, mortal."

He put a hand on her hip again as if staking a claim. "Morgan LaFaye tricked me from your side."

"And Queen Guinevere tripped you into her bed?" she asked drily. "Do you think me a child to feed me such tales?"

His eyes snapped with temper. "It's not what you imagined. I looked for you back then. I searched for months."

"And now?"

"I want you back." His grip tightened.

"I'm not who I was."

"You are. I felt your heart in your kiss. You haven't changed."

That wasn't true. This conversation had to end for both their sakes, so she aimed every word like an arrow. "This is who I am, Lancelot. Merlin's spell tore my people apart. The fae crave the souls of mortals to fill the void where our own used to be. We are the monsters Arthur's knights seek to destroy."

His lips parted as if to speak, but she pushed on.

"We won't stop hunting humans. We can still feel enough fear to survive the perils of the world, but nothing more. Feeding on souls makes us whole again, gives us back joy and sorrow, but the mortals die and the effect never lasts. Even so, it's easy to become addicted, needing more and more souls to cling to some semblance of who we used to be. That's how the queen buys our loyalty. If we invade the mortal realms there will be no end of humans to feed us. It will be our paradise."

She'd known herself too well to risk tasting such ambrosia, but she'd seen others fall prey to soul-thrall, living only to hunt. Once, they'd been honorable, valued friends. Now they were little more than beasts.

Lancelot looked as if he might be ill. "I know all that." He finally let her go.

"Then you know why you must forget me."

"But you're different." The words were firm, but somewhere in their depths she heard a plea for reassurance.

"Don't be naive." Nim turned and walked away.

This time he let her.

Barely able to breathe, Dulac watched the swing of her hips as she walked away. The sight of that very female motion, combined with the lingering taste of her lips, had him aching against his jeans. He ground the heels of his hands into his eyes, desperate to clear his thoughts from the fog of lust scattering his every last wit.

Dulac had sought her for so long. He'd searched before the demon wars and then after, when he'd discovered her castle had vanished from the Forest Sauvage. That had been a sure sign she'd left for the Hollow Hills, but he hadn't stopped even then.

Many of Camelot's knights had been wary of Merlin's sleeping spell, but Dulac had jumped at the opportunity to travel into the future. Nimueh was immortal. He was not. If Merlin's magic worked, the knights would rise healthy and in their fighting prime when the fae returned to the mortal realms. Then, after crossing centuries, he could take up his quest anew.

Of course there were risks—what if the spell had failed or Nimueh never came back? Still, the stone sleep was his best chance. Dulac had sacrificed all to come forward in time—his name, his lands, and his wealth. In the end, the gamble had been a success because now he'd found her.

Except Nimueh had just walked away. Walked. Away. Not a tear. Not a word of regret after he'd spent centuries as a piece of stone for her sake. Heat crept up his body, anger mixing with incredulity. His skin prickled as if he might burst into flame.

He watched her turn right and disappear into the night. She didn't go back to the celebration inside, which was as clear a message as any that she didn't want him following her for another round in the dance of emotional push and pull. Maybe she was as dead inside as she claimed.

But Dulac wasn't a boy or a new-fledged knight any longer, and he knew his lady. "I don't believe you," he said into the hot and sticky night.

This wasn't over. When it came to bed play, Nimueh was made of fire. Dulac had felt that same spark in her now, faint but no less real. His body remembered hers, every move of their familiar dance unlocking their treasured past in his heart and flesh as much as memory. Surely it worked the same way for her—it had to.

So why hide it from him? Had he so utterly destroyed her trust?

Of course he had.

A door inside him slammed shut, sealing off the pain beneath his anger. It had a poor seal, that door, and regret leaked around every edge of it. Dulac stalked back to the sidewalk in front of the hall, wishing he was still at the bar. He needed something to dull the roiling storm inside him—but he'd learned long ago there was no cure for the addiction named Nimueh.

Wedding guests lingered on the steps of the hall, vainly seeking fresh air. Just as Dulac put one foot on the stairs, the hooded fae hurried down and disappeared in the same direction Nimueh had just gone. Dulac narrowed his eyes, aware he'd allowed himself to be distracted from his original mission. Then again, now he knew it was Nimueh the hooded figure followed. Both his missions were the same. He waited a few seconds, then glided after them.

As if the fae sensed the knight's interest, he turned to

look over his shoulder. Dulac ducked into the shadows, swift enough to evade detection. But the fae had tricks of his own. By the time Dulac emerged from hiding, the fae had vanished.

Cursing, Dulac searched the street but both Nimueh and her tail were lost to sight. Nevertheless, Dulac pushed forward, going on instinct alone. Within a block, the condition of the neighborhood declined. Streetlights highlighted the faces of the buildings, picking out broken windows and peeling paint—and then the lights, too, were smashed. Fierce protectiveness rose in Dulac. What business would Nimueh have walking into a place like this? She should have been somewhere safe.

Scanning the street, and then a playground, Dulac looked around for his quarry one more time without success. Wind nudged litter down the gutters, the skittering noise loud in the darkness.

Dulac heard a cry and scuffle coming from a building site surrounded by a chain-link fence. Holding the knife in his teeth, he quickly scaled it and dropped lightly to the ground. It was darker here, walls of the neighboring buildings blocking most of the ambient light. He rose from a crouch, knife in hand and with every sense alert. Someone was panting hard.

The noise was coming from behind a half-built wall. Dulac approached silently, pausing every few feet to check for movement. He had hunted all manner of creatures in his time—demons, trolls and even a dragon—but modern weapons were just as deadly. He'd never had a bullet wound and had no desire for the experience.

When he slid around the corner of the wall, he immediately saw Nimueh huddled on the ground. Above her stood the male fae, his hood thrown back to reveal long white hair. The pale color was a stark contrast to his dark skin and bright green eyes. Dulac stiffened when he saw the fae had one hand on Nimueh's hair as if holding her in place. What chilled him most was the anticipation in the male's expression, as if he was going to enjoy killing her the way another would enjoy a gourmet meal.

"Hello, mortal," said the fae. "Have you come for the show?"

Chapter 4

Fury rose like an incoming tide. Even in the dark, Dulac could see Nimueh's features had gone sharp with fear. Somewhere along the line, she'd shed her high heels and her bare feet looked achingly vulnerable.

"Let her go," Dulac demanded.

"No," Nimueh cried, her voice cracking as she met his eyes. "Leave me. This is not your concern."

That just made him angrier. "You've always been my concern." He took a step forward.

"Don't!" she shot back, her eyes widening until he saw white all around the iris. "It's too dangerous. You don't understand any of this."

"Who is this man?" the fae asked in a bored tone.

Dulac took another step, calculating his odds.

Instead of answering, she attempted to writhe out of her captor's grip. Dulac closed the distance, but he wasn't fast enough. In the time it took to get halfway there, the fae's long fingers closed around Nimueh's throat.

Her attacker turned his head, the movement so grace-ful it was alien. The fae were elegant, long-boned and so slender they looked almost delicate. That was an illusion. They were tough as cockroaches.

"Use your magic!" Dulac demanded. She should have reduced her attacker to a grease spot.

She shook her head, struggling against her attacker's grip.

"She can't use her power," the fae said, sounding almost apologetic. "I bear the faery queen's amulet."

Dulac caught sight of a star-shaped medallion at the fae's throat. The last time he'd seen it, Morgan LaFaye her-self had worn it, the ruby gem brilliant against her creamy white throat. LaFaye never bothered with mere trinkets, so no doubt the gem had magical properties.

"Leave us, boy," said the fae. "I am on the queen's work."

He gathered up a fistful of Nimueh's dyed black hair and used it to give her a cruel shake. She gave a moan of pain. The sound was too much. Dulac sprang forward, every instinct honed to protect.

"Don't be a fool!" Nimueh cried, her voice half-strangled.

The fae raised a hand, releasing a thread of magic. Light twisted through the air, gone in a blink, but it hit Dulac squarely in the chest. A white-hot sunburst of pain dropped him to one knee. Every nerve blazed with elec-tricity, numb and raging by turns. Dulac tried to stand, but nothing would obey. Still, he got his feet under him, forcing his muscles to push through agony.

The creature's lips drew back. It was impossible to say what the expression meant—it wasn't laughter or fear or even contempt at Dulac's struggle. Nevertheless, he let go of Nimueh. She shot forward, diving under her attacker's arm.

"Go!" Dulac ordered. "Get out of here."

But the fae was too quick, grabbing Nimueh's ankle

to trip her. As she stumbled, the fae grabbed her arm and twisted it behind her in a brutal grip. She lurched to her knees with a shriek of pain. The fae dug his other hand in her hair once more, wrenching her head back to expose her throat. "Make another move, and I will punish her. She's already escaped me once, and I'm tired of hunting. I won't let her go again."

Dulac pulled himself to his hands and knees, every limb trembling with the shock of magic. He had a sudden memory of deep green silk bedding, Nimueh's long white hair spread across it, across his chest. He wanted that moment back so badly it hurt worse than anything the fae could conjure.

"What shall I do with you, mortal?" asked the fae.

In another being, the words might have been sarcasm, but the fae made it a problem of logic. Dulac studied him as he dragged one knee forward, setting off a fresh burst of pain along his limbs. If he could just get to his feet—the fae seemed to favor his right side, as if his hip had been hurt. That meant vulnerability. He could use it.

But the fae spotted his motion and flicked another spell his way. Dulac doubled over, too blinded by the hot fire in his core to even cry out—but his fingers clenched around the handle of the knife hidden beneath his coat.

Dulac lifted his head, ignoring the sweat drenching his body. Despite the sensation of claws tearing his flesh, he staggered to his feet. "You will leave her in peace."

The fae's expression hardened. "Don't presume to order me, human. I am something new in your world."

Dulac's vision swam, but he stood firm. "Where I'm from, the fae are old news." The words nearly choked him when an unbidden rush of memory constricted his chest. The first fae he'd met had been Nimueh. She had made everything new. "The Lady of the Lake is mine."

"You, a mere human, know the lady's true name?" A

blink of those cat-green eyes—as close to surprise as the creature could likely get. "So who are you?"

Dulac ignored the question, watching the enemy's every breath. It would be like their kind to toy with a mortal only to crush them when they tired of the game. Still, neither fae looked away from Dulac, as if he was the one factor that could tip the balance of fate.

"You must be one of Arthur's knights," the fae said slowly as he worked it out. "Are you the one called Lancelot? I heard the king has his champion wolf again."

Dulac frowned at the description. "And I heard your kind is skulking in the shadows. It seems our informants are correct."

"Not quite," returned the fae. "I do not skulk. Tramar Lightborn simply takes what he wants."

Dulac had heard the name before. Before Merlin's spell, Tramar had been a lord among the fae, famed for his wisdom and depth of learning. Was it possible this was the same man?

Tramar ran his fingers down Nimueh's face. It was a purely clinical touch, accompanied by a whispered spell. Nimueh trembled with what looked like genuine terror. A high, thin, keening sound escaped her lips along with a wisp of pale blue smoke. She began to shudder, the muscles in her neck corded with pain, the noise she made escalating to an agonized scream.

The sound tore through Dulac, but Tramar was deaf to it. His eyelids flickered, an ecstatic expression suffusing his features. When his gaze returned to Dulac's, there was mockery in them that had been lacking just moments ago. Real, savage emotion.

The emotion Nimueh should not have had to give.

"I didn't think she had any soul left to take," Tramar said with a slow smile.

Nimueh sagged in his grip, suddenly limp.

The sick feeling in Dulac's gut snowballed to rage. He jerked forward a step, the bone-crushing pain suddenly irrelevant—but it was still like forcing his way through solid brick. That single move had taken him within yards of the fae, but it wasn't enough. Dulac snarled, his voice dropping deep into his chest. "Step away."

"Oh, come, it's barely a sip and the queen will destroy her. Why waste it?"

That was too much. Dulac was human, with no magic, but he was Camelot's knight. With an act of will, Dulac shut down the pain in his body and sprang into the air. The fae's eyes widened in affront, but he was too surprised to respond in time. Dulac hauled him away from Nimueh, wrenching him off balance.

Nimueh fell to the ground, but the impact seemed to wake her. With no wasted movement, she covered her head with her arms and rolled away from the fight. Dulac wanted to check on her, but Tramar was on him again, forgetting his magic to deliver a cracking punch.

With a swipe of his foot, Dulac knocked Tramar to the dirt and gravel, planting a knee on his chest to keep him still. The attack was quick and brutal, leaving the fae no time to resist. Dulac's knife sliced through the chain of the amulet and kissed the soft flesh beneath Tramar's chin.

The amulet fell with a clatter and skidded into the shadows. Dulac paused for the barest sliver of a second. As far as he knew, fae did not age. There was no telling what wonders Tramar had seen in his long life, what knowledge would be lost with his death. But he'd learned in a few short weeks how badly Merlin's spell had destroyed the fae, and Tramar had tried to consume what was left of Nimueh's soul. That had earned him his death.

Tramar's eyes held Dulac's. There was understanding in those cat-green depths, and the fae gave the slightest of nods. Dulac saw bravery, but also relief. Perhaps the worst tragedy of the fae was that under the influence of a stolen soul, they knew just how far they'd fallen.

Dulac slashed the blade, quick and sure. The skin of Tramar's throat parted with a flare of red. Hot blood sheeted from the wound, slick against Dulac's fingers. The fae gasped once, and it was over.

The fae's body fell. Dulac remained where he was, breathing hard.

"Stand back." Nimueh's voice came from behind him.

He looked up to see her standing barefoot, her limbs smudged with dirt. Her eyes seemed too huge for her face, her cheekbones sharp against the frame of her coal-black hair. The buttons had torn from the tight skirt of her dress, giving him a flash of slender, olive-skinned thigh.

Though she shook with the aftershock of the fight, in every other way Nimueh seemed calm. She raised a hand, fingers spread, muttering words beneath her breath. The breathless summer night grew thick and close, almost as if an invisible fist were crushing them. Her hair fluttered around her face in a breeze that he couldn't feel. A faint blue glow gathered around her, sparking and twisting as if it were alive.

Dulac felt a faint pop in the air. A sudden wave of heat made him spring aside. Moments later, Tramar's body burst into white-hot flame, releasing an acrid cloud of smoke. They both stared at the fae's body for the few moments it took for it to turn to a smear of ash. He could hear her panting as if she'd run a race. "Are you hurt?" he asked.

"It doesn't matter," she replied.

He spun to face her and grabbed her shoulders so he could look her over, but he never made it past her face. Tears tracked down her cheeks. "You're in pain."

"It hurt," she said, her voice husky. "Losing my soul was agony the first time, like someone ripping my bones through my flesh. This time it was even worse. I knew what it would be like."

He pulled her close, needing to hold her even though she would surely push away. To his surprise, she simply rested her head against his chest, her faint exhalation almost a sigh.

They'd stood together this way once before, the morning he'd left her. She'd curled against him just like now, her hair the color of the palest dawn light and her eyes wet with a grief she'd refused to admit. *Go.* Her voice had been soft. *I cannot keep you to myself anymore.*

He'd never returned. Shame burned him like white-hot fire.

As if Nimueh shared that memory, she drew away, putting space between them. She shook herself slightly as if recovering from a temporary lapse. "I'm fine," she said coolly. "Thank you for your assistance."

The formal words checked him before he could gather her back into his arms. He bit back sudden anger. "Why was Lightborn following you?"

"The queen sent him to kill me." She met his eyes, her own defiant. "He's tried before. LaFaye blames me for her son's death. In truth, it was only partially my doing, but that does not matter."

He'd heard the story from Gawain, but it wasn't what he wanted to discuss now. "You're not safe. Eventually she'll send another assassin."

"I know."

"Nimueh," he said, the word turning to a plea.

A moment passed, the night falling into a hush so complete all he heard was his own heartbeat. He could sense the pull of Nimueh's presence, as if her blood and bones called to his. Perhaps it was mutual because, unexpectedly, she reached out her hand and clasped his. Her cool fingers were so slight they barely covered half his palm. He froze, certain that the smallest movement on his part would collapse the bridge she'd permitted between them. It was the first time since they'd met tonight that she'd reached out.

Dulac took a breath, but let it escape without speaking. Once, words had flown between them with barely a pause as if there wasn't enough time in all eternity to share everything they'd wanted to say. Now he wasn't sure what to say beyond the obvious: assassin, kill, danger. A barking dog could have imparted the same thing. He squeezed her hand gently, trying to give comfort.

She allowed the pressure, though she didn't return it. Then her fingers slid away and she took three quick steps, scooping up something from the ground. When it flashed in the errant light, he saw it was the amulet. She slid it into a pocket, then paused to regard him, her expression matter-of-fact. "Don't tell anyone this happened. Don't even mention you saw me."

It was then he saw the dark stain on the side of her dress. He hadn't seen blood on Lightborn's knife, but somehow she'd been cut. Adrenaline jolted him one more time and he lunged forward, but she was too quick, side-stepping him with fae grace.

"You *are* wounded." The words came out angry, but Dulac was past caring about manners. "You need a healer."

"Let me go. You've done enough." The words were quiet, her face utterly composed. "The only thing more you can do is keep silent, even to Arthur. A careless word will only help the next killer who comes looking for me."

He knew that already, and knew these days Arthur would be merciless when it came to any fae, even her. An overwhelming need to keep her safe sped his already pounding heart, but frustration made him savage. "Then tell me where you are at all times!"

Her brows raised. "Pardon me?"

"Don't be a fool. I can't protect you if I don't know where you are."

Her eyes closed as if gathering herself. "Goodbye, Lancelot."

There was a movement in the dark. By the time he realized she was leaving, he was alone.

That was all it took for Dulac's control over his pain to slip. The adrenaline left his body in a rush. Immediately, he collapsed, retching as the residue of Tramar's spell blew past his control. All the agony he'd pushed aside by sheer will flooded back with interest.

His body retaliated, lashing out through every nerve. Dulac rolled to his side, gasping and cursing under his breath. This punishment was the price of his gift—if that's what a person called his bloodthirsty urge to fight.

How long he sprawled there, he didn't know, but eventually Tramar's punishing spells dwindled without the fae's magic to fuel them. Only then did the pain fade.

Clammy with sweat, Dulac's skin grew cold, his shirt clinging to his back and chest. He raised himself on an elbow, shaking his head to clear it.

A jumble of ideas crowded in on him, but two stood out above all the rest. Nimueh still had a piece of her soul and Morgan LaFaye wanted her dead. He took a deep, shaking breath.

There was a reason he'd come through time. Nimueh needed him.

Chapter 5

Nim ran and ran *and ran*, her single thought, to put distance between herself and the scene of Tramar's death. The agony of having her soul ripped apart returned in a flood of nausea. She retched into the gutter, the wine she'd drunk coming back in a hot, acidic flood. But as soon as she could stand, she sped into the darkness again. If she'd had any doubts about leaving Carlyle, they'd vanished. Death she could face. She couldn't risk another attack like that one.

Miles passed before Nim slowed her steps. She wasn't sure where to go. She'd had to park some distance from the reception and had been on her way back to her car when Tramar had chased her. Now the car was miles in the opposite direction. Her shop and apartment were too far away to walk, and she'd lost her shoes. She didn't trust cabs or the bus—she couldn't bear to be enclosed with no way to run. If there were more assassins with more amulets, using her magic might well be a death sentence.

At that last thought, she came to a complete stop, her breath coming in short, sharp pants. The night had finally cooled, but her skin was slick with sweat from running. Making a slow circle, she looked around, considering her options. The street was deathly silent, empty but for the flickering aura of a slowly dying streetlight.

Her thoughts scattered, refusing to order themselves. Only one remained front and center. *I nearly died tonight.* Her hand went to her side, where a sharp pain clawed her. Her fingers came away warm and wet. She stared at the blood, briefly stupefied. She couldn't remember when the injury had happened. Maybe in those last moments, when her would-be killer had wrestled her to the ground. *Tramar.*

She hadn't known Tramar Lightborn had been the assassin following her for the last weeks, but when she'd finally seen his face, it had all fallen into place—his voice, his movements, even his scent. They'd played together as children, dunking each other in the icy streams of the Hollow Hills and chasing the goats that played among the gently rolling hills. Not that such bonds meant anything among the fae these days. He'd just tried to steal whatever traces of soul she had left before he killed her, and she'd just annihilated his remains. No thoughts of burial or mourning had crossed her mind, just a need to keep the human police ignorant and herself free from an accusation of murder. And Lancelot, who'd actually done the killing. She owed him that much protection for saving her life.

Nim searched her heart, looking for grief but finding only stunned silence. Her childhood friend deserved more, but she had nothing to give. *I'm sorry. I'm so sorry.*

Pain scrambled her thoughts. There was no way to know how deep the wound was, but it was bleeding freely. Healing magic wasn't her strength, and using it might beckon to a second assassin. Holding her side, Nim began to walk aimlessly, not knowing where she was going but aware it was stupid to remain in this seedy part of town. Her bare feet hurt, already scraped raw by the hard pavement.

Nim turned a corner, instinct guiding her toward the light of a busier street. She made out the sign of a liquor store, a late-night pharmacy and a diner. Like a moth, she craved the comfort the brightness promised. She clutched her side, the pain of her wound mixing with exhaustion. It felt as if she'd cried until her ribs ached even though she hadn't shed a tear.

A memory came uninvited: Lancelot, sitting on the dapple gray mount she'd given him, his face set in obstinate lines. He was lingering with her before a ride. He always did, except this time it was only for the moment it took to say goodbye. It was too short a time for everything she wanted to say.

So very brief for the end of everything they'd known together.

"I cannot remain with you," Lancelot had said to her, looking down from the tall steed. The sun had turned his hair to burnished gold, giving him the look of a warrior angel. "Camelot awaits. I can make a name there. I can become somebody."

As if he was nothing when he was with her. As if all their love was a mere ripple upon water. They had embraced and she had let him go, playing the generous lover. She'd refused to cry, at least until he was out of sight. Then she'd stood in that forest path, barefoot among the autumn leaves, and wept until she could no longer stand.

The image hit Nim like an electric shock. She reached out to brace herself against the side of a building, every nerve ending on fire. Even in her broken state, the pull of the past was intoxicating. She couldn't give in to it, and the fact that some corner of her wanted to made it all the more imperative that she leave. Lancelot would die to defend her, and that would destroy whatever was left of the woman she'd been.

Tonight's events meant she had to go *now*. She'd finally made contact with the individual who could make her disappear. Not just mundane practical aid, but the magical kind. There were only two people she knew with as much or more magic than she already had. One was La-Faye, and the other was Merlin Ambrosius, once enchanter to Camelot's king. Nim was one of very, very few people who knew Merlin still lived.

All at once, Nim realized what street she was on and where her feet had been taking her. Perhaps part of her had known where she was going since the moment she'd begun to run. Her contact wasn't expecting her until tomorrow, but he'd just have to deal with an early appointment.

An old-fashioned neon sign in the shape of a coffee cup blinked across the street. It marked the place where she hoped to find safety. Her fingers slipped into her pocket, fingering Tramar's amulet. At least she had a bargaining chip.

Nim pushed through the glass door of the all-night diner, an electronic chime announcing her presence. The place smelled the way it looked—tinged with decay and antiseptic at the same time, as if it couldn't quite decide whether to rot. There was only one patron at this hour, but that was on purpose. Merlin kept his office hours in the dead of night.

The waitress behind the counter looked up but didn't comment as Nim walked directly to the booth in the back. Nor did she so much as blink at the fact that Nim was barefoot and her dress soaked in blood. That said a lot about the clientele.

When Nim reached the darkest corner, she slid into the vinyl booth, her skirt catching on the duct tape that repaired the cushion. A dark-haired man already sat across the table, his chin resting in his hand. He had a lean build, but the play of muscles in his forearms spoke of a hidden strength. He looked no more than thirty, but Nim knew they were about the same age. Nim had been born a fae, but she had no idea how Merlin had achieved immortality and wasn't about to ask.

"You could at least look surprised." She grabbed a handful of napkins from the dispenser and pressed them to her wound. "Our appointment was for tomorrow."

He watched her wipe the blood from her hands. "And the other guy?"

"Lancelot killed him."

"So your path finally crossed with Dulac's, eh? That boy always had a way of complicating your day." Merlin leaned back and gave her an appraising look. "Love the battlefield chic."

"I need help."

"Ya think?"

"I need your kind of help."

The sorcerer narrowed his eyes, a challenging glint in their golden depths. "I don't *help* anymore. These days I'm a hired gun. Or wand, if you prefer to be literal about it."

Nim stared at the sorcerer, glad for once she felt nothing. She had every reason to hate Merlin—his bad judgment had destroyed the fae and Camelot both. Only her cold heart gave her distance enough to realize he wasn't actually evil. He'd been desperate, and she recognized a crumb of what might have once been pity inside herself. Otherwise, she would have burned him to ash before she'd even sat down. That would have been unwise, given how badly she needed his help. "Then I will pay you for your time."

With a grimace, he waved his fingers and she felt a

pulse of heat in her side. The pain eased and the blood stopped flowing.

"Thank you," she said, crushing the wad of bloody napkins in her hand.

"That was for old time's sake. The rest is on the meter." He picked up his cup, smelled it, then set it down again. "My clientele doesn't respect freebies."

"You must have interesting clients."

"I like them interesting. There's no point working for lightweights where all anyone wants is a unicorn that poops rainbows."

They paused while the waitress filled their coffee cups and left menus. "I wouldn't recommend the chili," said Merlin once they were alone again. "Last time it tried to grab my spoon."

The dimpled half smile would have been charming on anyone else. On Merlin, it was vaguely sinister. She wondered for a moment if she'd made a mistake coming here. Merlin was arrogant, bitter, and a schemer. These days, his customers came from a black magic underworld she could barely imagine. And yet, who else could she turn to who could actually help her?

"I'm looking to disappear. I need to be completely untraceable."

He tilted his head, looking very much like a curious crow. "Any particular reason?"

"LaFaye sent one of her personal assassins after me. Tonight he nearly succeeded. The next one probably won't miss."

He made a sympathetic noise. "The queen is nothing if not persistent. She enjoys her little games too much."

"I don't know how her assassin found me." She folded her arms, instinctively protecting herself. "I've only been back in town since last night."

Merlin finally tried a sip of his coffee, his mouth twisting in disgust. "You can leave Carlyle, run and hide on a desert island, but LaFaye's creatures can still track you. Hunting is their specialty and every magic user gives off a unique power signature the way a rose sheds its scent."

"Magic is traceable?" The night Lightborn had chased her to the warehouse, he'd mentioned tracking her. Then she remembered burning Tramar's body and silently cursed. Any magical bloodhounds in the area would surely scent that.

"It's the simplest way for the queen to find you," Merlin agreed.

"But that's not possible. I've not been using spells," she protested. "Not before tonight. Since I left LaFaye's service, I've been living the life of a human. No magic for months. Not much, anyway. Just a bit."

"Just a bit. To be sure." Merlin's smile grew rueful. "Out in the modern world, we're like chain-smokers down to the occasional cigarette in the bar. That doesn't mean we're not lighting up."

Unfortunately, it made sense. Nim lifted her chin. "I can quit completely." She sounded confident, but the idea seemed bizarre. Magic was part of who she was, as integral as the color of her eyes—and yet she'd done what she could to disguise that, too.

Merlin shook his head. "You've got too much power to stay off the radar. You shed it whether you're casting spells or not. Self-control won't be your salvation."

Something very much like panic bloomed in her chest. She could feel Tramar's grip on her again, sucking away everything inside her. "There's got to be a way."

"I can help you bind your power. Then you can leave town and live your life as a human for real. That's the only true way to disappear."

Nim fell silent. The enormity of what Merlin suggested

loomed like a forbidding mountain, poised to crush her. "I don't know."

"You can keep going on as you are," Merlin said reasonably. "The one advantage you have is assassins prefer to kill in private. Your business is probably safe because there are always staff and customers. Your condo—up to a point. Your real vulnerability is when you walk alone. LaFaye's bullyboys hunt like big cats, waiting for the ideal place to ambush their prey."

Nim buried her face in her hands, her battered body throbbing. Merlin waved away the waitress when she approached to take their food order. When Nim didn't say more, he leaned forward. "Safety is frequently overrated."

"I thought you could give me a different choice. A spell so LaFaye would look elsewhere or maybe a better disguise."

"Those spells mask your trail, but they don't eliminate it. Sooner or later they fail."

That wasn't what she wanted to hear. Nim picked at her hands, revolted by the blood still caked around her nails. "The fae can still feel fear," she said in a small voice.

He leaned forward, his expression uncharacteristically gentle. "I know. I've been told some fae still have pieces of their soul, as if shreds were left behind."

"Tonight he tried to steal what little I still have." She bit her lip, panic hot inside her.

"My poor lady."

She wasn't anyone's poor anything. She refused to be. She swallowed hard. "Can I unbind my magic if I choose?"

One corner of his mouth curled up. "Absolutely."

"Are you sure? I could unleash it if things got bad?"

"Of course."

She met his eyes. "Truly?"

"Truly."

"Then let's do it."

Merlin's smile faded. "Before we go a step further, answer me two questions. In the past, you've been Camelot's friend. Are you sure you want to leave Carlyle?"

"I've done what I can for Arthur. I helped Gawain destroy Mordred, didn't I? I made Excalibur, the only weapon that will kill LaFaye." Nim swallowed hard. "Morgan laughed to have the maker of her nemesis at her beck and call!"

"And?"

"I found Lancelot for Arthur. That's three things, a magical number by the rules of lore and magic. More than any loyalty demands. I'm done. Now that I'm in the crosshairs, the only thing I am is a magnet for danger."

Merlin folded his hands, his expression troubled. "I have one other question. Are you really so ready to surrender everything you are? Binding my magic would be my very last choice. I might live in squalor as a mercenary to the worst bottom-feeders of the magical realms, but I will not live a lie."

"That's your choice." Nim could feel Tramar sucking out her soul, the nova of pure agony stopping her heart. "I need to run."

Merlin nodded slowly. "If this is what you wish, I will do it. You can trust me."

"I trust you to earn your pay," she said sharply, weary of his attempts to counsel her. She took the amulet from her pocket and slid it across the table. "I'm sure you recognize this."

Merlin's eyes flared, the amber depths suddenly bright. "LaFaye's jewel." His fingers closed around the amulet. The chain clinked across the tabletop. "Are you sure you wish to part with this?"

"I'm trying to vanish. I don't think the queen's toys will help me become inconspicuous."

"Of course." He pocketed the amulet. "Do you want time to think this over, or to take care of loose ends?"

"I've been planning this for weeks. I don't need time."

Merlin rose, leaving money for the coffees next to his half-empty cup. "Then follow me."

He turned, not toward the door, but to the back wall of the diner. There was a framed poster of Elvis hanging against faded red wallpaper, but no exit Nim could see. Nevertheless, the sorcerer made an elaborate gesture in the air, and then stepped forward—and vanished as neatly as if he'd been sliced out of the world.

A faint internal tug reminded Nim of regret. There had been a time when magic was her calling, the one thing that defined her. And maybe once she would have fought for love, but that was beyond her now. These were just more losses in an endless string of goodbyes.

Nim followed Merlin into his lair.

Chapter 6

The next afternoon found Nim at her bookstore. Mandala Books rambled through an old house, piles of new and used volumes overflowing shelves and stacking the stairways like a literary avalanche. The place was bright and clean, but it was crowded. The store was filled with browsing customers and the scent of new ink as the staff unpacked a shipment of paperbacks.

Nim stood behind the front desk, her mind curiously blank after the barrage of unexpected events the night before. Last night's attack had been painful enough, but Merlin's spell had hit her like a cudgel. A pounding headache made her queasy, enough that all she wanted was to lie down and whimper. But there was no time to be ill—she was putting her escape plan in motion that very day.

The paperwork was in place so that Mandala Books would transfer to Antonia's oversight the instant Nim gave the word. In the little while she'd owned it, Nim had revived the business and wouldn't abandon it without a new caretaker. Jobs depended on the store, as did the many, many loyal customers.

She closed her eyes, her headache pounding as her thoughts scattered like loose marbles. Merlin and Tramar had played their roles in reducing her to a state of confusion, but she really blamed Lancelot. She raised a hand to her lips, fingertips brushing where the knight's mouth had touched hers. His breath had been hot, his kiss hungry and urgent. By all the stars, what had he hoped to gain with that kiss? Did he believe himself so fine a man that his caress could restore her soul after centuries of loss?

Arrogant fool. She pursed her lips, hiding the movement behind her fingers as she relived the moment. Then she dropped her hand, astonished by her sudden lapse into daydreams. She was overwrought, addled by trauma and Merlin's magic. She checked for witnesses but thankfully no one was looking her way.

The service desk sat opposite the wall painted with a huge, colorful image that gave the store its name. From there she had a view through the bay window that overlooked the sunny street. At that moment she saw Lancelot walk up the steps, wearing a faded T-shirt and jeans that hugged the muscles in his long, strong legs.

"No, no, no," she muttered under her breath as he sauntered in. How on earth had he found her store?

"Looking for something to read?" she asked in a bland tone.

"Are you a bestseller?" He leaned on the shelf beside her desk, seeming to take every inch of space around the desk. His T-shirt strained with the movement, showing off the thick muscles of his chest.

"What is that supposed to mean?" She performed a quick visual survey, determining that he was unhurt from the night before. Of course, Lancelot had always been the kind to hide his injuries out of an impractical manly pride. Once, it had driven her into a frenzy.

"You're the only subject I'm interested in at the moment," he said, drawing her gaze from his chest to his face. "Not my best opening line, but it's the truth. We need to talk."

He was so close, she had to crane her neck to look up at him. "Again? I thought you'd said your piece last night."

"Yes, again," he said, bending down to speak softly. "And it's about what happened last night."

"Why? As you can see, I'm fine."

He was looking at her the way she'd looked at him, checking for bruises—except his eyes heated as they traveled over her form. The corners of his mouth flattened in an expression she couldn't interpret. "We need to decide where we're going from here."

"I've moved on." She straightened the items on the desk, suddenly in need of order. "I can't go back to the Dark Ages."

His dark eyes flashed. "I'm not asking you to."

"Oh?"

"We can do better than that." He reached out, brushed the back of his rough fingers to her cheek. The contact was electric, sending chills all the way to her toes with a mere graze of skin on skin. That should have been impossible, given what she was.

Needing to take charge of the situation, Nim stepped out from behind the desk. "Let's have this conversation in private." She signaled to the staff member stocking books to cover the till.

Lancelot took a step back in response to her crisp tone, but followed her when she led the way up the stairs to a small office. She closed the door and turned to face him. "You saved my life last night. I salute your prowess," she said, deciding to be blunt. "I think that covers everything that needs saying beyond goodbye."

He looked uncertain a moment, but then seemed to re-cover. "I'd rather begin our recap with the fact that you kissed me."

Her breath caught, but she hid the reaction. "I think that was the other way around. You dragged me into the dark like an apprentice lad at his first May Day Fair."

"Perhaps, but you kissed me back."

It was a gentle tease and if she was utterly, mercilessly honest, she had to admit there had been a flash of feeling during that kiss. There and gone, it had passed as swiftly as the sun dancing off a blade—but it had happened. A strange, hollow feeling grew inside her, leaving her with the sense that she might fall into some inner abyss. "Don't waste your time."

His fingers skimmed over her shoulders, the touch be-ginning light and deepening to a caress. She spun away from him before he could see her shiver. She could feel his breath then, warm and strong on the back of her neck. Closing her eyes, she let that strength wash over her. She'd forgotten what comfort there had been in these moments where Lancelot had blotted out all the demands of the world. For a heartbeat, everything was simple, just the meeting of a man and his woman.

He turned her slowly so she faced him once more. When she felt his lips against her brow, she hissed in a breath.

"Hush," he said, his kisses brushing her nose, then her eyelids.

Her eyes automatically flicked open, needing to see what he was going to do next. His hands caressed her shoulders again, his skin pale against her dark olive com-plexion. She'd always found the contrast arousing. Lance-lot had been exotic, other—the only human she'd ever taken to her bed.

His warmth fanned across her lips, and instinct made them part. But Lancelot didn't crush her with his kiss this time. Instead, he continued his featherlight touches, teasing her until she leaned in to capture more of his mouth. Then, and only then, did he unleash the passionate eagerness she'd once craved. Her mouth opened under his, responding to his hot tongue. Granted permission, he plundered her.

A skitter of fear reminded her of being face-to-face with Tramar, his mouth just above hers. But this was the opposite of what he'd done. Rather than ripping out her soul, Lancelot was trying to make her whole. For a moment, she let him, waiting for a spark to ignite in her. It had been so long, surely she would combust in an instant. And yet—a ghost of sadness claimed her.

"Take your time," he said softly. "You're only just remembering how to be with me."

"Don't be arrogant." She pushed him away.

"I know the way your body bends into mine, the sound you make deep in your throat when you surrender."

"I didn't surrender. I don't." She stepped back to put distance between them.

"No, but you thought about it just now." His gaze grew bolder.

When he reached for her hand, she grabbed his wrist and pushed him away. "You aren't the first to get a reaction from me. It doesn't mean I'm whole."

His eyebrows rose. "Care to explain?"

"Prince Mordred enjoyed torture. For a moment, I remembered what it was to hate and now the Queen of Faery wants my head on a spike for betraying her son. So yes, I had an instant of caring. It will probably mean my death."

Clearly troubled, he considered her for a long moment. "That's why LaFaye sent Lightborn? Vengeance?"

"Yes." Nim leaned against the desk, glad of the support of its heavy oak. The nausea that had plagued her earlier roared back with redoubled force. "I knew it was coming and planned to vanish. If I'd been quicker about it, you and I would never have met."

The silence that followed pushed at her like a physical force. "You ran last night," he finally said. "I could have helped you."

"No," she said again. "I didn't stay the lonely fae woman you met at the edge of the lake. I don't need you." More to the point, she couldn't depend on him. One day he'd leave again and the lack of a soul wouldn't matter. She wouldn't survive it.

"Nimueh." He reached for her, but she stepped back out of reach.

"Please go," she said. "This discussion is pointless."

A tiny claw seemed to catch at her voice, but not so much that the words sounded anything but cool reason. Confusion crossed Lancelot's face, but it quickly froze into a mask she knew too well. She'd finally managed to push him away.

"Do you not trust me?" he asked, his voice gone hard.

"You would never betray me. It's not in your nature," she said, and then remembered Guinevere. There had been plenty of rumors about Lancelot and the queen. "I mean, you wouldn't turn me over to LaFaye."

The lines around his mouth deepened as if he'd read her thoughts. With a muttered curse, he turned and stalked to the door. Nim sagged against the bookcase, watching his broad, strong back. Unfamiliar tension crawled through her chest until she could not breathe. Lancelot had always pushed her to impossible places, good and bad.

He'd just reached for the handle when the door swung open from the other side.

In a temper, Dulac barely jerked to a stop before he mowed the newcomer down. The bride from the wedding stood in the doorway, wearing an expression no newly-wed woman should ever wear. With a muttered apology, Dulac stepped aside. It spoiled his grand exit, but something had happened and intuition told him he needed to know what that was.

The bride glanced up at Lancelot, her blue eyes growing large before her gaze shifted to Nimueh. "I need to talk to you."

"Antonia," Nim said, a faint edge of surprise in her voice. "You should be leaving on your honeymoon."

"I can't." The words were grim.

Dulac watched Nimueh's reaction, struggling to be objective about what he saw. As with the other fae, her expression was oddly flat. The flow of normal emotion created thousands of barely seen muscle movements—ones that he'd only noticed now that they were missing. And yet, as she gave a slow nod to the bride, urging her to continue, he was certain Nim cared. He hadn't lied about feeling the heat in her kiss.

"I can't leave." The bride—Antonia, he reminded himself—paced the small workroom, her arms hugging her chest. "My cousin Susan didn't come home last night."

"I spoke to her," Nimueh replied. "She was the redhead with the violin."

Dulac searched his memory, but found nothing. He'd only had eyes for Nimueh.

"Are you sure she's not staying with a friend?" Nimueh asked.

"Susan's not like that." Antonia shoved a hand through her riot of fiery curls. "Not that she's a saint, but she's not stupid. She would have left a message if she went home with someone. The police told us it's too soon to say she's missing."

Nimueh cast a glance at Dulac. He could tell she was making up her mind what to do. She'd always been elusive, a scholar more likely to retreat than engage in life's battles, but people had always turned to her for thoughtful advice. Evidently, that at least hadn't changed.

"What do you need me to do?" he asked. Whatever she said, he was still hers to command.

When Nim frowned but didn't answer, he turned to Antonia. "Do you have any idea where Susan might be?"

"I talked to her friends already. After the wedding reception, the diehards went to the White Hart."

"The bar downtown?" Nim asked.

Dulac frowned, remembering what Gawain had said. There had been problems there before.

"Susan's bandmates saw her in the parking lot around two o'clock," Antonia continued. "One moment she was there and the next she was gone. Her car is still there. She'd left her violin on the hood. That's how we know something's wrong. She'd never leave her instrument sitting out where it might be stolen. It's her baby and the most expensive thing she owns."

Dulac drew closer, folding his arms. He was next to Nimueh now, their shoulders nearly touching. "Go on."

"Right before that she was talking to a pair of strange-looking young men."

"What do you mean by strange?" Nimueh asked.

"Tall, with their hair bleached white."

He exchanged a glance with Nimueh. *Fae.* He did a quick calculation. Tramar would have been dead by that time. This was a different pair and from the sound of it, they were hunting. A young, pretty human female would be a choice target—sport and a soul to drink in one convenient package.

Nimueh's fist clenched in the fabric of Dulac's sleeve. "Please give us a moment," she said to Antonia in a voice that brooked no argument. "Wait for us downstairs."

Confusion settled over Antonia's features, but she left,

closing the door behind her. Nimueh turned to Dulac. "You were leaving."

"I was."

She pressed her hands to her temples, as if her head was aching. "You should have left this room before Antonia came to me just now. I should have left Carlyle before you found me here. I desire nothing more than to disappear from sight, and yet at every turn I find you back at my side."

He folded his arms. "The forces of lore and magic seem to want us together."

She gave him a dry look. "Either that or you simply will not go away."

"Admit that you need my sword. I'm a knight and there is a job to do."

"Yes." She closed her eyes. "I need your help. These hunters hurt my people."

The words might have confused someone from the twenty-first century, but Dulac understood. The Lady of the Lake protected those who served her, no matter what century it was. Anyone who touched her staff or their families was asking for swift retribution. Beneath the disguise she wore—so plain, so banal, so *human*—he could see the shining creature she'd been, the sorceress and lady of a white stone castle deep in the Forest Sauvage.

Time meant nothing in that moment, and he was again the penniless young knight who had adventured from France into the wilds of the Western Isles. He'd been nothing—desperate to make his name and restore the honor of his family. His armor had been so dented and mismatched he'd been called "the ill-made knight."

One day, he'd gone deep into the Forest Sauvage and there he'd found a lake as still as glass and crowned with mist. He had stood on the shore, his old horse cropping the long, lush grass, when a silver boat had come soundlessly across the water, barely a ripple creasing its surface. And then he had beheld the Lady of the Lake, sitting in the prow and wrapped in a cloak of gray, her long white hair unbound and flowing like a second cape. All Lancelot's cares had melted away beneath a wave of dumbstruck awe. He'd never seen a fae before. After Nimueh, he would have sworn he'd never seen a female. She'd eclipsed every woman before and since.

And here she was again, at her best in defense of someone she cared for. The trials she'd suffered hadn't changed this one essential thing. This was the lady he knew.

"A human won't survive the loss of her soul. The pain alone—" Nimueh broke off, leaving Dulac to imagine what she might have suffered the night before. "The pain alone will rob her of reason. Fae sometimes keep their victims alive for days, drinking them a sip at a time so they can savor the rush of sensation. Death will only be the last torment this young woman suffers."

She stood with her fists clenched as if holding something back with sheer will. Dulac would have called it grief or fury, but she would deny emotion and he didn't know what to believe. He would reach her far more easily with a practical solution. "Where is the White Hart?"

"Across town. It's near an abandoned house the neighbors say is haunted. I would say it's haunted by rogue fae and we should start looking there."

"Wouldn't that be the first place Susan's friends would go? It's an obvious hiding place."

Her face was set and pale. "All the more reason to get there first. We will survive an encounter with hunters. Ordinary humans will not."

The "we" wasn't lost on him, but he kept his expression cool. She'd given him an opening and he wouldn't ruin it by spooking her now. He pulled out his smartphone—as marvelous a device as anything Merlin had ever dreamed up.

"What are you doing?" Nimueh asked, almost with suspicion.

Lancelot tapped his contact list. "I have a few friends who jump at any chance to rescue fair maidens. They would never forgive me if I kept this all to myself."

Chapter 7

The Price House, also known as the most haunted house in Carlyle, looked precisely the way Nim would have expected. It dated from gold rush days and had three stories fronted by an impressive porch. Time had left it sagging, with much of the ornamental scrollwork rotted away. Even in broad daylight, the place looked forbidding.

She parked her Audi S3 sedan down the block. Lancelot sat in the passenger seat, his long legs looking cramped despite the roomy interior of the sedan. She studied his handsome profile for a long moment, wondering at his ability to overset every plan she made. If he'd shown up at the bookstore an hour later, she might well have been on her way to the airport. Instead, here she was miles from where she had intended to be and sitting outside a supposedly haunted house containing an unknown number of murderous fae.

"What now?" she asked.

He held up his smartphone, reading what looked like an

entry from an online encyclopedia. "It says here the original owners were great collectors and after their death the house was turned into a museum. Then it went bankrupt and was sold to a land developer who in turn lost all his money in the economic downturn of the 1980s."

"I'm not sure how that helps us."

"Neither do I, and yet there is something bewitching about the amount of useless information these little devices can provide." He tucked the phone away, his movements as graceful and precise as a hunting cat's. The closer Lancelot came to a battle, the more he took on the predatory aura of a lion. She knew without asking that he anticipated a fight.

"I'm going to look around," he said, getting out of the car. "My friends have to cross town. They won't be here for a few minutes."

Nim stayed where she was, the experience with Tramar chaining her to her seat. "Be careful."

Lancelot circled the car and opened her door. "I know you want to keep out of sight of the other knights, but until they arrive you're coming with me. I'm not leaving you alone on a deserted street."

He was correct. Many of the knights knew her face, and she didn't want gossip leading the queen her way. Furthermore, Nim didn't want to leave the safety of the Audi, but she accepted his large, strong hand and got out of the car. As soon as she was standing beside him, she knew it was the right decision. He was a knight, and his physical presence was as good as a shield—but more than that, he radiated the will and confidence she couldn't seem to find. Everything would be better with him by her side.

The house was on a large lot, but it was one of a row of vacant, crumbling places waiting for bulldozers. The opposite side of the street was nothing but empty fields, and the White Hart the nearest business beyond that. It was little wonder that the fae had chosen this place—there were no neighbors to speak of for several city blocks, and yet there was hunting enough in the crowded apartment complex a bare mile away. There was privacy and opportunity both.

As they drew near their target, Nim stretched her magical senses, probing for signs of life. It was only after a fruitless attempt that she remembered her magic was bound. *Stars!* A sense of helplessness sucked the breath out of her. She was safe from detection, but she had no more power than the victim she hoped to rescue. Sure, she could undo the binding, but then she'd be visible again and waste the value of LaFaye's amulet. Nothing seemed to be a good solution.

She reached instead for the Smith & Wesson tucked at the small of her back, touching it for reassurance. Her other hand reached out, her knuckles brushing the folds of Lancelot's coat for the same reason. He made her feel physically safe.

Lancelot was a consummate fighter, the best anyone had ever seen—even from the moment he arrived outside her castle in the Forest Sauvage. Mortals had sometimes wandered by her lake, and she'd given them a meal and a bed for the night. Lancelot had repaid her hospitality with a demonstration of his fighting skills. It was all he'd had to offer.

It was then she'd seen something special in the young knight with the bad armor. As a noble, it had been her prerogative to offer him a place in her household. She'd given him a fine horse and fine weapons, taught him languages and educated him in the ways of the court. By the time he'd left her, he'd been a paragon of chivalry.

They had not become lovers at once. Not, in fact, for some time. She was a creature of the mind, given to books and spells and slow to trust the needs of the flesh. But while she'd shown him the intricate world of the intellect, he'd guided her to the blazing fires of mortal passion. She had learned the difference between existence and life.

No, Nim corrected herself, Lancelot was far from safe, for she'd never been content with anyone else ever after.

He stopped, catching her hand. Nim's thoughts returned to the here and now and the moldering mansion straight ahead. The broken windows looked down at them like squinting eyes.

"Won't there be guards watching the street?" she asked, although as soon as she said it, she guessed the answer. These weren't LaFaye's personal assassins. These fae weren't even professionals—these were trash. Soul addicts tended to hunt at night and sleep off their fevered madness during the day, oblivious to anything but the rush of stolen emotion.

"We'll soon find out if there are sentries," Lancelot replied lightly. "I see a single front entrance. I'd like to find out what's in the back."

With that, he glided down a crooked wire fence that ran between the derelict houses. Nim followed, careful not to lose her footing on the lumpy ground. There was a garden at the back that had been swallowed by a tangle of wild blackberries. Lancelot crouched in the long grass, pulling Nim down beside him so he could keep his voice low. "Two exits at the back. One looks like it leads into the cellar."

A figure passed before a main-floor window. A tall, thin figure with white hair. She heard Lancelot suck in a breath. He'd seen it, too. They'd only guessed that Susan was held here, but they'd been right about the house being a haven for rogue fae. So far their predictions had held true.

Nim studied the place, trying to figure out the layout inside. There had to be fifteen rooms in a place of this size. They could imprison a human almost anywhere inside. Then movement drew her eye up to a second-floor window—the only one that still had curtains. The sash was up and the hot summer breeze was stirring the light panels, tossing them wide to show a glimpse of the derelict room beyond.

"In a house with barely a chip of paint left, why the curtains?" she asked. "Is there something special about that room, I wonder?"

"Do you believe they're holding Susan there?"

"I don't know. The second floor is more secure, but an open window is not. It's worth investigating."

He shook his head. "The house is full of dry rot. Climbing in or out of there would be risky."

She turned to meet his deep brown eyes. "And waltzing through a house full of fae criminals is not? Look at the advantages. If we go in an open window, we don't need to pick the lock."

One corner of his mouth curled up. "I'm more likely to carry the day when I'm not falling from twenty feet up. Even the brickwork around this place looks like it would crumble under my weight."

"I'm lighter. I could do it."

He frowned, but in a considering way. He'd never underestimated her abilities. "I'm sure you could, but even if those fae aren't like Lightborn, they're dangerous."

And I should be sitting in the airport by now. But this time, the thought had less power over her. Her fear had faded because she was there for a good reason and Lancelot was a solid, steadying presence beside her.

Nim was wishing for binoculars when she saw something move behind the lace curtains. It was impossible to see what it was, just a streak of moving color. Her acute senses had nothing to do with magic and everything to do with her fae blood, and binding her powers hadn't dulled them. Still, they had limitations.

She strained to catch the movement again, afraid her mind was supplying images she wanted to see instead of what was truly there. Then a feminine voice splintered the afternoon heat—a muffled cry of protest, barely audible even to fae ears.

Nim wheeled to Lancelot. "I'm going in."

He grabbed her arm. "Wait. The other knights will be here any minute. There's no need to risk yourself."

"You have no idea what losing your soul is like," she said, her voice a bare whisper. Tension thundered in her ears, but the image of the girl in the yellow dress blazed through her anxiety. "She's just a young human. A minute is far too long."

Nim pulled away from him and ran to the side of the house, keeping low. She reached the foot of the wall, looking up to see the curtain billow out against a cerulean sky. To her left was a drainpipe, but it was covered in rust. To her right was the chimney, the mortar crumbling from between the bricks. She dug her fingers into the chimney and began to climb, the soft soles of her sneakers gripping the bricks with ease.

She moved in near silence, her agility and strength greater than a human's even without her powers. It didn't take long to scale the first dozen feet. A quick glance over her shoulder told her Lancelot was guarding her ascent, his long knife in one hand and a gun in the other. The sight of him made her climb faster, eager to finish the job and get them all out of danger. She'd reached the sill when she heard the slam of a door and a sudden movement on the grass below. The urge to look down was like a blade against her spine, but she dared not waste the time. If someone saw her clinging to the bricks, they would shoot.

She drew level with the window and reached out for the sill. A stick propped up the sash, so she was careful not to disturb it as she steadied herself to look inside. However, when she put weight on her outstretched arm, her hand came away with a fistful of dust and splinters. The frame was crumbling with age and neglect. Lancelot had been right about the risk of climbing.

She scaled another few feet and this time hooked a foot through the window, using an awkward lunge to crawl through the opening. She knocked the prop holding up the sash and the frame dropped on her shoulders with a vicious thump. With the wind knocked from her lungs, Nim slithered onto the grimy floor.

The room was empty of fae, but neither were there prisoners conveniently awaiting rescue. She cursed softly, but was distracted by sounds of fighting rising from the yard outside. As she jumped to her feet, she glanced outside to see men running, some with swords, others with guns. When she recognized Gawain, she knew reinforcements had arrived. She pulled back from the window, keeping out of sight.

Now it was up to Nim to do her part. She took a second, slower look around, wrinkling her nose at the smell of ancient filth. There was no furniture except for an old mattress on the floor, a blanket rumpled at its foot. Nim stepped forward and pressed a hand to the mattress. The room was warm, but this was damp with sweat. Someone had been there, and recently. A pair of bright yellow shoes—the same shade as Susan's dress—were carelessly tossed in a corner.

Nim started to rise from her crouch when she felt something beneath the blanket. She pulled back the cloth to see a chain of dull silver ending in a broad cuff. That answered why it had been safe to leave a window open.

Was this where the fae kept their humans until it was time to feed? Was the cry she had heard Susan, as the girl was unchained and taken away for another session of unthinkable torture?

The image that formed in Nim's mind obliterated everything else. She drew her gun and glided toward the door, wincing when a floorboard creaked. She reached for the brass handle, turning it slowly. It was unlocked. She listened, leaning toward the crack as she opened it an inch. There were plenty of sounds, but they were all coming from outside. She let the door drift open, willing the hinges not to creak.

When she reached the corridor outside, it was empty but for stairs leading to the rooms above and below. Where had they taken Susan? It had to have been just minutes ago. Nim listened to the sounds around her. There was fighting downstairs, spilling in from the yard. Not the first place she'd take a prisoner. She glanced up, but the condition of the ceiling said there'd been considerable water damage on the third floor, perhaps from a leaking roof. She'd try her luck in the immediate area first.

Six doors faced onto the hardwood hallway, including the room Nim had just left. A few stood open and one was missing altogether. Most of the rooms were little more than stinking burrows, telling the tale of how far these fae had sunk in their addiction.

The fourth room she peered into was different. The window had been boarded up, but a single candle threw a pool of light over the space. Some attempt had been made to furnish it with a sagging sofa and a moth-eaten rug. Unfortunately, what it had acquired in fabric it had gained in the stink of mildew. Nim stifled a sneeze.

One of the shadows moved. A male fae rose, holding Susan to his chest. Nim couldn't tell if he meant to protect her or use her as a shield, but when she looked into his eyes all became clear. His expression was filled with fury— and that was only possible if he'd drunk from her soul.

"Who the stars are you?" he rasped. He was shaking,

a telltale sign of the damage addicts suffered. Next on the list was incurable madness.

Nim kept the gun to her side, unwilling to risk shooting Susan. The violinist looked barely conscious, as if she would collapse if her attacker released the arm he clutched around her waist. The fae himself looked barely able to stand, overcome by the emotions swirling inside him.

Nim kept her voice soft and calm, but she knew better than to beg him for Susan's life. If the fae had still possessed a better nature, he wouldn't be there in the first place. "I'm here to save you."

"Oh?" he scoffed.

"From dishonor," she said in the same even, implacable voice. "You blacken our people's name."

"Does it matter?" His lip curled. "They call this house haunted. What are we fae but ghosts?"

His barb struck home, echoing Nim's darkest thoughts. But she took a step forward, knowing every inch closer to her target improved her aim. "Even so, remaining true to our best selves is the test of our worth."

Fine words, considering the suitcases already packed and waiting at her condo. They were both running in their own ways, this man with his addiction and Nim with her plans to vanish. They were both running to meaningless ends. The thought made Nim falter, and the fae must have seen it in her step.

He thrust Susan forward. The girl stumbled forward, but Nim's reflexes were too swift. She pushed Susan onto the sofa and stepped aside in the same moment. Susan fell hard into the dusty cushions, but now Nim had the opening she needed.

She took aim, but was a split second too late. The fae had a gun, too.

Chapter 8

They both fired, and though the fae's hand shook, his aim was good enough. Hot pain scored Nim's shoulder the same instant as she fired.

The fae stumbled backward, crashing into the furniture. He hung there, clinging to the jumble behind him for a long moment. Finally, he collapsed a bit at a time, first dropping the gun and then folding limb by limb until he sank to the filthy floor. Nim stumbled forward, picking up his weapon and thrusting it into her belt. There was a neat hole in his forehead, assuring her that he was dead. She refused to look at the mess on the wall where he'd been standing.

Only then did she look down at her own wound, feeling a wave of sticky heat rise to her skin. It was the second wound in two days, but thankfully it wasn't deep. She bled, but the bullet had only scored her upper arm.

"What happened?" demanded Lancelot.

She spun to see him filling the doorway. Someone had

brought him an ax, and he was covered in dirt and blood, his hair slicked back from his broad forehead. He'd lost his jacket, and his heavily muscled arms glistened with sweat. Tension slipped from Nim's shoulders, making her wound throb afresh as her muscles released. There was no doubt that she could have got Susan out of the house on her own, but now that Lancelot was here everything would be so much easier.

"I found her." She pointed to the couch.

His gaze was slow to shift from her bloody arm to Susan's prone form.

"I'm fine," Nim said. "She's alive."

"And he's not." Lancelot nodded to the body of the fae. "That was a clean shot."

With some surprise, Nim felt a pang of regret. "Perhaps it was a mercy." Yet those words tasted false, so she tried again. "It was a tragedy."

Working quickly, Lancelot thrust the ax into a leather hanger strapped to his belt and carefully rolled Susan over. As Nim had suspected, she was gagged with a strip of cloth. Nim loosened the knots, cursing the fingers of her left hand. The wound was making them clumsy.

"There's fighting on the stairs," Lancelot said, his tone brisk. "I had to fight my way up here. We can't descend carrying an unconscious girl."

Nim finally got the knots undone and pulled off the gag, wincing at the angry marks the bindings left behind. Susan didn't revive, even when Nim tapped the girl's cheeks. "Stars!" Nim cursed. "After what's been done to her, there is no telling if she'll ever wake up, or if she'll be right when she does."

She met Lancelot's eyes, nearly falling into their deep brown depths. There was sadness there she'd never seen before. Whatever he'd endured since they parted had left traces behind. She looked away, the room suddenly feeling too small.

"A house this size would have had servants," she said. "Perhaps they had a back staircase for the staff to move about the house. We could take her out that way."

Glad to have a concrete goal, she returned to the hallway. Lancelot followed, Susan draped in his arms. Nim forced open the remaining doors. The smallest was in a recessed niche off the main corridor, and the settling house had jammed it shut. One slam of Lancelot's boot sent it crashing open.

It was indeed another staircase, but the opening showed a cobwebbed nightmare. Nim could almost hear the scuttle of spidery feet in the yawning blackness. "This looks old. It might not be safe," she said.

But then they smelled smoke. "Fire," said Lancelot. "This place will go up like paper."

Nim looked over her shoulder and saw flickering light in the direction they'd come from. "There was a candle in the room where I found Susan. It must have tipped over in the fight."

Even as she watched, the flames licked the dry, crumbling wood outside the room. Lancelot was right. The old place would go up in minutes, and the fire was between them and the main exit.

"Go," he said, his voice firm. "We don't have a choice."

One hand held up to protect her face, Nim took a step into the stuffy blackness. The stairs creaked ominously beneath her foot. "I don't like spiders," she said.

"I know."

She could hear Lancelot's feet searching for the steps behind her. Although she had better night vision than a human, she was all but blind once they were halfway down the old staircase. How he managed was a mystery. Once or twice she heard a scrape against the wall as he misjudged and Susan touched the plaster.

And then she thought about what she'd said. She wasn't supposed to like or dislike anything. And yet—a cobweb snagged over her hair and she frantically flicked it away— she really did *not* want to encounter anything with more than two legs. She felt it with an intensity that went beyond a fae's self-preserving fear.

She coughed, smoke sticking to her tongue and throat. It was too dark to see how thick it was, but she could feel the rising temperature around her. She'd lost any sense of how far they'd come, but it was plain they had to hurry. Her thoughts were interrupted when her foot plunged through the wood of the staircase. She threw her weight back, hoping to retreat to the last step, but it gave as well. Shards of wood stabbed her ankle as she pitched into empty air and tumbled over and over into the claustrophobic dark.

Nim slammed to the tile below, instinct alone making her scramble to get out of the way of the falling chunks of wood and plaster. By the time she gathered her wits, she was on the fringe of the battle raging in the kitchen. She could just make out the combatants through the smoke. Fae and knight were savaging one another in a fight so brutal the fire barely seemed an annoyance.

Lancelot landed behind her, cursing loud and long enough that he had to be mostly undamaged. She turned to speak to him but nearly came eye to eye with Arthur Pendragon. She spun away, ducking Arthur's notice. All her fears of LaFaye surged back, but they weren't alone. Since waking, the king had treated magic users with suspicion and the fae without mercy. If he caught her, he'd kill her on sight, especially in a skirmish like this. Using all the stealth and speed she had, Nim fled the burning house.

* * *

Dulac landed with a crash, his shoulders colliding with hard tile. He'd been trained to roll out of a fall, but he had a hundred-odd pounds of deadweight in his arms and lumber crashing down around his ears. He might be forgiven for bad form. He got to his feet, shaking himself free of debris and looking around for Nimueh. At least there was light here—enough to see his troubles weren't over. He might have only fallen six feet, but he'd gone through the steps and onto the kitchen floor. The smoke was thick here, and so was the fighting.

Susan was a limp bundle at his feet. He picked her up again and charged for the door that stood open to the yard. More men were fighting out here in twos and threes, but the smash of weapons was quieter than before. Where there had been a dozen fae against half that number of knights, Dulac saw only a handful of the enemy still on their feet. He jogged away from the burning house, cursing the hot cinders that floated from the roof. Smoke was leaking from the broken shingles and pouring from windows where the glass had been smashed. He set Susan on the grass.

The next moment, Nimueh was beside him, bending down to examine Susan's still form. Dulac studied her a moment, watching the way she moved. Nimueh had always been graceful, but now she was filled with the quick energy he had only rarely seen in her, as if a taste of danger had been an invigorating tonic.

"Are you hurt?" she asked.

"No," he lied, ignoring the bruises he'd have the next day. He put an arm around her, giving in to the need for touch. He could feel her bones move as she reached around to touch his hand. She seemed so fragile. "And you?"

"I'll be fine." She looked into his face then, close enough that their noses all but touched. Her eyes were bloodshot from the smoke, her skin smudged with dirt. "You don't need to worry about me."

"I always do." His chest ached with more than the abuse he'd just taken. "I know you're an enchantress of remarkable power, well able to take care of yourself. Yet you just about stopped my heart when you ran to climb up the house. I need to keep you safe, even if you don't need me to do so."

Her lips parted as if she were about to speak, but she didn't. He was left staring at their soft, plump contours, tasting them in his imagination. He was about to steal a kiss when she put a hand against his chest. "Don't." It wasn't the time or place, but her downcast eyes said her reluctance was more than that. He was wearing down her resistance, but she'd reached her limit of intimacy for right then.

She looked up, her gaze flicking to his before it darted away again. "Susan needs a hospital. Even if doctors can't heal her soul, they can tend her body."

Frustration burned worse than any sword thrust, but he kept his answer brief and to the point. "I can carry her to your car."

"No. If we take her to the hospital, the staff will ask too many questions we can't answer with honesty."

"Are you suggesting that we leave her here alone?" he asked.

Nim shook her head. "I hear sirens far off, but they are coming in this direction. They will bring help."

Dulac listened, but his human ears detected nothing. Still, it was no surprise the neighbors had called in the disturbance. They might be too far away to hear gunshots, but the smoke from the fire would be visible.

"I'll stay," Nim said, "but the knights should leave. A woman is less likely to arouse suspicion than a man with a war ax."

"No," he said automatically. She was the one trying to keep out of sight, and getting her name on a police report was a bad idea. "You go. I'll meet you at your car." With that, he straightened and surveyed the scene.

The fighting had ended. Two of the knights, Hector and Beaumains, were hauling the last of the fae bodies into the burning house. The way the fire was going, it would provide an excellent funeral pyre.

King Arthur stood dangerously close to the conflagration, hands on his hips and breathing hard. Though he was covered in blood and his red-gold hair darkened with sweat, it was easy to see that he was the king. From the set of his head to the way he planted his feet, his posture spoke of a man who dominated his surroundings. And yet, the weariness Dulac saw was real, too. Arthur was as much one of the knights—working and fighting shoulder to shoulder with them—as he was their leader. That was one of the reasons he ruled them without question.

Except for Dulac. Their relationship had always been more complicated, but since coming to this new time and place, Dulac had done his best to keep peace with his king. He approached Arthur, hoping that streak would continue.

"There is an innocent who needs medical attention," said Dulac.

"Who is it?" Arthur replied, his eyes fixed on the kitchen doorway. He visibly relaxed when Hector and Beaumains emerged without their burden.

Some of the knights had scrapes and cuts, but none were seriously hurt. The fae had been badly armed and weakened with soul-hunger, and the only firearm he'd seen had belonged to the male Nimueh had killed. Nevertheless, crazed fae were dangerous enemies. This part of town would be safer with the house and its occupants gone.

"I found the young woman inside," Dulac replied. "I pray we got to her in time."

Arthur made a noise of agreement and followed the direction of Dulac's hand as he pointed toward Susan's still form. Nimueh had disappeared, and he waited for someone to ask about her—but no one did. In all the confusion, she must have slipped away unseen. *Good.*

"Did you know the victim was here?" the king asked. "Or was the fact that she was rescued a happy accident?"

The question didn't surprise Dulac. He'd been vague about the details and silent about Nimueh when he'd called. "I met someone looking into the disappearance of a young relative from the White Hart. The girl was seen speaking to fae moments before she vanished. Details of her story pointed to this place."

Arthur's blue eyes narrowed. He suddenly seemed less pleased than he had a moment before. "And so you decided to investigate?"

"For the girl's sake, yes."

"Then these fae broke the law of lore and magic," said the king. "Ordinary humans should never have known creatures of the shadow realm were hunting here."

"It was a good raid."

The king rounded on him, temper flashing in his gaze. "As happy as I am to rid the world of this place, you should not have undertaken this single-handedly."

Dulac frowned. "I called for assistance."

"You called Gawain, not me. An entire house of rogue fae merits a conversation first. We don't have so many knights that we can take careless risks."

Dulac drew himself up. "And yet the girl was saved and the fae are dead. It appears that we won."

Arthur's jaw bunched, reminding Dulac of his father. Arthur was Dulac's senior by only a few years, but authority made him the parent. Unfortunately, Dulac had never been an easy son to any of his fathers.

Dulac looked pointedly at the burning house. "Our

numbers have grown. We can take these larger targets now."

Arthur paused. Dulac could hear the sirens now.

"That was not your decision to make." The king took a deep breath. "What if I had let this place remain untouched for reasons of strategy you did not know?"

Dulac's temper lunged like a snarling dog, but he held the leash tight. "I would ask you what that strategy was and why I did not know of it until now."

"Perhaps you did not need to know." Arthur's expression darkened. "You are an accomplished general, but you do not understand this world we're in. Not yet. There is a reason I am king. It is my job to understand and lead."

"And mine simply to kill where and when I'm told?"

"You're the well-honed blade I draw when necessary. Weapons don't make strategy."

And weapons didn't get a say in how they were used. Morgan LaFaye wasn't the only ruler with personal assassins; Arthur had unleashed Dulac on Camelot's enemies time and again. "I am more than just a sword."

"I need you to do as I say." The king's cold blue gaze was hard to hold, but Dulac refused to look away. They had been the best of friends once, until Arthur's jealousy over Queen Guinevere had taken root. From that point forward he'd taken out his fury on Dulac in a hundred small ways.

The heat from the fire licked the side of Dulac's face, burning in its intensity. Something popped and sparks flew up into the hazy afternoon blue. It was dangerous to remain so close to the fire, but Dulac would not look away from the king. Not even the attention of the other knights, their curiosity equally uncomfortable, could make him back down.

The sirens cracked the tension, blaring louder now. Arthur gave a quick gesture of dismissal, turning his back to Dulac. "Go. It is time we left this place."

Dulac took a last look at the burning house. By the time the fire engines arrived, there would be nothing left to save.

Turning his back, he went to wait with the injured girl.

Chapter 9

Nim waited by the car for half an hour before Lancelot slid into the passenger seat smelling of smoke and in a bad temper. "Let's go," he said.

Without argument, she complied. She'd bandaged her wound with supplies from the first aid kit she kept in the car and the injury didn't hurt enough to interfere with her driving. She pulled away from the curb and sped down the street.

Lancelot gripped the door handle, seeming to brace himself against the motion of the vehicle. It had been the same when they'd set out for the Price House. Lancelot had a way to go before he was completely comfortable with his new surroundings.

As the buildings slipped by in a blur, the late afternoon heat shimmered in a yellow haze. Just when they were turning the corner, an ambulance flew by. Nim followed the vehicle with her gaze, wondering how Susan fared. The young woman might live or die—and Nim hoped it would be nothing in between. Even in the best outcome, Susan would bear scars on her soul. Nim wished she could help, but she had too much damage of her own to understand how.

As they drove, Lancelot remained silent. Only the tight angle of his jaw revealed the temper he ruthlessly controlled. She knew that look—one of disappointment and anger that said he'd just had an argument. It was astonishing how after all this time she still remembered every one of his expressions.

The idea made her tongue-tied, cautious of conversation that was supposed to be just the surface of a deeper territory that they'd once intimately shared. She was afraid he might peel back her words to find nothing underneath—no soul, no heart, no meaning. Nothing but a ghost of herself stubbornly clinging to survival because she didn't know how to give in.

A ghost, like the fae she'd killed that afternoon. The memory nauseated her.

It was some time before Nim trusted her voice to be cool and collected. "You looked angry when you got into the car," she said. "What happened?"

"Arthur," he said, his tone flat. "Hurtling through time hasn't changed him. He needs to get drunk more often. Perhaps he'll relax."

"Did you expect him to be different in this time?"

"I didn't expect old arguments to travel with us."

Nim decided to leave that statement alone. Arthur's biggest complaint was over Guinevere, and that was one topic she refused to discuss. "I take it you stayed with Susan yourself. I saw the other knights leave before the fire trucks arrived."

"I stayed," Lancelot replied, finally releasing his death grip on the door handle. "I waved the firemen over."

"Did they question you?"

"I didn't give them a chance. They didn't get a good look at me. They were focused on Susan."

Nim cast him an assessing look. "Are you certain?"

"Yes." Dulac shifted in the seat, his big body seeming to hunch against the confines of the car. "Why should I have to worry about being identified? The fae were the criminals. Is there no reward in this time for dealing out justice?"

Nim returned her gaze to the road ahead. "That's the kind of question that never has a satisfactory answer."

He looked out his side window. "There is much about this time I don't understand."

Nim was tempted toward sarcasm, but held her peace. She knew Lancelot wasn't simply grumbling; he actually wanted to find logic in the universe so he could make it better. He didn't deserve her cynicism.

She pulled up to a stoplight and signaled to turn. "I called Antonia and told her that we'd meet at the hospital. Right now I'm taking you home. We can't arrive in a public place covered in soot and blood. That would inspire questions."

"Your home?"

His voice held surprise. It was a mark of trust for a fae to open her doors to a mortal. She'd done that for him once before, but then he'd trampled her gift by walking away. No one else would get a second chance, but today he'd been there when she needed him.

And, though she wouldn't admit it, she was afraid to be alone in her empty condominium. As Merlin had said, it was only safe from assassins up to a point. She hadn't expected to return for one second longer than it would take to put her suitcases in the car.

The light changed and she urged the Audi forward. "After you risked your life to help Susan, the least I can offer is a place to clean up."

"I am always at your service, my lady." The formal words brought back memories, like the wild, sweet sound of a far-off fanfare.

She pulled into an underground parking lot. From there, she led him to an elevator that took them to the fifth floor. Dulac followed her down a narrow carpeted hallway and waited while she unlocked the door of her suite.

"How do you find it living in a building filled with so many humans?" he asked in a low voice so that no one would overhear. "This is like a small village stacked together under a single roof."

"Actually it isn't," she replied, unlocking a second and third dead bolt. "In a village everyone knows their neighbors' business. Here I could raise a dozen demons and no one would notice as long as I kept the smell down."

Lancelot looked up and down the hall as if he was unsure what to make of that. Then Nim invited him inside, trying to visualize her place through his eyes. Her castle in the Forest Sauvage had been a confection of white stone and purple-veined marble, every room filled with objects of rare and colorful beauty. There had been a living tree made all of silver with leaves that chimed whenever a breeze stirred the branches. There had been carpets so thick the cats had to lift their paws high as they padded from room to room. But what she thought of now, with Lancelot there, were the beds—so soft and luxuriant some days she would lie down and lose the will to rise again. Or, at least, that's how she recalled the days and nights when he had been there.

"This is very different," he said. Indeed it was. It said everything about what had happened to Nimueh, and she knew it.

The suite was spacious and scrupulously clean, but it was all sharp angles and almost entirely white. She found the sterility restful because it didn't demand an emotional response. It was also so impersonal that it made the notion of walking away from it easy. "It was the show suite," she explained. "I bought it furnished."

"Ah," he said, eyeing the barely cushioned couch with suspicion. It had spindly black legs that gave it the appearance of being emaciated, as if furniture could starve. If someone with Lancelot's bulk sat on it, there was a reasonable chance it would collapse.

"Come into the kitchen," she said, taking pity on man and couch both. "I don't keep much food in the house, but I have brandy. I think we could both use refreshment after this afternoon's business."

Lancelot followed, his tread sounding heavy on the tiled floor. There hadn't been a man in her place since she'd moved in, and he made the room seem insubstantial. Suddenly she wished for a few more comforts. Before the wars, fae had always been perfect hosts.

She took two glasses down from the half-empty cupboard and poured them each a measure. When he reached for it, she saw the slight hitch in his movement. "You're injured."

"Not so much." He drained the glass in one swallow.

She pushed the bottle his way, leaning against the counter. "You always say that. You'd say that if you'd been chopped into bite-size nuggets, deep fried and served with dipping sauce."

He gave her a curious look. "What?"

Nim realized his acquaintance with fast food had to be mercifully limited. "My apologies. It was a tasteless reference."

He narrowed his eyes. "Was that a pun?"

"I would have to possess a sense of humor to jest." But she had meant it. It was a bad joke, but she was rusty after centuries of being deadly serious. Why Nim was suddenly poking fun at Lancelot was a mystery. She just knew she wanted to, and that made her feel oddly exposed. She didn't normally *want* anything but she was overtired and clearly not herself.

He was still looking at her with suspicion, so she kept her face sober. "Show me your wound."

"Take care of yours first."

"I had time to bandage mine. You go first."

He poured and drank another glass of brandy, but then pulled off his T-shirt with the unconscious ease of a man utterly comfortable with his body. Nim blinked. She couldn't help it—only a lifetime of hard physical activity produced such perfectly proportioned muscles. He had the deep chest and broad shoulders of one trained with lance and broadsword, but his overall physique was lean, with no unnecessary flesh. Like a fine horse or fast car, Lancelot was built for speed as much as strength.

Nim leaned in to examine the nasty bruise forming on Lancelot's shoulder. The dark musk of his scent drew her closer as old instincts stirred to life. She brushed her fingertips over his purpling skin, feeling the heat. The gesture was meant to be clinical, but instead it was deeply intimate. They had been too much to each other, and the memories pressed on her with the iron grip of regret. She cleared her throat. "I'll get you some ice."

"You've always done that for me," he said.

"Get you ice?"

"No—yes. Yes, but more important, you see what I need. Not what I say." His dark eyes searched her face.

"You need to learn to say what you need. We'll all be less confused."

She moved swiftly, all but diving for the refrigerator behind him. She needed to put physical distance between them. She needed those images from the past—Lancelot on the practice field, in her bed, standing as she had first seen him with a wild hunger for experience awake in his brilliant, mortal gaze—to vanish back into the mists of time. But when she turned back, a bag of frozen blueberries in one hand and a towel in the other, her old life confronted her one more time.

She bit her lip, stifling an exclamation. His back was to her, the broad span of his shoulder blades bare. She'd forgotten the map of scars that ran from the base of his neck to his waist, slashing across his skin like the trail of savage claws. Or maybe she'd blocked it out.

Lancelot's back was a ruin of scars left by a sword belt. He'd come to her that way, savaged by a father he'd been desperate to please. As a child, Lancelot had been too young to bear the weight of his father's sword or his father's wrath and yet he had been expected to do both. The harder he tried, the more old King Ban demanded. That heartbreaking, heartbroken thirst for excellence had started the future champion of Camelot on the road to greatness, but that foundation automatically had cracks of self-doubt. She'd tried to mend them with kindness, but she couldn't give a father's love. Not for the first time, she wondered if that was one reason Lancelot had left her to join Arthur's court. He'd still had something to prove, even if his father was dead. What better patriarch to serve than a king, even a young one?

He moved then, scattering her thoughts. It was time to stop dwelling on things she couldn't change.

"I'm glad you're here," he murmured. "Have I said that yet?"

"And I am grateful for you. I owe you many thanks for helping when I asked." With brisk motions, she wrapped the towel around the berries and pressed it to his bruise. "I'm being a terrible hostess. Why don't you get cleaned up? There's a shower through there."

She pointed to the bathroom, one in a trio of identical white doors down a short hallway. The Lady of the Lake was a water fae and the Jacuzzi tub—along with the building's swimming pool—assuaged her need for cool, wet places. Lancelot obeyed her directions with a bemused smile, taking the ice pack with him. Unfortunately, he opened the wrong door. He'd started to close it when she saw him pause, then let the door swing wide to reveal her luggage waiting just inside the bedroom door. "Your suitcases are packed," he said, his voice quiet. "You're leaving."

She could hear the words he didn't say—that she was leaving him when they'd just found each other again. The accusation was more potent than any show of temper. Nim's lungs were suddenly stiff, every breath an effort. "I told you before. LaFaye knows where I am. She won't stop sending her assassins."

His expression was steady, his eyes fathomless. "I can protect you."

"There's no need."

"No need?" He closed the bedroom door as if erasing the existence of her packed bags. "I searched for you. I left Camelot and lived like a wild man in the woods, seeking you in every glen and shadowed thicket of the Forest Sauvage. They thought I'd run mad. Perhaps I did."

Nim was confused. "When was this?"

He tossed the ice pack aside, apparently done with finding comfort. "Before the demon wars. Your castle had disappeared. Even your lake was gone."

"I went back to the Hollow Hills, Lancelot. You said you'd come back to me, but even I could only believe a lie for so long. I went home."

"I didn't lie. I came back."

"You were too late."

"No, I'm not," he said. "I just had to wait a very long time to find you."

She stiffened, pushed beyond endurance for the day.

"Enough. You left me. Maybe you left to serve the king, but you finished by loving the queen."

She'd tried to find him in Camelot, but it had only served to show her how much she didn't fit in. The visit had started well. Arthur had welcomed the Lady of the Lake with great honor, as befitted her rank and accomplishments.

And then everything about the visit went wrong. Guinevere was little more than a child, with a bell-like voice and a fretful pucker between her golden brows. Nimueh saw at once how matters stood between the queen and Lancelot. Guinevere could not do without him, and he raced to tend to her every whim.

Nimueh had left Camelot at first light.

Now Lancelot shook his head sadly. "I became a pawn in a very complicated game. I was a country boy overawed by the brilliance of Camelot. I made a lot of mistakes."

All the while that he'd been speaking, he'd come toward her with the grace of a stalking cat. There was no hesitation, none of the diffidence she remembered in her young knight. This was an older Lancelot, and his expression held no apologies. He took her arms, holding her in place. "Don't go."

She was still sorting through his explanation. Parts of it made sense, but she'd believed in his betrayal too long to revise her thinking so soon. "You left Camelot to look for me?"

"I did. In the end, I walked away from the Round Table. I only went back to Arthur when the war came and I couldn't find you. Whatever my feelings for the king, the mortal realms needed my sword."

"It doesn't matter what happened before," she said, knowing that wasn't true. "In any event, I can't stay now."

"Trust me, you can."

Trust the man who had abandoned her? "No."

The past was only one problem of many. Sooner or later the faery queen would send another assassin, and even if Nim had bound her magic, they could find her if she remained in Carlyle. Lancelot would fight for her if she let him, but that wasn't an acceptable plan. No one fought Nim's battles but Nim.

And yet her brain was moving too slowly to fully grasp those thoughts. Lancelot's gaze was hypnotic, his deep brown eyes pulling her into dangerous waters. "Give me a chance to change your mind."

"No."

As if she hadn't spoken, he leaned in to kiss her. Instinctively, she pulled back but there was nowhere to go. He'd pinned her against the wall and now his hands were braced on either side of her while his body blocked her in. She'd let herself be stalked and trapped. When she began to squirm away, he pressed closer until his bare chest was against her front, his heartbeat hammering against her ribs. It was as if he was trying to fill her with his spirit to make up for all she'd lost.

His breath was hot, his lips soft. "Stay. Give me one day to convince you. No one will come for you for another twenty-four hours."

"How do you know that?" It sounded reasonable, but there was no reason why it should be true.

"Because we just gave the queen something else to think about. The reason Arthur is annoyed is because right or wrong I just kicked over a wasp's nest."

And he'd done it because she'd asked him to. She suddenly saw the enormity of it—it was one thing to patrol and stop a fae in the act of a crime, but today they'd executed fae in their own home. Morgan would have to protest, and Arthur would be forced to answer. No wonder the king was perturbed—but Lancelot had still taken the risk to please her.

And he was right. LaFaye would be distracted for at least a day.

He kissed her again, his palms caressing upward from her hips, up her ribs and finally cupping her breasts with reverence that left Nim shattered and hungry with a single touch. Lancelot didn't make love, he worshipped.

Nim's defenses crumbled away. "One day." Stars, she hoped she hadn't just sealed their doom.

Chapter 10

"It's not fair," complained Gawain through Dulac's smartphone. "Back in the day we killed the dragon and people gave us wenches and mead. Now we kill the dragon, bury the evidence, and we have to show up for work or we get sacked."

"Not to mention the dragon welfare activists," Dulac replied. The comment earned him strange looks as he came up to the huge, arched gate of the Medievaland Theme Park. Happily, Nimueh was at his side, and anyone with eyes in his head was soon admiring her instead.

"Is that a thing?" Gawain asked suspiciously. Dulac noticed that his friend had picked up a great deal of slang from his twenty-first century witch. "Because if it is, the activists have never met a real dragon, much less hugged it."

"I have no idea. I'm here. I'll see you in a minute." Dulac ended the call and slid the phone away. The gate guard recognized him and waved him through the entrance. The evening sun slanted a golden glow over the brilliantly colored pavilions of the park, but the heat hadn't abated one bit. It was nearing seven thirty.

The kiss he'd shared with Nimueh had been long and tender, but he had pushed matters no further. He was coaxing her back to him, and that took skill and patience. Too much too soon would only hurt his cause, and twenty-four hours didn't give him room for setbacks. All he needed was to convince her one day should become two, then four, and then forever.

After he and Nimueh had cleaned up, they'd gone to the hospital to check on Susan. They'd met Antonia there, who'd been tearfully grateful but uncertain about Susan's future. At least the young woman was safe and with her family now.

Dulac's phone chimed a reminder from his pocket. He didn't need to look at it to know what it said. "The show starts soon," he said to Nimueh. "I'll take you to the stands and then I need to get ready."

"Do you really have to take part in the performance?" Nimueh said incredulously. "You've fought a battle and your shoulder is hurt."

Dulac looked down into her questioning gaze, so strange behind the dark contact lenses. He might have said the fight at the Price House was barely a warm-up for a hardened warrior, but decided that sounded less than humble. "The people like to see the jousting, and the money they pay provides an honest living. Besides, the practice keeps us sharp."

Nimueh's beautiful mouth pressed into a thin line. "But your injury gives you pain."

"I've fought with far worse. This is mere play. It's nothing like a real fight." He was glad of that. Lancelot was a warrior of renown, but he didn't take bloodshed lightly. However, the twice-daily tournaments at Medievaland were a game he was fond of winning. As headliners, Gawain and Lancelot usually took the heavily attended evening shift with the best crowds.

"You *want* to do this!" she said with disbelief. "That is hardly logical. You could injure yourself further."

"It would not serve us to cancel a sold-out performance. The police will be curious about the fire. The fae will eventually notice a fringe group of their own are missing. It is best that everything appears normal."

"Very well." Her words were still clipped, but he could see from her expression that she understood. "There is a modern saying that the show must go on."

He kissed her forehead, grateful that she was being protective. It was a good sign. "I'll be careful."

She pushed him away, but her touch was light. "Go. You'll be late. I can find my own way to the stands. It's crowded enough that I'll be safe."

"I'll come find you as soon as I'm done." He kissed her lips this time, letting the moment draw out like sweet honey.

Nimueh pulled back with a gasp, her eyes intent. "If your lance is as practiced as your seduction, no one will be left standing tonight."

"That's the plan."

"Then if you must fight, you will wear my token." Suddenly brisk, she pulled a gold ring from her thumb and pressed it into his palm. "A gift from the fae once guaranteed good luck."

Wearing a lady's token into battle was an old tradition. Whether she was a lover or a patroness or merely someone a knight admired, accepting it was akin to an act of fealty. If he wore Nimueh's ring, he pledged himself to her service.

"I will wear it with honor, my lady." He brought the ring to his lips, then slid it onto the smallest finger of his right hand. The ring was an intricate, twisting design that reminded him of ivy—clearly fae workmanship.

"Then, sir knight, I will cheer you to victory." She gave him a sidelong look. "Go, then, and amaze us all."

So dismissed, Dulac set off at a jog. Unfortunately, the summer crowds of tourists made quick passage through the park next to impossible. He dodged around the lineup for jalapeño dragon fries and down a row of artisans displaying their wares in rustic-looking booths. There were knifemakers, bakers, leatherworkers and dozens of others, all dressed in medieval costume. Every merchant was thronged with enthusiastic shoppers.

Dulac doubted most of the fairgoers understood how little Medievaland represented accurate history, but he didn't care. Fantasy had its purpose. As long as people left their cares at the gates and were happy for a while, that was all that mattered.

Once free of the market stalls, Dulac sprinted across the field toward the tourney area. The basic structure was an oval amphitheater with raised seating on all sides. The central field could be converted for any number of purposes, from archery contests to plays to concerts. Today, its full length would be used for jousting. Dulac heard the roar of the crowd and put on an extra burst of speed.

He bolted past the stand selling tourney souvenirs—wincing at the *Lance-a-lot* cartoon T-shirts—and skidded to a halt in the secure area where the knights and horses armored up. Gawain was there, his shaggy dark head bent as he checked his horse's hoof. The animal was caparisoned in scarlet and gold, and from the excited swish of its tail, it knew it was about to perform. The big destriers, with their feathered fetlocks and proudly arched necks, were almost as popular with the crowds as the knights.

Gawain looked up, his eyes bright with mischief. "You

and I are riding against each other. Ready to take a seat in the dust?"

Dulac patted the horse's neck as he returned Gawain's grin. "Unlikely, old friend. Lady Luck is turning her smiles my way."

With that, he left his friend and found Sir Gareth Beaumains, who was Gawain's youngest brother. Beaumains had once been Lancelot's squire and had taken on that role again for the evening. Chatting cheerfully in the locker room, the younger knight helped him into his gear with the efficiency of long practice, then left to ready his horse. As Dulac waited near the tourney ground, one of the Medievaland employees wearing a page uniform bustled up carrying an armful of roses, each tied with silver ribbon. He passed one to Gawain and then to Lancelot. The petals were a red so dark they appeared almost black.

"Who is this from?" Dulac asked.

"From a fan. There's one for each of the knights," the page said in a harried tone. "She was most specific that you got them personally."

Dulac set his on the table holding bottles of water and snacks for the competitors. He was wearing his lady's token and would not accept that of another. For his part, Gawain held his bloom between thumb and forefinger, casting it a suspicious look. "Where I come from, one does not accept gifts from mysterious ladies without checking for witchcraft."

A young woman with a long, fair braid plucked the flower from Gawain's hand. "Then it's a good thing your intended is a witch."

Gawain moved to snatch it back. "Be careful, Tamsin!"

Laughing, she danced back a step, not taking him seriously at all. "I'm not sure I approve of fans giving roses to my man!"

"Don't you think I deserve adoration?" asked the dark-haired knight. "Am I not the very picture of chivalry?"

"I think you're arrogant enough without slavering females falling at your feet."

Gawain cocked an eyebrow at that. "Fie, woman, would you have me grovel?"

"Keeping you humble is a monumental job, but someone has to do it."

Gawain kissed her cheek with a long-suffering air.

Dulac watched the lively exchange with a smile. Tamsin was the historian at Medievaland, but she was also a powerful witch and healer who had discovered how to bring knights out of the stone sleep, Dulac included. But more important, she was a good mate for Gawain. Not every woman would be strong enough to match his stubborn will, and even fewer could make him laugh that way.

One of the other knights arrived to help Gawain don his armor. Temporarily abandoned, Tamsin turned to Dulac. "Gawain's glad to have you back, you know."

Dulac nodded. "He shows it by the brotherly blows he gives me on the practice field every day."

"That's my sensitive, new age man." Tamsin gave a cheeky smile. "They say emotional memory is stored in the body through trauma. Gawain just wants to be in your thoughts."

With that, she left. Dulac frowned, pondering her words. Tamsin had meant them as a joke, but the modern study of the mind intrigued him. Dulac's body had endured much, both bad and good. Were his father's beatings stored in his flesh? Were Nimueh's caresses? The idea made his mind race, considering possibilities he hadn't known existed before that moment. Was the memory of his love somewhere inside her, too? Could he use that to call her back to him?

Dulac was still turning that over in his mind when, a few minutes later, he mounted his big bay and moved into the starting position. The area that had been set up was about 160 yards long and thirty yards wide. Down the center was the tilt, a fence about five feet high meant to prevent a headlong collision between the two riders. This modern setup was, in his opinion, almost ridiculously safe. In fact, the first few bouts would be no more than passes with a lance. Hand-to-hand combat between opponents would come later, and the free-for-all melee was saved for the grand finale of the show.

Dulac studied the noisy crowd through the raised visor of his helmet. They'd taken to holding up banners with phrases like *Go Gawain* and *Arthur is King*. Today someone had *Love Me Lots Lancelot*. He was tempted to roll his eyes, but he owed respect to anyone who sat in the hot, dusty stands just to see him ride. He looked for Nimueh and found her sitting near the very top.

The emcee's voice boomed over the loudspeakers. "To the north in the red armor we have the Scottish Scourge, Mighty Sir Gawain riding Gringolet and hungering for revenge. His opponent to the south and in the blue armor is the undefeatable Sir Lancelot du Lac on his steed Bucephalus. Hold on to your hats, folks, this is the grudge match you've all been waiting for!"

The crowd cheered. There was no grudge, but this was a show and the two knights did their best to look appropriately fierce. Dulac never underestimated Gawain as an opponent. Dulac had greater skill with a lance, but Gawain had a way of getting creative that landed the unwary in the dirt. The Scottish knight took a theatrical bow from horseback, ostentatiously thrusting the rose into the crest of his helmet.

"Are you ready?" cried the emcee. The audience packed into the outdoor auditorium roared their approval.

Dulac closed his visor and took his lance from Beaumains. His shoulder protested, but not enough to change his mind about fighting. The weapons they used at Medievaland were wooden, tapering to a hollow point over an eleven-foot length. The butt rested in a hook on Dulac's breastplate called an arrêt, which held it steady while hurtling at his opponent at breakneck speed. Much of this was new innovation to Dulac, but the principles were the same as he had learned as a boy—ride very fast and hit your opponent with a long pointy stick.

Dulac dipped the point of his lance in salute to Gawain, who returned the gesture with a jaunty air. The marshal gave the signal and they urged their horses into the charge. Speed was important, but so was the smoothness of the horse's gait and the strength to hold and guide the unwieldy lance. It was all about hitting a very small point at just the right moment. In Dulac's mind, it was mathematics in motion, a problem that he had to solve before the fluid properties of time and space eluded him. Emotion had no place in it. The trick was to be relaxed and willing to wait until the last moment when he raised the tip and knocked his opponent's shield as neatly as a hawk striking its prey.

This bout was no different, though it was all in fun. Through the slits in his visor, he was aware of Gawain barreling down on him, his horse's scarlet caparison flying in the wind. The pounding of his own mount's huge hooves was deafening, his breath heaving within the confines of his padded helmet. He was also acutely aware of Nimueh in the stands, watching him and deciding whether he was worthy of her trust as a protector and a man. But long practice had taught him that doubt and distraction were his enemies. The only thing that mattered was the geometry of distance and angle and the instinct to lift his weapon at the exact moment it was time.

He did. The lance hit with jolting force and he braced himself, using the design of the jousting saddle to keep his seat. He heard the crack of splintering wood and Gawain flew from Gringolet's back, landing in a cloud of dust. A jolt of exaltation soared through Dulac. Lady Luck was indeed smiling on him. It was all he could do to stop himself from twisting in the saddle to reassure himself that Nimueh had witnessed the blow.

Dulac trotted Bucephalus around the tiltyard, lifting his visor to see the crowd waving their signs and cheering. Gawain picked himself up and shook his fist theatrically, swearing to get his own in the next round. It was all a good-natured fairy tale.

Dulac reined in before the emcee, making a final salute before leaving the field to prepare for the next round. When he lifted his eyes, a flash of silver and red caught his attention. When he looked again, he involuntarily recoiled. His horse pranced, picking up on his dislike.

A woman sat near the emcee's booth, holding a bouquet of the roses with the silver bows. With a flick of her long, elegant hand, she threw one at Dulac's feet. A page ran out, picking it up and raising it to Dulac, but he could barely convince his hand to take it. He had no choice. In front of an audience, he could not afford to be discourteous.

But he could not stop his pulse from galloping with dismay. Another might have called the woman lovely. Her fine, pale face was framed with masses of loose black hair that hung to her waist. Though her mouth was a touch too wide, her eyes were large and gray, almost luminous in their clarity. Her tall figure could have graced any painting or any runway she cared to tread. She was, after all, the Queen of Faery.

Morgan LaFaye smiled as if she'd just caught all of Camelot in a trap.

Chapter 11

Nim cheered the spectacle below, raising a triumphant fist as Lancelot knocked Gawain from the saddle.

She yelled and pumped her fist to fit in with the crowd, but in truth there was something contagious about being one of a sea of voices all roaring enthusiasm—and she relished the secret knowledge that this unparalleled warrior wore her token and fought in her name. It had been a long, long time since she'd had a knight to cheer on.

Now she clapped along with the rest as Gawain picked himself up for a bow. Lancelot was playing his part, too, making the destrier rear and prance. He looked her way just once, catching her gaze for a fleeting instant. Even over that impossible distance, she thought she read concern there.

Centuries had passed since anyone had turned their heart and mind to her welfare, and it put Nim off balance. Did she even deserve such care? Nim hadn't been forced to look within for years, hadn't had to weigh and measure the worthiness of her thoughts and actions. By the mere fact of its existence, Lancelot's regard challenged her to be the best version of herself.

Nim craned her neck to see the scene on the field more clearly. Something had gone wrong—she could tell by the way Lancelot had suddenly stiffened. She leaned forward, following the angle of Lancelot's gaze. A moment later, the popcorn she was eating turned to ash in her mouth.

"Oh!" she gasped, breaking into a coughing fit as she inhaled a kernel.

Morgan LaFaye was there! Nim automatically shrank back in her seat, her skin suddenly icy with alarm. She shoved her bag of popcorn aside and grabbed her purse to leave, but then forced herself to be calm. Morgan wouldn't openly attack—not with so many witnesses—and neither could Arthur strike her. The queen's appearance here and now was carefully chosen *not* to result in open hostility.

Even so, Nim's first instinct was to check Merlin's binding spell, testing it with her mind. There were no cracks and no unraveling seams. As Merlin had promised, the protective shell around her magic was complete and she should be well off the radar. So then, if Nim wasn't the immediate target, what was the queen doing here? Could she have found out about the Price House incident already?

Nim watched with bated breath as Lancelot took his place to fight a second opponent. His movements seemed almost slow, as if every muscle was coiled with shock and anger. Oh, Morgan had played her game well, if she'd meant to torture the knights! The show had to go on. Medievaland could not close just because Morgan LaFaye had turned up.

Nim watched Lancelot intently for any sign his shoulder was bothering him, but saw no weakness. His next bout was against Sir Palomedes, the Saracen knight of Camelot and a formidable master of the tiltyard. Palomedes seemed relaxed, and so could not have seen the Queen of Faery. The audience cheered as he hoisted the black-and-white checkerboard of his shield. In another moment, the horses were hurtling forward like graceful thunder.

This time, things did not go so well for Lancelot. He looked her way again, and that destroyed his timing. He brought up his weapon an instant too late. The tip broke against his opponent's shield with a sharp crack, but Palomedes kept his seat. Meanwhile, the Saracen delivered a perfect strike, which sent Lancelot reeling. Nim was on her feet with the rest of the crowd. Lancelot dropped the butt of his lance and grabbed his saddle for support, barely staying on his horse. The crowd made a sound of confusion—a roar of delight at such an expert blow, but also of dismay at seeing a favorite brought low.

And then Palomedes fell from the saddle, arms wheeling. Nim gave a cry of surprise along with the rest of the crowd, but then berated herself for her lack of faith. Lancelot never failed to unseat his opponent—although his distraction had nearly cost him the bout. Palomedes picked himself up and bowed. The crowd gave him a round of applause for his brave showing.

"There you have it, ladies and gentlemen," crowed the emcee. "Sir Palomedes has been defeated by Medievaland's reigning champion, Sir Lancelot!"

Lancelot righted himself in the saddle, but now she could see his shoulder had reached its limit of abuse. She made a soft noise of concern as he stiffly pushed up his visor. No doubt LaFaye's presence had distracted him. She sucked in a breath, tension aching through her whole torso as her hatred for the faery queen found new dimensions.

Lancelot wouldn't ride again that day, and he was clearly too hurt to participate in the melee. He proudly straightened his spine as he left the field with a last farewell wave to the fans, but she knew he would die before admitting to pain. Nim took advantage of the standing ovation, shouldering her purse and edging her way along the bleachers to the stairs. She had to know just how badly he was hurt.

When Nim reached the ground, she circled behind the stands and made her way toward the stables. Mobs of enthusiasts were crowding around the souvenir stands, and she had to wait for the right moment to slip past security and into the performers' area. The locker rooms were past the stables and to Nim's right. She stopped and listened for voices, but all she could hear was the echoing drip of water from the showers. She tread softly over the tile floor, rounding the corner of the battered lockers. Lancelot sat on the wooden bench, an ice pack abandoned on the bench beside him. Above the scarred and sculpted muscles of his back, the bruise she'd seen earlier was now a vibrant shade of plum. He gingerly tugged a clean T-shirt over his head, swearing softly under his breath.

She sprang forward. "Let me help you with that."

Lancelot spun and stood in the same movement, one arm stuck halfway through the sleeve. He pulled it through with a grimace. "What are you doing in here?" His voice was low and tense, but he reached out with one hand and drew her close. "You're trying to stay out of sight, and a beautiful woman stands out in a men's locker room."

She welcomed the contact, finding she needed to touch him before she was sure he was safe. His eyes were wild, the fever of combat still simmering in their depths. She cupped his face with her hands as she'd done so many times long ago. "How badly are you hurt?"

"I'll be fine. Beaumains brought me ice." Trouble clouded his eyes. "It was my own fault. I saw—"

"I saw LaFaye, as well," she interrupted, smoothing his hair with her fingers. "You looked my way. You shouldn't have done that."

"I suddenly wondered if you were safe. In that moment, Palomedes was the lesser threat." He released Nim from the embrace, but she clung a moment longer, wanting to bury herself in his scent of soap and clean cotton. When she finally stepped back, she felt blood rush to her cheeks. This neediness wasn't like her.

"We have to get you away from Medievaland," he said.

Nim tensed, knowing that was logical but wishing he'd said something else. "I would have liked those twenty-four hours where you tried to convince me to stay."

He put a finger under her chin, turning her face to his. His expression was very male, his eyes dark with meaning. "That still stands. I just meant that you should leave the park while LaFaye is here."

"And where should I go? Where is it safe from the queen of the fae?" She'd put her suitcases in the car when she'd left the condo, thinking a hotel might be safer. That seemed flimsy comfort now.

"You're safest wherever I shall be."

The words were simple, but they brought an ache to her chest. His steady brown eyes held hers, seeming to urge her to believe the sincerity of his vow. Her mouth went dry, her pulse quickening. "That's going to put you in danger."

"I'm going to keep you close."

Nim blinked, for once not sure what to do. She was used to steering her own course and had the resources to do it. All the education, riches and beauty of a fae noble had been hers from childhood, not to mention the power bestowed by magic. Even now, she had a plan in place to save herself—but she would end up alone. For once, that wasn't enough.

Lancelot had always been the uncontrollable factor, the element she couldn't provide for herself. He completed her. If she meant to keep him, she had to revise everything she'd assumed about the immediate future. Twenty-four hours suddenly wasn't enough.

She kissed him, surprising him enough she heard the intake of his breath. She savored that spice of the unexpected, along with the warmth of his lips. Then she gathered her wits, finding a shred of her usual cold reason. "I'm going to leave now, when it's busy and I can lose myself in the crowds. You follow when the show is done. If we leave at different times, we'll be less conspicuous."

"We should stay together."

She waved a hand. "No, we should leave one at a time. Until we know why she's here, we should take no chances."

Lancelot reached into his locker and pulled out a set of keys. "Then go to my place and wait for me there."

"Your place?" She took the keys reluctantly as he gave her the address. Despite what she'd just said, she had a sudden dread of parting from him, even for an hour. The sight of the queen had shaken her more than she'd known.

His mouth curled in a lopsided smile. "I have dreamed of you there, eating my food and sleeping beneath my blankets."

"So I am merely there to fulfill your fantasies?" she asked archly.

His eyes filled with fierce protectiveness. "A knight fights best in his own castle."

"I don't want you to fight for me," she said, though the stars knew that was only a half-truth. "I fight my own wars."

"Then call it an alliance," he replied. "Neither of us needs to fight alone this time."

"An alliance." She liked the word. "Very well. That has potential."

He cocked an eyebrow. "I'm all about possibilities."

Nimueh left moments before the locker room filled with knights. Word of Morgan's presence had spread like burning oil, and Lancelot could hear the roar of angry male voices echoing on the tile like thunder. Most were stopping just long enough to ready themselves to patrol the park for fae. Yet Lancelot listened with only half his mind. In the few minutes Nimueh had been with him, everything between them had changed.

His lady had agreed to wait in his home without an argument. It made sense, given the grave situation. Still, Dulac had been a little amused by her solemn acceptance of his door keys, as if they were the means to enter an enchanted realm instead of a messy town house.

Perhaps it was the newness of the situation. Always, their meetings had been in her territory, her castle and with her rules. She had been the mistress and Lancelot her protégé. Now he was taking care of the fiercely independent Lady of the Lake. A rush of pride chased through him. It was a privilege he'd worked long and hard to earn.

It was one he'd all but thrown away once upon a time.

Come with me, Arthur had said so long ago. *A man like you needs to rattle about the world a bit. Try his strength in real combat. You can't find out what you're made of if you hide behind your mistress's skirts.*

But I love my Lady Nimueh, Dulac had replied with all the earnestness of the young.

In the next instant he'd seen something in the king's eyes—a flicker of jealousy. But he hadn't understood the expression for what it was—evidence that a man could be High King, with all the realm at his feet, and still feel empty for want of love.

You should love your king just as well, Arthur had said in a teasing tone. *You should love me first and better. I will show you such adventures as you will never know here. I will make you part of a brotherhood of knights as has never walked this earth before and you shall win fame for*

*your feats of arms. No softhearted woman can make you
a warrior of renown.*

To be fair, Arthur had kept his promises. He had made
Dulac a knight of the Round Table and they had adventured through the mortal realm and beyond. There were
no words to describe the bond Dulac felt with his fellow
warriors. But he could not deny that he'd sacrificed his
love for Nimueh to become a feared soldier. His father
would have approved of the trade, but Dulac regretted it.
He owed the king his duty, but he'd let his heart slip away.
In the end, he'd had nothing left that mattered.

"Dulac?"

He snapped back to the present to find Gawain standing beside him, a grim look darkening his face. "Yes?"
said Dulac.

"Arthur's called a meeting in the clubhouse." Gawain
cast a glance at the other knights, keeping his voice low.
"You and me. We need a plan to deal with our unexpected
guest. Come when you're done here."

Gawain left, and a minute later Dulac left the crowded
locker room. Dulac wanted to go home to be with Nimueh, but dealing with LaFaye was the priority for her as
well as Arthur. Filled with purpose, he stepped into the
performers' area.

The show was done and the seats were emptying out,
the merry chatter of the patrons disembodied in the gathering darkness. The lights of the theme park twinkled where
the midway's Ferris wheel and roller coasters swooped into
the sky. That was the last part of Medievaland to close,
but it was also the farthest away from the buildings Arthur claimed as his headquarters. If anything happened
at their end of the park, the public was safe.

"That was quite a blow you took," said a voice at his
elbow. It was LaFaye.

Chapter 12

Dulac stared with cold, sharp horror. It took all his self-possession to cover his surprise, but he wasn't fast enough. The Queen of Faery's smirk said she'd seen it. He cursed silently, hating that he'd given LaFaye even that much of himself.

"Madam." Dulac made his best bow. "It's true my opponent nearly bested me today."

LaFaye's lips curled. "Humility from Lancelot of the Lake. These new times are strange indeed."

He wasn't sure how LaFaye had crept up on him, but then she was—whatever she was. The queen carried fae blood, but the old royal families had intermarried to the point no one could accurately draw a family tree. Even King Arthur had fae and witch ancestry, though it was generations back. What mattered was that Morgan LaFaye hadn't been touched by the soul-stealing spell that had devastated her subjects, but she was fae enough to use their magic with ease. And, she believed Arthur Pendragon was an upstart who had stolen the crown of Camelot. She wanted it back.

"How may I be of service?" he asked.

LaFaye studied him. There was something odd about her large gray eyes, as if they caught the light like a cat's. It made the skin between his shoulder blades crawl.

"Take me to your king." She looped a hand over his elbow as if they were strolling into a feast hall.

Her touch made him shudder, in part because he did not want to be mistaken for her amour. A glance told him that they were alone, but he didn't trust the evidence of his senses. Right about now the place should have been filled with knights cleaning up from the melee, but he saw and heard nothing. "Have you put a glamour on us? Are we invisible?"

Morgan LaFaye smiled, showing small white teeth. "You did not wear my rose today."

Withholding an answer was her way of establishing control. He decided to play along. "I did not know it was you who sent it."

She laughed, tilting her head back. He could not help but see that her throat was smooth and white. The curves revealed by her low-necked dress were generous though her arms and waist were small. Then again, poisonous fruit was often beautiful. "Putting my name on the flower would ensure you would crush it under your boot heel. Don't be diplomatic, Lancelot. I know you loathe me. It's part of your job as the king's loyal wolf."

"Then, as a loyal wolf, I ask you to swear on your powers that you will abide by the rules of hospitality from this moment until you leave the park grounds. You will not harm anyone, nor cause them to harm themselves or another. You will do your business without magic, trickery or sowing discord. You will not damage or steal anything. You will behave as a guest should and in turn you will be treated as one, without discourtesy or harm. Swear this, or I cannot take you to Arthur."

"You demand much of a queen," she said, a dangerous tone creeping into her words.

For an instant, Dulac felt the cold grip of nerves—but he would be far more worried without LaFaye's promise of good conduct. "By the rules of lore and magic, I demand what I must."

She hesitated a long moment. An oath upon her powers was a serious contract that even LaFaye could not break. To do so would compromise her right to rule as well as her ability to work magic. Her eyes grew hard with displeasure. "Very well. By the rules of lore and magic, upon my powers I swear all that you demand."

Without saying more, he gestured her toward a two-story service building behind the tourney grounds. She walked at his side with perfect ease, clearly confident. He longed to snap her slender, pale neck but it would do no good. Only Excalibur could kill her. Determining what LaFaye wanted was the sole course of action that made sense.

They mounted the steps to the building, their feet loud on the hollow wood. He held the door. "After you, my lady."

With another smile, Morgan LaFaye entered the building Gawain had dubbed the Camelot clubhouse. The building was utilitarian, with a kitchen, bathroom and meeting area on the main floor. Upstairs was an office and an infirmary or sleeping space when needed. It was a far cry from the sumptuous halls of the old Camelot, but it had quickly become the hub of their universe, all the same.

Only Gawain was there, sprawled in an ugly overstuffed chair and with his feet on a low table. He was reading a magazine, the cover featuring a half-clad woman draped over a motorcycle. LaFaye's glamour had to be gone, because Gawain raised his shaggy dark head, surprise blanking his expression. "What's this?" he asked, dropping the magazine and grabbing a knife from his belt.

"A visitor for the king," Dulac replied quickly, holding up a hand as he felt the queen tense. She'd sworn to behave, but self-defense was beyond her promise.

"No need to sound so formal," the queen said with a snarl. Her polite mask dropped as she looked at the dark-haired knight, hatred plain in her eyes. "Sir Gawain and I are old friends."

Gawain's expression clearly said otherwise. Reluctantly, he sheathed the knife. "I will announce your arrival." With that, he stomped up the stairs.

The faery queen finally released Dulac's arm, leaving him with the urge to brush off the last traces of her touch. She wandered about the room, examining everything, until Gawain returned and gestured for them to follow.

The first room on the right was the office. A city map was taped to the back wall with colored pins indicating all the places where enemy fae had been seen. Facing the map, a large whiteboard was usually scrawled with clues to the location of the missing knights, but it had been erased. There was no telling what LaFaye might do with the information.

Arthur sat behind a battered desk piled with file folders, the overhead light glinting on his red-gold hair and neatly trimmed beard. Excalibur leaned against his chair, unsheathed and ready to hand. The Queen of Faery's face darkened the instant she saw it. She would never be entirely safe as long as her kinsman had that sword.

The king rose and Gawain took a position to Arthur's left, Dulac to his right. Shoulder to shoulder, they presented a solid front to LaFaye.

Her gaze locked with the king's. "No doubt you wonder why I'm here."

"To kill me?" Arthur asked, almost indulgently.

"That would be pleasant," said LaFaye. "Destroying you is my fondest wish."

Both Gawain and Arthur reached for weapons, but the Queen of Faery waved them off. "Sir Lancelot made me swear parley. You cannot do me harm. Unfortunately, I can't hurt you, either. We will have to content ourselves with words."

"Then please, sit," Arthur said with a wave toward a threadbare visitor's chair. "Would you like refreshment? I can have coffee sent up. Wine? Soft drink?"

LaFaye ignored the offer. "I have come to protest the murder of my subjects this afternoon. Even if they have fallen prey to soul-hunger, they are mine to punish."

She took a deep breath as if reining in her temper. Arthur waited, not stirring a muscle. Their attack on the Price House was within the rules, but LaFaye would know that. The king wouldn't apologize or explain.

"Furthermore," she went on, "one of my personal servants was murdered last night. We were bonded. I felt the flicker of his life force as it was snuffed out."

"I take it you refer to one of your personal assassins," Arthur said slowly. "I believe they are the only servants bonded in that way?"

She shrugged, finally subsiding into the chair with graceful ease. "Do his duties matter? He was mine. Moreover, he possessed a valuable jewel that belongs to me. I want it returned."

Dulac kept his face neutral. He still hadn't told anyone about Nimueh, much less her assassin. He wasn't about to apologize or explain, either—not until Nimueh was safe.

"I know nothing of your servant or your jewel," Arthur replied. "However, one courtesy demands another. By the rules of lore and magic, if you sent an assassin into Carlyle, you should have consulted with me first. This town is my territory."

"Is it?" she replied with a serpent's smile.

"Of course it is," the king replied, taking his seat in the desk chair as if it were the great lion-headed throne of yore. "The heart of the magic that carried Camelot through the centuries is here, in the Church of the Holy Well that stands at the center of Medievaland. Carlyle is the new Camelot. Here is where I renew my rule of the mortal realms."

Coming from anyone else, the declaration would be grandiloquent nonsense, but Arthur spoke with the authority of a king. If anyone could turn back the fae, he could. That raised Carlyle from an insignificant tourist trap to the nexus of the battle between human and fae. Dulac watched the queen's face and saw the flicker of frustration as her gaze traveled once more to Excalibur, the one weapon that kept her at bay.

"Then I shall consult you now. You have a fugitive in your *territory*—" LaFaye put sarcastic emphasis on the word "—that I want returned. Harboring her is an act of war against my crown."

Dulac stiffened. *Nimueh.*

"Who is it?" Gawain asked, his brows drawn down in thunderous temper. He stood against the wall, arms folded as if to keep them from reaching for the queen's throat.

"The Lady of the Lake," LaFaye said with a curl of her lip. "Nimueh forgot her manners when she helped you murder my son."

"I wouldn't call it murder," Gawain said evenly.

Her gaze threatened to reduce the knight to a smoldering grease spot. "We are enemies and this is war. You live because we have agreed to parley. However, I cannot say there was betrayal on your part, Sir Gawain. You've never pretended to be my friend."

"But not so with the Lady of the Lake?" Arthur propped his chin on one hand, his air deceptively casual. Dulac knew the king well enough to know it for an act.

"I made Nimueh my advisor. I trusted her to keep my son safe. Instead, she did all she could to destroy him."

Dulac shifted uneasily. He doubted Nimueh had volunteered for the post.

As if reading his thoughts, LaFaye turned his way, her lips parted as if she might smile—or perhaps bite. With her, either was possible. "Beware, sir knight. Your lost love has grown a treacherous streak. She is not the noble soul you remember."

A sound came from Dulac's throat, as if he meant to curse or growl but instead did both at once. Arthur gripped his arm. "Peace, Dulac."

LaFaye's eyes narrowed. She'd scored a hit and enjoyed it. "I'd thought the rivalries of our youth were over, but it seems Nimueh still harbors dreams of my destruction. As the current phrase goes, the gloves are off. I want her in my dungeons."

"No!" Dulac snarled. He could hear the pulse roar in his ears and realized he was halfway to seizing LaFaye, parley be damned. His fingers curled into fists.

"No," Arthur said, holding up his hand for silence. "I will not permit it. The Lady has done nothing to harm me or my people."

"That is a foolish move," LaFaye said, her tone sharpening. "First you refuse the return of my jewel, then you murder my subjects, and now you harbor a traitor who betrayed the Crown of Faery. I demand compensation."

"Finally we get to the point of this meeting. What do you want?" Arthur asked in a flat tone.

"Excalibur," she replied.

"We could deliver it directly to your heart." The words were out of Dulac's mouth before he could bite down on them.

Arthur's look was acid. "You may not have my sword."

The queen rose in a liquid movement. "Then bring me

Nimueh. I would like her alive, but I will accept her head. If you do not, I will unleash my armies on Carlyle. You are far from finding all your men, Arthur. You know as well as I do that in a war with the fae, your knights—your friends and only companions on this earth—are too few to do anything but die with courage."

Sweat was starting to bead on Arthur's temples. "And if I agree to this you will simply attack anyway."

"True." Her smile was poison. "But I will give you a year of peace. Think of what you could accomplish in that time. You could find the rest of your men. You could find magic to undermine my schemes. You could finish cementing an alliance with the witches. In other words, you could scrape together a chance of survival."

LaFaye's voice wove around them, every word nudging and molding the truth until what she said seemed entirely reasonable. Dulac had fallen under its spell before, when the queen—then plain Morgan LaFaye—had put him in Guinevere's path, moving him into place like a pawn on a chessboard.

She made a sweeping gesture around the room. "What kind of a king would throw away all the mortal realms to save one soulless fae?"

"What kind of a king betrays an ally?" Dulac shot back.

Arthur touched his arm again, demanding silence. Then he drew a breath and addressed LaFaye. "I must think on what you have said. Give me until the dark of the moon to decide what course I must take."

The queen inclined her head. "The new moon is two days from now. Why should I give you that time?"

"Because if you do, I will give you an answer that is to the point. If you rush me, I will tell you whatever it takes to put you off." The king folded his arms as if making himself comfortable. "Let's not play games, Morgan. Neither of us has time to waste."

She clearly hadn't been expecting this tone. Anger flared across her features. "Very well. But be prepared to make your answer, King of Camelot, when the hour comes. And if you answer the wrong way, be sure there will be consequences."

With that, she left in a swirl of skirts.

They remained utterly silent until her footfalls had descended the stairs and the screen door had slammed shut. Then both knights rounded on their king.

"We cannot do this," Dulac protested.

"This isn't our way," Gawain said to Arthur. "You know Nimueh saved Tamsin and me from Mordred. We would never have found your tomb without her aid."

Arthur bowed his head. "The Lady of the Lake is a fae. Once she was a friend to Camelot, but she has been changed by Merlin's spell. And there is truth in Morgan's words. We are not strong enough to face the fae armies yet."

"We have Excalibur," said Dulac.

"We have one weapon Morgan fears. That is our only advantage."

"We have to find another answer," Dulac insisted.

"That's why I asked for time." Arthur frowned. "Do we know where Nimueh is?"

"No," said Gawain. "She disappeared after Mordred's death. Obviously, she's hiding from her queen."

"Then we must find her."

"Why?" Dulac asked suspiciously.

Arthur massaged his forehead, as if a headache was brewing. Tension and fatigue dragged on his features. "Regardless of how I answer that, the first step is to determine where she is. You knew her best, Dulac."

"I will not hand Nimueh over to LaFaye."

Arthur's pale blue glare could have cut glass. "Your task is to set aside your personal history and do your sworn duty." The king's demand was a physical thing, pushing against Dulac's anger like a closed fist. They had clashed like this before, but there had never been so much at stake.

"I will fight for you," said Dulac. "I will shed my blood to guard the mortal realms, down to the final drop. But I will not help you destroy an innocent."

"The lady hardly qualifies as an innocent."

"That does not make her fair prey."

Arthur raised his eyebrows, comprehension dawning in his face. "You already know where she is."

Chapter 13

"I left then," Dulac said, leaning against the door of his home with a mix of relief and foreboding. "The only surprise was that Arthur let me walk away."

The words hung in the darkening room. His place was a small two-story town house not far from Medievaland. He'd only been in it a few weeks, and it was far from luxurious or even properly furnished—but it was private. He wanted that seclusion now, with his lady.

Perhaps he had even chosen it with her in his thoughts. The glass patio doors of the living room looked onto a wild garden with a rocky slope beyond. The interior was wood and stone, with a fireplace and a thick white rug before the hearth.

"Arthur guessed that you know where I am?" Nimueh said with narrowed eyes. She stood in the living room, backlit by the one table lamp in the corner. The summer evening was finally growing dark.

"I didn't tell him." He heard the defensiveness in his voice.

"No, but you were never a great liar. It's one of your best qualities."

She ducked her head, the bobbed black hair swinging forward to hide her face. He hated the false color. He hated the contact lenses more. Nimueh should never have to hide.

"You say the queen wanted her jewel?" she asked.

"Tramar Lightborn lost it when I killed him. I saw you pick it up."

She seemed surprised that he had noticed that detail. For an instant, he thought she would deny taking the jewel, but she shrugged. "I did."

"Perhaps if you turn it over?" he began, but she shook her head.

"I don't have it any longer. I traded it away that night."

"What for?"

Nimueh hesitated. "A way to hide from LaFaye's assassins. The fact that I'm still alive to tell you is proof that the bargain wasn't wasted."

That raised a thousand more questions, but he stayed focused on what mattered most. "We have two days before the queen wants an answer. How do I put you beyond her reach?"

The words had an effect he didn't expect. Nimueh swayed on her feet, then seemed to crumple onto the battered brown couch. She covered her face with her hands. "I thought I could run and hide. Now—I don't know. If I vanish, what becomes of Camelot? If I don't vanish…" She trailed off with a helpless gesture.

"I don't know," Dulac replied, suddenly awkward. He'd never seen her so lost. He eased onto the couch beside her, wrapping an arm around her shoulders and pulling her into his chest. "The only certainty is that I won't let her have you."

With a sigh, Nimueh pulled away. "That's selfish."

"No, it's practical. Even if Camelot hands you over to buy a year of peace, will that prevent our destruction? Or are we stronger with you at our side? If we start sacrificing each other, LaFaye's brand of cruelty has won. That's hardly a victory."

She looked at him sharply. "What are you proposing?"

"You stay here with me. We hide or we fight, but we don't surrender."

She stared at him, her brows drawn together. "Do you seriously mean that?"

It was a ridiculous question, but she clearly spoke from the heart.

"Of course," he answered, because she obviously needed to hear it. "I'm at your side, Nimueh. No exceptions."

The corners of her mouth jerked downward and for a moment he thought his supposedly soulless fae was about to cry. His heart seized and he reached out, but she raised her hands. "Wait."

Dulac stopped. "What is it?"

Her breath had gone ragged. She wiped her face with her sleeve and looked up, shaking her hair into place. "I need a drink. Please."

The agitation in her voice was oddly beautiful, a sign of the emotions he had longed for. He hid a smile behind an obedient nod. "Right away."

Dulac retreated to the kitchen, which was the most neglected room in his new home. Gawain's witch, Tamsin Greene, had equipped it with the basics. It was a kind act, but he had barely opened the cupboards since. However, a few bottles of wine reclined in a folding wooden rack on the counter. He grabbed one, drew his boot knife and attacked the foil top.

The business of uncorking the bottle gave him a moment to gather his thoughts. He missed true silence, without the constant hum and rumble of traffic and appliances. He preferred firelight to the harsh glare of electricity. He missed the clean bite of truly fresh air. And yet he was where he had chosen to be, with Nimueh in this new world. It was up to him to adapt. It was up to him to keep her safe and make this reunion work.

He poured the wine into two glasses, slightly reassured by the heady smell of the red vintage. Wine was at least a little bit the same as he remembered it, but the glasses were impossibly fine, so delicate he feared crushing them every time he picked one up. In his day, goblets were of metal, heavy and durable. Good in a fight, like him.

But Nimueh was, at the moment, as breakable as the glasses. It was plain she was recovering her emotions—more each time he saw her. The flatness was leaving her expression and her voice. What did that feel like? Chaotic? Painful? Strange? His mind—so attuned to war and conflict—said that they should be making battle plans against LaFaye. His instincts warned him Nimueh needed a moment of tranquillity.

He picked up the glasses and went into the living room where Nimueh reclined on the couch, her face drawn with exhaustion. Taking the wine, she moved her long legs so he could sit down. "Thank you."

He sat, leaning back so he could look at her. She'd obviously retrieved her suitcases from the Audi because she'd changed her clothes. She was wearing leggings and a long blue sweater, her feet bare so that he could see the long delicate bones.

"Your toenails are painted bright green." He found the sight amusing and faintly disturbing at the same time. "It reminds me of a mer-creature I once knew. She ate a lot of raw fish."

Nimueh tucked her feet out of sight beneath her. "It is

the fashion," she said primly. "Part of hiding as a human is behaving as they do."

"And painting your toes is a mark of humanity?"

She sipped her wine. "It is never one thing you do or don't do. It is the accumulation of a pattern that people notice. Humans are smarter than one might think."

"Surely you jest," he said drily, taking a swallow of the wine and setting it aside.

She gave him a look he remembered well, part scolding and part indulgence. She'd left the contact lenses out to reveal the emerald brilliance of her eyes. Up close, he could see the iris held a dozen shades of green rimmed in deepest black. In the darkness, they refracted light like a cat's. No one would mistake them for human, but he found them unbearably beautiful because they were hers.

He slid his hand over her ankle, circling it with his broad palm. Her dark olive skin was silky and warm. Her body held such delights, such secrets he'd taken joy in discovering. Then he thought of what Tamsin had said about memory and emotion stored in the flesh. If that worked with negative experience, did it work with pleasure, too?

"What are you doing?" she demanded, her foot shifting so those bright green toes peeped out again. He was starting to get used to the look.

"I'm petting you," he said, sliding his hand over the curve of her calf. Her soft gray leggings molded to her shape, leaving nothing to the imagination. Modern clothes had their advantages.

"Why?" she demanded, her glass clutched in both hands.

"To awaken your flesh. It remembers that you want this." His hand reached her knee, but he went no farther, just started the motion again.

She stilled, her brilliant eyes growing wide. "How dare you tell me what I want."

"I dare because you need me to," Dulac replied.

"I'm not like I was," she said quickly. "I'm a book with half the pages missing."

"But I remember the story. I can fill it in." His hand curved over her knee, cupping it gently before his fingers eased along the slender arch that ran outside her thigh and toward her hip. When he reached the hem of her long sweater, he simply carried on, pushing it up as he went. "Do you like it when I do that?"

She drank down the wine in one long draw and set the glass beside the couch. "Yes."

Nimueh shifted so that she leaned against him, her weight against his chest. Dulac slid his arm around her shoulders, pulling her close. "I'll take you in pieces if I have to. Whatever you are, I want it."

"Why?"

He thought he saw tears in her eyes and he scrambled for an answer. "I don't have a single reason. In truth there are too many to count."

"Tell me one. I won't believe you any other way."

"You were the first real family I had."

She looked up, searching his face. "What do you mean?"

"You know where I came from," he said softly.

His father had been King Ban of Benoic, one of the thirteen kings conquered by Camelot to stop the many small wars tearing the land apart. Endless fighting had left Dulac's country poor, with barren fields and no one left alive to plant them. Hunger and sickness took the few who were left, including his mother. King Ban, however, would never abandon his pride.

The only thing a man needs to know is how to use his strength, Ban had told his son. *The rest comes naturally once you've made it clear who is in charge.*

The soldier—or son—who failed to excel in battle felt Ban's lash. Dulac learned the arts of war with almost supernatural ease, but that only made his father demand more. Some days the dried blood made it impossible to remove his shirt, much less fight, and the cycle of pain would begin again. It was clear to all that defeat had turned the king's mind, but none would interfere with the right of a father to raise his heir.

The torment only ended when his father's enemies—spurred on by yet another meaningless dispute—burned their home to the ground and his father's corpse with it. From a hilltop too far away to ride to the rescue, Dulac had watched the flames with a mixture of relief and despair, for he had nothing but the armor he stood in. After the ashes were cold, he had ridden away to seek his fortune. He knew nothing but killing, but he was very, very good at it. Wars needed soldiers, and war was never hard to find.

How little had he expected to find love and kindness instead.

"I could barely write my own name when I met you," Dulac said now, "and yet you never made me feel small."

"You were never small. You've always been twice my size."

With that, she bit her lip. In another, the gesture might have been saucy, but with Nimueh it was an expression of suppressed fire. He picked her up, setting her in his lap. She settled in, bracing her hands on his shoulders as he slid his hands under her sweater to span her waist. He felt her muscles flex as she bent forward to kiss his brow. "I don't know why you don't find a good mortal woman. There is a world filled with females who would be eager to please you. I am a bad bargain."

"Is that so?" He ran his thumbs over the curve of her ribs. The touch made her sway forward, arching into it like a cat. He slid one hand higher, finding nothing but Nimueh beneath the sweater. His hand cupped her breast. The soft, generous weight was familiar and filled him with re-membered longing. He'd missed her so much.

"I wish you would smile," she said.

"I will when you do."

"Then make me."

Dulac had the sweater off her before she could protest. Wordlessly, she shook her hair back into place and leaned forward, taking his mouth with hers. Her first kiss was tentative, a brush of heat that left him hungry. The second ripped a growl from his throat as she plundered his mouth, her tongue seeking his. He sank back until his head rested on the cushioned arm of the couch, Nimueh leaning for-ward so their lips did not part. The taste of her was like wild berries, sweet and tart at once. She nipped his lip, a tease with just enough bite to send a prickle down his neck. There was nothing tame about Nimueh, however carefully she hid her nature in books and formulae.

"What could another woman give me that you cannot?" he whispered. It was more like a groan.

She sat back on her heels, looking down at him from under slit lids. The room was dark, the only illumina-tion the single lamp and the stray light creeping in from the kitchen. It made her eyes flash like winking gems, mysterious and strange. "Safety. She would bind your life around with garlands of comfort and surety. She would keep your hearth and home and fill it with kindness. Your future would be known and beloved, a tale well told and filled with love and laughter. I foresaw this future for you in my gazing crystal, long before you went into the stone sleep. I hoped you would have found her before now. Per-haps you still can."

"She sounds marvelous. A paragon. Undoubtedly a good wife and mother."

"Many long for a crumb of such happiness as she could give."

"Who is she?" he asked.

"I do not know. Magic rarely works in specifics."

"Well," said Dulac, "when we find her we should introduce her to Beaumains. She sounds like his type. Or maybe Palomedes. For all his talk of quests, he likes his domestic comforts."

Nimueh let out an exasperated breath. "Why not you?"

"I have you."

"I am fae."

"The fae love ardently." He pushed a lock of hair from her eyes. It was thick and springy, full of life. "I have tried mortal women and found them wanting. You are my first and only real love. I swear this."

A moment passed during which neither said a thing. Then Nimueh caught his hand, bringing it to her lips. Her breath was hot, sending a surge of electricity along his nerves. With her eyes closed, she gripped his fingers as if he were a lifeline and the only thing keeping her from a fall into darkness. "I shall try for you. I shall try to be the woman you want and need, but I can promise nothing."

There was no more he could ask. He cupped her cheek and she leaned against it, a pucker between her fine eyebrows. Slowly, slowly, she sank down until she rested against his chest, their legs tangling together on the couch. Her fingers gripped his shirt in a tight fist as if he might escape. Strangely humbled by her surrender, he wrapped his arms around her, holding her close. He could feel the beat of her heart, quick and urgent as a fine trembling ran through her, as if she were a bowstring drawn tight.

She was afraid, but he knew it was not simply of Morgan LaFaye.

Chapter 14

Nim dreamed, and it began beautifully.

It had been a brilliant April day when the procession from Camelot had ridden into Nim's part of the Forest Sauvage. The green meadows were starred with wildflowers and the treetops filled with joyous birdsong.

First, she had heard the silver bells hung from the horses' bridles, and then the lilting voices of the minstrels. She'd been picking herbs, but put down her basket to search out the unexpected visitors.

Nim had been startled to see it was the royal court from Camelot. Arthur had ridden at the head of the party, resplendent in scarlet silks. He'd been little more than a youth, his face still shining with an open innocence that he'd slowly lose as the years passed and the crown grew heavy on his brow. But back then, his merriment was almost childlike, yearning for laughter and the wonders of magic. Knights and ladies followed the young king two by two, each one in costly finery and dazzling jewels. They were the handsomest company Nimueh had ever seen.

"Where do you go, King of Camelot?" Nimueh had asked. "May I offer you bread and wine?"

"My kinswoman tells me there is a mighty warrior beneath your roof," Arthur answered. "I would make him my sworn knight."

The sun hung in a clear sky, but Nimueh felt its warmth no longer. "Who is this kinswoman and how does she know my affairs?"

"Her name is Morgan LaFaye," said the king.

That was the first time Nimueh had heard of the woman who would someday become Queen of Faery. Still, the name stirred a dread premonition. With a cold feeling in her stomach, Nimueh invited the king and his company to feast with her, sparing nothing that might tempt the appetite or slake the courtiers' thirst. There was honey wine and wild game, exotic fruits and sweetmeats fragrant with spices. But she warned Lancelot to remain in his chambers, so keeping him away from the king. She could not admit the truth to herself, but she loved Lancelot too much to risk that he might leave her.

The moon had risen and the guests were yawning when LaFaye at last crossed the feast hall to sit and speak with Nimueh. "For shame," said the dark-haired sorceress, "you keep your warrior hidden."

"How do you know of him?" Nimueh asked.

LaFaye lowered her lashes. "I have some small skill in magic. I asked for a vision of the mightiest warrior in all the land, and my spell led me here."

Something in the young woman's manner put Nimueh on alert, but she would not be rude to a guest. "It was very clever of you to find my hero, but I am not ready to let him go."

Morgan LaFaye set a pale hand on Nimueh's sleeve. "I

entreat you to reconsider. With Arthur, your warrior will be knighted and earn a name of great renown. It would be cruel to deny a young man his destiny. Love is not love if it holds its object too tight."

Shame filled Nimueh, burning her cheeks a dusky rose. Lancelot yearned to make his fortune and restore his family's good name, and the king could give him that chance. LaFaye saw her embarrassment and shook her head, jeweled combs winking in the masses of her dark hair. "Ah, my lady, the fae are so jealous of their mortal servants."

"Lancelot is no servant."

"Isn't he?" chided Morgan. "Then bring him here and let him decide his own fate."

Nim woke with a start, her heart pounding. She was disoriented, half in the past and—well, in truth she didn't know where she was. Morgan's smirk seemed to hang in the darkness around her, mocking as a sense of dread ruffled the hairs along her nape.

It was a dream, she told herself. That was what they did, clinging and trailing cold fingers down a person's mind. She hadn't dreamed since… She couldn't remember when.

Nim's fingers explored, finding a bedsheet beneath her hand. It was a long, tense moment before she fought free of the dream and recalled the night before. She and Lancelot had kissed until fatigue and wine had won out. They had fallen asleep on the couch and, at some point in the night, he had carried her upstairs to his bed. She'd taken off her clothes but he'd let her sleep, rightly guessing she needed comforting more than sex. She lay next to him now, curled in the soft sheets. The night had finally grown cool, but Lancelot was a long line of warmth at her back.

That heat was a detail she'd forgotten about him, but she burrowed into it now, listening to the slow rhythm of his breaths. He'd draped an arm over her waist, one big hand curled loosely before her. Slowly, not wanting to wake him, she brushed her fingers against his. Touch revealed so much—the callus where he held his sword, the fine lines of scars, the broad strength of his palm. He'd killed with those hands far too often, but few knew how capably he could comfort. Those who only saw the swordsman in Lancelot missed the best part of him.

She slid her fingers between his, barely able to fit his massive grip. They had so much history, even long before the night she had dreamed about. He had come to her when he had just crossed the threshold into manhood. Young Lancelot had been oddly innocent and world-weary at the same time. He'd been a challenge to teach until she'd won his trust and then, as the years passed, he had begun to teach her. Nim had been young then—at least by fae standards. She'd never experienced a mortal's love, or indeed much romantic love at all. Lancelot had been a revelation.

The memory, which should have been a comfort, made her muscles stiffen. Waves of apprehension coursed through her—there was no other name for what she felt. She had changed since the days of her castle in the Forest Sauvage. True, her ability to experience emotion was gradually returning, but she wasn't sure why it was happening, much less why now. Was it Lancelot and all the memories he brought with him? Or—more likely—exposing herself to more of Merlin's magic?

Whatever the reason, experience had reforged Nim, but she had no idea of her new shape or purpose. When her new self was finally revealed, would Lancelot still want her?

He'd left her once. Nim squeezed her eyes shut. Without feelings, she'd experienced a kind of deathly peace because nothing ever mattered. A tiny part of her missed that stability. The little bit of emotion she'd regained already had her tied in knots.

Lancelot's hand squeezed hers, letting her know he was awake. Welcoming the contact, Nim turned in the circle of his arm so they were face-to-face. Automatically, her hands went to his chest. She seemed unable to stop herself from touching the hard ridges of muscle every chance she got.

"You're petting me," he murmured.

"Are you complaining?"

Instead of answering, he slid a hand to her hip, his palm warm and pleasantly abrasive. He hooked her knee, drawing it over his thigh so that the space between them disappeared. Then he found her mouth with his. The closeness, the touch reawakened memories of nights long ago—and memories of joy. A hot, aching pressure grew inside Nim's chest, threatening to suffocate her, but at the same time making her spirit soar. She felt giddy, tears burning and an urge to laugh competing until she had to break the kiss and gasp in a great lungful of air.

"What is it?" he asked, concern softening the words. "Are you well?"

"I think I'm happy." Her words sounded small and bewildered.

"Good." He kissed her temple. "You're out of practice."

She was, and she felt clumsy and stiff with the experience, as if all her protective armor had been stripped away. Numb was predictable. This was most certainly not.

Nim put a hand to his cheek, her fingers exploring the shape of his cheekbone. The touch should have been natural, but voices chattered in her mind, wondering if she was moving too slowly, or if she should hold herself back. Suddenly she, an ancient fae, felt as awkward as a teenager.

"Hush," he murmured. "I can hear you thinking."

"I can't help it."

"I can." With that, he rolled onto his elbow, leaning over her until she had no choice but to lie back on the pillow.

He traced the curve of her breast, cupping it with exquisite care. Yet, for all his gentleness, there was a burning possessiveness in the gesture, as if he was measuring the territory he meant to reclaim. He slid his thumb around the nipple, rolling it until it ached. Instinctively, she pushed into his touch, needing the pressure to still the electric need pulsing through her. She pressed against him until she could feel every beat of his heart.

She slid a hand toward his shaft, which lay hard and thick against her hip, but he pushed her hand away. "No, this time is about you."

"I don't understand."

"Trust me."

This time his kiss demanded more, his tongue teasing until a spark caught fire deep in her belly. She shivered as his long, rough fingers glided to the inside of her thigh, working their way up and up until they found the cleft at the top. Nim inhaled sharply as they stroked the curls and folds of her, working that burn of need until she squirmed restlessly beneath him.

She had remembered his touch, but as a faded image of the original. Now brilliant reality came crashing back, primal and demanding. A desperate sound tore from her throat as his finger slipped inside her, reawakening sensations she'd long believed lost. She felt the slide of wetness as she pushed up, greedily seeking more.

"That's it." He stroked and coaxed, sliding in a second finger as her hips rolled, questing for resistance. She was on fire, burning and imploding at once. Nim dug her fingers into the hard flesh of his shoulders, wanting him inside her. Darkness rose, a yearning to claw and bite to get her way, but he had her firmly under his control.

Nimueh hated it. She hated him for making her desire him so completely. She adored him for the same reason, needing him never to stop. Her emotions were new and raw, vulnerable as fledglings.

It was too much at once. She shuddered, the world turning dark and blindingly bright at once, smashing conscious thought to splinters. Her back arched, straining against Lancelot's solid form as ecstatic release swept through her after centuries of nothingness. Nim cried out, a brief exclamation of shock and relief, and then she could say no more as her body wrung every last drop of pleasure from the moment. Consciousness flared and splintered, tearing her mind wide open.

When she finally fell back, the room spun. After so long, her every nerve was overwhelmed.

Lancelot bent and traced her forehead with soft, barely tangible kisses, lingering against the closed lids of her eyes, her nose and finally her lips. They weren't kisses to arouse, but to reassure and seal the experience with meticulous care. He seemed to know she had experienced as much as she could take that night. Any more, and she would shatter completely.

"Will you sleep now?" he asked softly.

"I don't know." Languor melted her bones, but she was still strangely wakeful.

"What kept you up?" His fingers rested lightly on her forehead, as if he could feel her thoughts.

"I dreamed of LaFaye. I dreamed of the night she convinced me to introduce you to Arthur."

He made a considering noise. "She persuaded me that going with Arthur was the only possible future for me. It took me a long time to understand Morgan was playing a complicated game and I was just a piece on the board. I'd seen the brutality of war and the savagery of my father, but I'd never experienced that kind of cunning. I was clay in her hands."

"So was I," said Nim with brutal honesty.

"That's the past. This is the future." Lancelot leaned over, pressing his lips to her temple. The touch settled her and she curled into his chest, basking in the male warmth of his body. She fell asleep.

Nimueh dreamed again.

In that dream Nimueh awoke in her castle in the Forest Sauvage. It was early, the sky still pearly with a false dawn. The first thing she felt was the cooling place in the bed beside her. Lancelot often rose before her to go for a ride, but that morning felt different, as if a storm hung in the air. Panic touched her and she grabbed her robe, running over the flagstones of the castle floor in her bare feet. When she reached the door, she hesitated, looking out into the morning mist limned by the first rays of morning. Then, obeying only her troubled spirit, she sprinted forward.

Outside, the grass was heavy with dew and it was easy to see which way he'd gone. She found Lancelot at the edge of the woods, astride his horse and staring down the path where Arthur and his courtiers had ridden away a month before. Lancelot had stayed with her out of loyalty, but the seed of his future had taken root. He dismounted when he saw her, guilt plain on his features.

The look seared her, branding her as a selfish, controlling creature. He'd come to her like a sculpture half-carved and unfinished. She'd smoothed edges and shaped what she could, but her work was done. It was natural that he had to find his own way from here.

And yet her heart would surely break. She clutched her robe tight, an ache in her throat beginning to build. "Go. I cannot keep you to myself anymore."

He closed his eyes, so still he seemed an artwork instead of a man. "I wish the king had never come."

So do I, she thought, but she had to be better than that for his sake. "I will keep you in my heart." Her voice broke on the last word, destroying all the dignity she'd held around her like a shield.

"I'm so sorry." Lancelot grasped her then, holding her so hard she could barely breathe. "Please understand that I will never have a chance like this again."

Never was such a mortal word, filled with urgency and doom. Her world was forever, with all the loneliness that implied. He kissed her mouth and then the tears from her face, his caresses stiff with misery. Loss shattered her resolve. "Don't go."

"I'm sorry," he said, finally pulling away.

"I'm sorry," he repeated, mounting his horse.

"I'm sorry," he said yet one more time as he crushed her heart.

He rode away and never looked back. Nimueh stood and watched him go, her bare feet chilled by the morning dew.

Chapter 15

Dulac rolled out of bed before registering the fact he was awake. He'd learned to be instantly alert on the battlefield, but this time the enemy was no horde of goblins or shrieking Northmen. This time his foe was an empty bed. The sheets were cold where Nimueh should have been.

He pulled on his jeans and hurried downstairs to the kitchen, cursing his shoulder as he struggled into his shirt. He found Nimueh sitting at the wooden table. As if the sight of him filled her with anxiety, she rose as he came in. She was neatly dressed in a blouse and slim denim skirt, her legs and feet bare, but dark circles underlined her eyes. She'd pushed her fingers into her hair, leaving it wild. He was reminded of a windblown bird, its feathers too broken to fly.

This was a different Nimueh than he remembered. The lady he'd known had never faltered—at least not until that last day when he'd left. He'd hoped never to see that look on her face again, but this was perilously close.

He took a step toward her but she tensed. "Did you still have trouble sleeping?" he asked.

"I had more dreams," she replied, wrapping her arms across her stomach. "Did you know the fae don't dream anymore?"

"Then it's a good sign that you had them."

"I would have said yes until last night."

Her tone left little doubt it had been a nightmare. "What did you dream about?"

She didn't answer. Giving her time, he went to the sink and began making coffee. He'd discovered he liked the dark, strong brew and today he had a feeling he'd need it. The silence dragged from seconds to minutes.

"When I fell back asleep, I dreamed about the day you left to join Arthur." The words rushed from her on a single breath. "I've always remembered how much you hurt me but this time I remembered how I hurt you, too. That was worse."

Dulac flipped the switch to start the brew, but he'd lost interest in beverages. Iron bands of tension gripped his chest. He'd heard the expression about the elephant in the room, and this was theirs. That elephant was standing on his lungs.

He turned to face her. "That was long ago. Longer even for you than for me. Don't bind us to the past."

"I don't have anything else to go on."

"Then believe this. I have never loved anyone but you, but you made that very hard to prove. You would visit Camelot, but I'd never learn you were there until you were gone. Then I would try to visit you, but you kept the castle hidden from me."

He saw her flinch. "I was angry."

"Why? I was trying to keep us together. You made it impossible for me to see you alone."

"There was Guinevere." She seemed to choke on the name.

And there was the elephant's mate. Dulac was speechless, not because he had no answer, but he was so unutterably weary of giving it again and again to those who refused to believe the truth. But Nimueh had not asked until now, so he owed her the story. "It was not what you think."

"What do I think?"

"The same thing Arthur thought. The same thing everyone believes. That we were lovers."

"And weren't you?"

"No." He reached for his sword hilt as if it were a comfort object, but found he was wearing only jeans. He folded his arms instead. "No."

"But she was as lovely as a May morning. All the poets said so."

Nimueh was jealous. He could hear it in her voice. He hoped that meant she still wanted him. If that was true, maybe she would be willing to sweep away this barrier between them.

"Guinevere was lovely," he admitted. "I was dazzled by her, as I was dazzled by everything at Camelot. It was so much larger and richer than my father's castle, and so full of people and feasts and tourneys and wonders. Arthur—the high king, no less—offered me friendship and praised my feats of arms. For a young knight, that was a heady brew. I lost my way for a time, but I swear to you I did not lose my honor."

"Arthur swears you did."

Dulac hung his head. "The lies about myself and Guinevere were repeated over and over—by Morgan, by Mordred and eventually by everyone. What was he supposed to believe?"

"He was your friend. He should have believed the truth."

As she should have believed the truth, but he did not

say it. Nimueh had been alone, abandoned by him, and letting rumors work on her imagination. Pointing that out wouldn't heal this breach. They both bore some of the blame.

"Arthur couldn't afford to believe me. That would have been an admission that his great, royal marriage was a simple, everyday failure. Betrayal is much more stylish." Lancelot sighed. "Arthur knows the truth, he simply doesn't want to face it."

"I don't understand," said Nimueh. "He lost you as a friend."

"The wedding was a foolish business. Arthur admired Guinevere's beauty, but they had met only once before, when the wedding contract was signed. A high king consolidating his power over thirteen fractious vassals has no time for courtship, and poor Gwen was homesick and bored. I knew what it was like to be alone at a strange court and showed her what courtesies I could."

"And she fell in love with you," Nimueh guessed.

"No." Dulac leaned against the wall. "It was never so simple. Perhaps at first she saw me as a romantic figure, perhaps not. Guinevere was barely sixteen and sold for her looks and breeding to a king who barely remembered he had a bride."

"Of course she wanted someone to rescue her."

"Hardly." Dulac felt a spike of temper, even after all this time. "Gwen wanted revenge. She wanted to make Arthur jealous. It would have been ridiculous except it worked."

Nimueh sat slowly, folding her hands in her lap. "When did you figure that out?"

"Too late. I believed her lonely and felt sorry for her. You see, we had common ground. People only saw her pretty face and my mighty sword arm. We made it our business to see the rest of each other."

"You were friends?"

"Yes. I took her riding, read to her, and showed her how to fly her falcon. We talked for hours."

Silence fell except for the hiss of the coffeemaker as steam collected and fell on the hot plate. "That is sad," Nimueh said at last. "For their marriage, I mean."

"Arthur and Guinevere never learned how to love one another. I became a weapon they used in their endless fights. When I finally saw how things stood, I left the court. I wanted no part in their misery."

"I thought Arthur sent you away."

"I left," he said, anger rising at the memory. "Camelot paid the price for our collective folly. The king couldn't afford to take his mind from running the kingdom, and in the end Gwen and I were the ultimate distraction. Things fell apart. That was the work of Mordred and Morgan, you can wager upon it."

Nimueh simply watched him with grave green eyes.

Dulac cleared his throat. "That was the fall of Arthur's reign. It crumbled when all anyone could talk of was the royal scandal. At the height of his fury, Arthur threatened to burn Guinevere at the stake. Then, for better or worse, we went to war with the demons instead."

Nimueh sat back in her chair. "You're right. Arthur wouldn't have believed such lies if he hadn't felt guilty. He knew he was in the wrong."

Dulac held her gaze, all but losing himself in those brilliant green depths. "Then you believe me?" He needed her to say yes. His fists clenched, holding back the need to grab Nimueh until she absolved him.

"I believe you about Guinevere," she said, the words hushed.

The elephant crushing his lungs vanished, and he hauled in a deep breath. "Good."

"But you still left me for Camelot. Now Arthur wants

to give me to LaFaye. How do I know you won't choose him again?"

"I will show you why." He was done talking.

Nimueh's eyes went huge and wary as she rose from her chair. With her messy dark hair, the effect was waiflike, as if she had never been a grand lady of the fae.

The kitchen was small, and one stride was enough to close the distance between them. The wall was at her back, trapping her in place. He put his hands on her hips, stroking the silk of her skin above the rough denim of her skirt. The contrast of texture lit a fire in his blood and a pleasurable ache began to pound low in his belly—but he knew he had to take this slowly. He pressed his lips to her forehead, making the gesture almost a benediction.

"Do you believe me yet?" he asked.

Her eyelids fluttered closed, then snapped open to catch his gaze. "Keep going. You've only got twenty-four hours, remember?"

"Then don't interrupt." It wasn't easy to hold the green fire of her gaze. Her power wasn't just magic; it was Nimueh herself. Instinct told him he had one chance to reclaim her, one chance to do what he had traveled through centuries to accomplish.

He grasped Nimueh's hips and lifted her. She gasped, hands bracing against his shoulders, but he sat her on the table, putting his body between her knees. The table behind her was clear of dishes and debris, but then he hardly ever ate there. That meant eating alone, and he was done with solitude.

With unmistakable intent, he lowered his lips to hers. Nimueh stiffened, holding back until finally his will prevailed. As if coming to a decision, she released a breath and allowed her mouth to soften under his. Dulac leaned closer, drinking her in at his leisure. The kiss went straight to his sex, but he forced himself to be patient. Taking his time, he trailed kisses down her long, graceful neck, tasting her pulse with his tongue. Her crisp white blouse set off the rich hue of her skin, enticing him to explore the arch of her collarbone and the valley beneath the V of her prim cotton top. But the more skin he claimed, the more he desired.

He reached for the tiny buttons of the blouse but she was there first, her long fingers deft. Whatever decision she'd made, she'd made it completely. The garment parted with a rustle, unveiling a dainty confection of white lace. Dulac groaned in approval, but she unhooked the bra and let it fall before he had a chance to fully study its effect.

The loss didn't matter. Nimueh herself was revealed, the dark buds of her nipples ripe against the smooth globes of her breasts. She arched her back as he bent to take her in his mouth, a moan coming from low in her throat. The sound spoke to the primitive male inside him, making him go hard. He moved to the other breast as she shivered beneath him, cradling his head until he'd teased her to a tight peak.

Dulac spoke better with action. He needed her to stay with him, needed her to know that he had always wanted her and that nothing had changed. Perhaps it was working. Nimueh was flushed, her expression at once aroused and furtive. With a darting glance, she parted her lips as if to speak, but gave a quick shake of her head as if falling in with his silent conversation. Then she was eagerly working at his waistband, giving her own message loud and clear.

"Gently," he admonished.

She flicked him a look from beneath lowered lashes, her expression coy. Those long, clever fingers slid his zipper down, and Dulac's mind went blank as his erection sprang free. Nimueh stroked his length, her nails lightly teasing. "You still seem to have at least one point to make," she whispered.

"Come here," he said roughly, words almost beyond him. Uncertainty flickered in her eyes. He didn't need an explanation. She was groping her way back to herself, lost in the maze of sensory give-and-take. She slowly slid off the table, obeying his command with a trancelike air. He stepped out of his jeans and then they were face-to-face, almost touching. He traced her collarbone with one finger, following where it dipped toward her breasts. "Take off the skirt."

Mechanically, her eyes locked with his, she undid the top buttons and let it fall. Her obedience gave him a sense of power, but he knew it was only temporary. This moment would end. Whether he kept her afterward was what mattered. No, whether she *wanted* to stay was what mattered. Nimueh could not be kept like a piece of art, however much he might want it.

He took both her hands, leading her from the kitchen to the living room, where the patio doors were open to let in the warm morning breeze. No neighbors could see in and they could see no other dwellings. This space was utterly their own. The filmy curtains billowed, sounding the wind chimes, and Nimueh closed her eyes. The air was not as fresh as it was in the woods, but it still carried the scent of the garden. When his feet reached the soft throw rug before the fireplace, he stopped and pulled her down to the floor.

Dulac had been right to appeal to her senses. As soon as Nimueh spread herself out on the thick white fur, she stretched like a cat, sensually and slow. He devoured the sight as he lowered himself to all fours above her. The only garment she wore was a tiny triangle of silk, and he soon dealt with that. He caged her with his limbs, the soft breeze caressing his shoulders as he bent to kiss along the midline of her lean stomach, working his way down to the curls at the peak of her thighs. She buried her fingers in his hair, kneading and tugging at him as he readied her for pleasure. When she pulled him to her to kiss his mouth, their tastes mingled salty and sweet.

"Whatever happens, know that I'm yours," he told her.

"Then remind me who I am," Nimueh whispered. "You're the only one who knows this piece of me."

Her words conjured emotions Dulac couldn't begin to name, but they were sweet and painful at once. They were everything that he had lost and hoped to regain, and everything she had been to him before he had known her true worth.

"You remember," he said. "All that's inside you."

He eased inside her slick heat with care, holding back lest his eagerness make him rough. She was tight, her body yielding slowly but deliciously as he thrust a little at a time. She writhed under him with small, needy moans.

The sensation of being with her was familiar but not. He knew the scents and softness of her body, but he had changed as much as the world around them. Innocence was long behind him, and his heart far harder to unlock even to himself. But still, if he had kept a piece of her—this intimate experience, this private pleasure—she'd kept a piece of him in turn. Being with Nimueh was everything he remembered and far more precious for having waited so long.

Chapter 16

Nim drowsed in Lancelot's arms, deliciously limp after the onslaught of desire and sensation. They were still on the floor, tangled together on the soft, fluffy rug. She could tell by his slow, regular breaths that he was asleep, his arm curled around her possessively. Through slit eyes, she studied his hand and forearm, the dusting of hair dark gold against his pale skin. His fingers curled loosely, but the thick muscle of his arm spoke of ready strength. She wanted to trace the line of bone and sinew with her fingertips, but she didn't dare. Lancelot never slept deeply and the slightest movement would break the spell.

Summer breezes stirred the curtains, caressing her bare skin and letting the sunlight play against the white ceiling. As the filmy curtains moved she caught glimpses of green and brilliant pink blooms that soothed her fae nature. Lancelot couldn't have chosen a better oasis in the city if he'd searched with her in mind. Maybe he had.

But the certainty of his affection only made her more

confused about what being together meant for them. Oh, what he'd said before this seduction made sense. Nim believed his explanation about Guinevere. The truth in his voice and manner had been plain, and she knew not to doubt his word in a matter of straightforward facts. Lancelot was incapable of an outright lie.

Nim remembered the painfully young queen all too well, the girl's pretty face frozen into a tight mask of determination. Was it any wonder Guinevere had used a handsome, kind hero to survive a court full of strangers and a disastrous marriage? Nim could not blame either of them, as much as she had to fight her own jealousy. In any case, she could afford to be generous. Guinevere had turned to dust centuries ago.

Nim studied the light dancing across the room with every flutter of the curtains. She loved this room with its comfortable furniture and ordinary, human clutter. It had everything that was important to make a home. Something she'd not had for a very long time.

Something that should not be hers at Lancelot's expense.

Lancelot should turn her over to Arthur, but he wouldn't—and that was a breach of his sworn duty. *Is it fair to ask him to choose between his king and his lady?*

She should have asked that question back in the Forest Sauvage. He needed to earn his way in the world, even if losing him tore her in two. She should let him go now— he could find the good wife she'd seen in her vision and live out his days in happiness. A bittersweet ache lodged in her throat.

All at once staying still was impossible. She wormed her way out from under Lancelot's arm. He rolled like a lazy cat, yawning and stretching every limb. Against her will, her eyes fixed on his naked form, every hollow and valley highlighted by the summer sun. He was breath-taking.

"What gives?" he asked sleepily.

The phrase struck her the wrong way. *I gave. I gave you everything but it wasn't enough to save our love. You left and I changed.* She swallowed back a sudden sadness, certain that their time together wouldn't last. How could it, when it meant compromising his duty?

"I'm taking a shower." She needed the comfort of the water on her skin. It wasn't her lake, but it would have to do.

"Very well." His eyes darkened, clearly anticipating a soapy playtime.

"I need a moment alone," she said, trying not to see his expression falter. "I won't be long."

Nim left before he could respond, gathering her clothes and going upstairs to use the en suite shower. After turning on the water, she caught her reflection in the mirror and was almost startled by the green of her own eyes. She'd grown used to hiding behind brown contacts.

Experimentally, she tugged at a strand of her hair, aware her naturally white roots were showing. She missed the long waterfall of pale locks that had been one of her best features. She'd cut and dyed them when she'd gone into hiding after Prince Mordred's death. Suddenly the loss of her true appearance galled her beyond reason. LaFaye had taken Nim's appearance away along with her freedom, her emotions, and her safety.

Disgusted, Nim turned away from the mirror and stepped under the hot spray to wash. Now here she was poised to give up again, to let everything Lancelot was trying to give her slide away. Was she letting him go for his own sake, or was she running? Was she letting LaFaye win once more? The worst thing was she didn't know. Her new, raw emotions were tangled together in an ugly mess.

Long ago, it was only after Lancelot had left her that she realized what it was to be lonely. Now she could feel the shadow of an empty ache biding its time, waiting for her to make a mistake so she could learn that lesson all over again.

She was impossibly confused.

Nim turned off the water and grabbed towels, wrapping herself in one and her hair in another. She opened the bathroom door to find Lancelot sitting on the bed. He was dressed in fresh clothes, his hair damp from the downstairs shower.

"Something's wrong," he said. "What is it?"

The question caught her off guard. "I was thinking about the first time I came to Camelot."

He nodded, his expression growing grim.

"Every time I tried to speak to you, the queen called you to her side," Nim said. "She didn't like to share."

He dropped his gaze. "I did not love her. I told you that."

Nim rushed on, interrupting. "Merlin was just as bad. I'd heard of him, but I'd never seen his like. Everything he did flashed or sizzled, exploding into doves or sparkles of color. The court lapped up his spectacles like children at a fair. Then he challenged me to a duel of magic, but I declined and said such displays were beneath me. The truth was that anything I did would have seemed dull and I couldn't bear to lose. I was afraid of the court's contempt."

Lancelot took her hand, pulling her down to sit next to him. "What does Merlin have to do with anything?"

She wasn't sure. Words were simply tumbling out unbidden. It was as if she was pulling threads together, realizing to her surprise that they made a pattern. "Everything. It's the same as my hair."

He blinked. "Pardon me?"

"I lived alone in the forest. When Merlin asked me to show my magic, I ran instead of showing who I was. Perhaps I would not have won, but I could have stood up to him. Instead, I walked away."

"And?"

"I'm still hiding and in disguise."

Lancelot wrapped his arm around her bare shoulders. His touch reminded her that all she had on was a towel. "What are you saying?" he asked.

"I don't know. I'm going in circles. I should let you go but I don't want to give you up. I wish I could say that I'd changed by becoming less selfish, but I think I got angrier instead. I don't want to run anymore. I want to fight La-Faye and take back my life."

Lancelot gave one of his very rare smiles. It began in his eyes. They seemed to change color, growing more golden even as his cheeks creased, fine lines fanning out where the sun had weathered his face. And then the rest of it came—all teeth and a soft, deep chuckle from deep in his chest. Nim burst into tears—not from misery, because his happiness had swept that away in an instant. She was simply, utterly overwhelmed by everything she felt for him.

It seemed so strange to cry after so long—the hot, messy physicality of it, with burning eyes and throat and ribs aching from her sobs. The last time she'd cried like this had been during the wars, when she'd said goodbye to her castle and gone back to the faery homeland in the Hollow Hills. Everything had paled after that, as if she'd crossed a boundary to a kind of grief that tears couldn't touch.

But now she was back and her emotions were out of control. The physical act of weeping had no dignity—the hot tears and aching throat, the fact that her breath seemed to have broken into jagged, painful sobs. "I'm sorry," she gulped. "I don't understand why I'm doing this."

She pulled the damp towel from her hair and pressed it

to her face. But she couldn't stop. Everything she'd stored up—all the fear of her time with Mordred, the torture she'd witnessed, the degradation of her people, the sudden dizzying pleasure of finding Lancelot again—it was all coming out now. It was as if her emotions had been building up and up, not so much extinct as repressed. As they found their way out from the bottom of her soul, she felt desperately vulnerable.

"Hush," Lancelot murmured, hugging her close. The gesture was undemanding, the kind of comfort that invited her to snuggle into the crook of his shoulder and weep her fill. She buried her face in his chest while his big hand cradled the back of her head, the other smoothing the damp strands of her hair. Despite his gentleness, Nim was mortified. She was the ice-cold Nimueh of the Lake, wearing nothing but a towel and her nose was running like a leaky faucet. The embarrassment only made her cry harder.

With his free hand, Lancelot found a box of tissues and put it beside her. He pulled one out and dried her face with tender care, blotting one cheek, then the other. At first it was pointless because she kept crying, wave after wave of pent-up distress letting go, but he kept at it. Finally she was exhausted, the sobs fading to hiccups and then to nothing. She sagged against him, wrung out.

"Feel better?" he asked, brushing a kiss against her temple.

"I do." Her ribs hurt and her eyes were sandy, but she felt transparent, as if there was nothing left of her but a glass vessel where her flesh should be. All the grief and all the anger she hadn't been able to acknowledge for so long had finally been put to rest. She felt utterly, completely cleansed.

He kissed her lightly on the lips, a promise of more comfort, more warmth. Nim melted, dark heat gathering

inside her. She put her hands against his chest, barely resisting the urge to dig her fingers in and cling there for
dear life. He smelled of clean soap and freshly laundered
cotton. The sheer masculinity of him was a drug.

Then his smartphone buzzed on the dresser, skittering
sideways like something possessed. With a curse, Lancelot
lunged for it and glanced at the screen. "It's Arthur." He
thumbed the screen and put the phone to his ear.

Instinctively, Nim pulled her towel tighter. The bubble
of their privacy faded even as Lancelot's expression grew
darker. He rose from the bed, his energy seeming to coil.
Without hearing a word of what Arthur said, Nim knew
there was trouble.

"An attack? Or was it a warning?" He listened a moment longer, his gaze finding Nim's. "I'll be right— Hello?
Hello?"

He ended the call and slid the phone into his pocket.
"The call dropped. Something's loose at the theme park.
They think it's an animal, and not a natural one."

Nim rose from the bed. "A creature of LaFaye's?"

"Arthur thinks so. It would be a coincidence otherwise."

"Of course." Regret hardened in her chest. It was the
first time she'd been emotionally alive in so long, and
Lancelot was about to leave her alone. Logic said he had
to go, but it stung.

He pulled on his boots. "It's already attacked a security guard."

"Then you had better go."

He cupped her face in his hands. "I'll be back as soon
as I can."

He kissed her again, sweetly and yet with a touch of
lust that said he meant to keep his word. Nim pulled on
clothes and followed him downstairs. She got to the living room in time to watch him pull weapons from a chest.

He slid his great sword with the ruby-studded hilt into a sheath that hung down his back. He had heavy leather guards called vambraces buckled around his forearms, and knives for his belt and boots. The last thing he added was a Smith & Wesson. His fingers moved quickly, strapping them on and then slipping on a leather coat to hide them. He would be hot, but he would need the protection of the leather in a fight.

"Be careful," she said, thinking of the smile he'd just given her.

But her words seemed to dissolve into nothing. In another minute, he was gone, leaving her alone.

Nim stopped herself before she trailed him to the door like a housewife waving her man off to work. Instead she poured a mug of the cooling coffee and forced herself to swallow it. Lancelot had left her behind because she couldn't go to Medievaland, not with Arthur under pressure to turn her over to LaFaye. That was as it had to be.

Nim's restraint lasted less than a minute. She slammed the mug down and stared out the window. The day was getting hot, the sunlight taking on an aggressive hue that matched her mood. She folded her arms, replaying the conversation she'd had with herself in the shower. Yes, she was in hiding and ready to run for a good reason. But was this how she wanted her future to go?

She was the enchantress, and yet here she was hanging back while mortals chased a magic beast. By choosing to hide she'd given up her power in every possible way. *Of course* it was impossible to impact her own fate if she refused to act, to be quiet and hope her enemies never noticed she was there. She had always claimed that she fought her own battles, but was that true? How much fighting had she done lately?

Anger bubbled through her like champagne. She dug

her fingers into her hair—the hair that wasn't her own—ready to tear it out by handfuls. Maybe she wouldn't be the same Nimueh she'd been before. Maybe how she changed was up to her.

Nim chose to be stronger. She would fight.

Chapter 17

Dulac's home was close enough that he could run to Medievaland in under ten minutes, but he took extra time to dodge down alleyways where few would notice a fully armed knight on the move. Even this close to Medievaland, running armed to the teeth would attract unwelcome questions and that would only delay him more.

When he arrived, the park looked bright and sparkling in the early morning sun, its flags and pennants snapping in the breeze. Gawain met him at the gate, looking grim. He had a massive yew longbow and a quiver of red-feathered arrows slung across his back.

"Explain what happened," Dulac demanded. "Arthur didn't give much information when he called."

Gawain shot him a dark look. "I'm surprised he gave you anything but a smack to the head after you walked out last night. You can't talk to a king that way, not even Arthur."

"There will be time enough to debate my disobedience later."

"I hope you're right about that. There's a wee hungry beastie on the loose."

Dulac didn't like the sound of that. "How wee?"

"The only good thing is that the park isn't open yet," Gawain said. "We can teach it manners before the tourists arrive."

Gawain led the way into the park with a purposeful stride. The clock on the church tower said it was seven thirty, earlier than Dulac had realized. His stomach reminded him that he hadn't had breakfast yet. "So what happened?" Dulac asked, catching the tantalizing scent of coffee on the breeze.

"Apparently the night watchman heard something around dawn. A stray dog or raccoons, he thought, until it tried to eat him."

"Are you sure he wasn't just drunk or scared?"

Gawain shook his shaggy head. "The man has teeth marks in his flesh the size of a bear's. It chased him down to take a bite. This isn't a case of some poor creature wandering in from the forest and needing a ride home. It was nasty."

Dulac grunted his understanding. "Description?"

"It had big teeth." Gawain shrugged. "That was all the man remembered. He ran to the clubhouse and woke Beaumains and Palomedes from their drunken stupor. Their accounts aren't much more reliable."

It wasn't unusual for the younger knights to sleep onsite. "So what are you and I doing here? Two experienced warriors should be enough to clear out any vermin."

"Try again." Gawain's disgust was clear. "One by one we've been calling in the knights. All of us together haven't been able to take care of it. No doubt that's why Arthur finally called you. So far we've been able to keep everyone else off the grounds, but sooner or later the staff will stop asking questions and demand to be permitted on-site."

And modern humans would not understand this kind of danger. "So I'm the exterminator of last resort?"

Gawain gave him a crooked grin. "You're good with dragons."

"You think this is a dragon?" Dulac stopped in his tracks. He definitely needed coffee.

"Hard to say." Gawain grabbed Dulac's sleeve and pulled him along, taking a path between the brightly colored merchant tents. "Only the watchman has actually seen the thing. We've just heard the roaring."

"LaFaye left us a present." Dulac made it a statement, not a question.

"Unfortunately, I think you're right."

They'd reached the edge of the midway, which sat on the far side of the park from the tourney grounds. The rides and shooting galleries were silent and still, the great metal structures rising into the sky like enormous frozen beasts. Despite the broad daylight, the effect was eerie.

Gawain stopped before the metal turnstile that led to the rides. He put his hands on his hips, his expression grim. "We've lost cellular reception, so coordinating the men isn't as easy as it might be."

"Magic." Its presence interfered with a lot of technology. That explained why Gawain had met him at the gate, and why Arthur's call had dropped earlier.

"We think we've trapped the beast somewhere in the midway. The lads have set up a perimeter. They can hold it if you and I go in and do the hunting."

Dulac nodded, his mind already calculating a plan of attack. Full armor and a battle charger would be a nuisance in the narrow, congested landscape of the midway. He didn't need much more than what he'd brought with him. He pulled the sword from the back sheath with a hiss of leather and steel. "Let's do it."

Dulac didn't have any experience with fairgrounds beyond Medievaland, but to him the place was endless—a sprawl of walkways, concession stands, and monstrous contraptions with names like Dragon's Tail and Spear of Doom. The rides circled a long narrow lake dotted with slides and wading pools and surrounded by lush greenery. The power must have come on with a timer, because the central fountain was already splashing in noisy plumes. A fine mist cooled Dulac's face, welcome relief from the rising temperature. Gawain fell into step beside him, watching the grounds to the right while Dulac scanned the lawn to the left. The fun house squatted there, gaudy and crooked. Nothing moved. He turned back to the water. Nothing—until a flock of sparrows exploded from the canopy of branches that trailed in the water.

With no need for words, the two men bolted, Gawain taking the path to the right of the water, Dulac sprinting straight ahead. Something was beneath the surface of the lake and swimming fast. Silver ripples marked its arrowing wake as it disappeared beneath a veil of weeping willows. Dulac ran, boots pounding on the carefully swept walks. Kiddie swings and recycle bins flashed by, reminding him of the toddlers meant to play in this park.

The sight spurred him on, making him push even faster. Camelot's presence—and by extension his own—made this town the fae's first point of attack. That made defeating LaFaye and all her armies personal. No one would suffer because Dulac lived in Carlyle. This was his town now.

Across the water, Gawain stopped, planting his feet and drawing his massive bow. Three arrows thrust into the water, one after the other with incredible speed. They were too close together to tell which one struck first, but a whoosh of water sounded and a snarl of pain cleaved the air. Dulac skidded to a stop as something leaped to the shore. The trees blocked his view, but he got an impression of a green and burgundy hide. Whatever it was looked about the size of a pony, but it was much faster. Even as Gawain loosed a fourth arrow, it was bolting across the lawn, a streak of clawed limbs and whipping tail. Dulac charged after it, knowing it would take time for Gawain to catch up. He didn't relish the thought of cornering the beast alone, but they couldn't afford to lose it in the maze of the park.

With the unerring instinct of any creature under attack, the thing aimed for cover. The nearest cave, complete with a twisting waterway and convenient hidey-holes, was the Tunnel of Love. Dulac mentally cursed as the beast slithered inside. Dulac hated the tacky place to begin with, and in these circumstances it would be a death trap. He paused at the entrance, casting a quick glance at the waterway with its tiny, two-person boats meant for snuggling lovers. The scene was eerily quiet. Normally there would be music and the hum of equipment, but the ride's operators had not yet arrived for the day. That was good—silence meant Dulac could rely on his hearing.

He sheathed his sword, deciding the tunnel was too narrow for the long weapon. Drawing his hunting knife with his left hand and his Smith & Wesson with his right, he stepped into one of the small boats and from there hopped onto the narrow walkway that ran at the base of the tunnel wall. The path was meant for service workers, not broad-shouldered warriors carrying weapons, and Dulac had to turn sideways and creep along with his back to the fake stone wall. To his relief, it was not completely dark. The timer that had started the fountains must have turned on the dioramas inside the Tunnel of Love.

Dulac made it to the first turn and crouched, making himself as small a target as possible. Surprise was his only advantage, but most creatures had an excellent sense of smell. The small breeze was in his favor, but was it enough to hide him? Possibly. The air was dominated by the stink of something green and heavy with magic, much like rotting lilies. A suspicion formed in Dulac's mind and he inched forward again, rounding the corner.

There was a diorama built into the far wall, so brightly lit that it made him blink. The figures were poorly done, the work clumsy and unimaginative. Dulac ignored it to concentrate on the shadows beyond. He thought he heard a splash and froze, listening closely to the lap of water against the boats.

He waited until his legs began to cramp, but heard nothing more. Silently, he ghosted forward, working his way through the twists and bends of the ride and ignoring the bright tableaux as they loomed up on either side. Each one depicted famous lovers. Many he did not recognize, but a few he did. Tristram and Isolde. Paris and Helen. Dido and Aeneas. Whoever had designed the ride had harbored a grudge against happy endings.

He had to keep his mind on the job, but the tunnel worked against him, the last turn putting him all but face-to-face with Antony and Cleopatra, their tale one he knew well. The workmanship was better here, the Egyptian queen almost lifelike as she reclined on her bed, the poisonous asp at her breast. The great Roman general lay slumped in his death agony.

Dulac always counted Mark Antony an idiot for getting himself killed and, worse, failing to keep Cleopatra safe. But now he had more sympathy for the pair. Love and duty were not always easy to reconcile. Even now, Dulac was keeping Nimueh from his king and hoping against hope all would end well.

Maybe it would. After all, Arthur had let Dulac walk away last night. Proud and difficult as he was, Arthur was a good man who could be a friend when it counted. It was that simple decency, as much as any grand vision, that held the remnants of Camelot together. But how long would that last in the face of LaFaye's threats?

Something lunged from the darkness. Reflex made him duck. Dulac caught a flash of red eyes and fired the Smith & Wesson, getting off two shots. He sucked in a breath, hoping for a reprieve, but he was disappointed. Rather than making the beast back off, the bullets just enraged it.

It pounced forward, landing in the water, but with its front feet planted on one of the tiny boats. Dulac braced himself, ready to fire again, but the thing merely studied him with glowing scarlet eyes. It had neither fur nor scales, but something in between. At first glance it looked like a large lion or tiger, with a red-and-black mane that faded to a bright green body and whiplike tail. But it was not an animal. It was made of green vines twisted together to give it the semblance of bone and muscle. The beast was entirely made of petal, leaf and savage thorn.

Dulac took these details in without allowing himself the luxury of shock. He was ready when the creature launched forward with a massive spring that brought it nearly on top of him. Dulac fired again, but the bullets passed through the beast's body without doing any real harm. It had no vital organs to destroy or blood to spill. He dropped the useless gun and shifted the knife to his right hand.

The beast lashed out a paw. Dulac raised the knife, but with feline quickness, the claws trapped his arm and it lunged to bite. Dulac twisted away, catching a glimpse of the long, savage fangs the security guard had compared to a bear's. He wasn't far wrong. Dulac felt the scrape and the sticky wetness of the creature's maw, but he sprang sideways, landing in one of the boats before its jaws could close on him. From there, he leaped to the opposite ledge, putting at least a scant few feet between them. The move reversed their positions and now Dulac stood with his back to the exit of the tunnel. He balanced on the balls of his feet, ready for their next encounter.

The beast pounced again, this time hitting his chest. Dulac flew backward, only the water saving him from a brutal collision with the cement. The beast was on top of him, its weight crushing his lungs. The smell of it was at once intoxicating and revolting, and when it opened its mouth, Dulac gagged. Water washed over his face, obscuring his vision. Its long fangs streamed with pale green ooze like sticky sap, its tongue the vivid green of rotting leaves. As it reared its head back to strike, Dulac drove his long knife into the roof of its mouth. It crunched as it punched through the beast's head, and he slashed with all his strength toward the thing's throat. The effect was immediate. The beast jerked away, bounding backward with green liquid coursing from its mouth. Dulac scrambled to his feet, still clutching the knife.

Eyes burning, the beast screamed in pure rage, sounding more like an eagle than any cat. Triumph and dismay pounded through Dulac. He'd hurt it, but now it was furious. Despite himself, he took a step back. The sun streamed in just behind him, and he needed the sanity of that light.

The creature prowled forward, tail whipping in anger. The water barely came to its belly, the boats mere stepping-stones in its path. Its head hung low, green drool dripping from its jaws. Dulac's muscles twitched with tension as he backed away. The beast's red eyes fixed on the knife that had hurt it. Suddenly a paw batted out, slamming Dulac's injured shoulder. The lancing pain drove Dulac to his knees and the thing snarled in triumph, closing in. That was its last mistake. Dulac drove the knife deep into its fiery red eye.

As he drove it home, he pushed up to free himself.

The beast fell backward, its huge head lolling as the eyes dimmed, the spark in them guttering to nothing. Dulac got to his feet, suddenly aware that he was freezing cold from the water.

Gawain appeared, breath heaving from haste. His face twisted in disgust. "That thing smells like compost."

"I'm not sure it's dead yet," Dulac warned, drawing the long sword from his back. There had been no room to fight with it in the tunnel, but it had its use now. "Stand back."

He brought the long blade down, severing the head with a crunch. Instantly, the body shriveled, the twisted vines and pulpy leaves withering and shrinking until it looked like no more than twigs, and then dried grass, and then nothing at all. The water carried away the last shreds of it and the two knights stared at an empty space.

"I heard the gardeners complain about the weeds," said Gawain. "I never imagined this."

Chapter 18

When Nim arrived at Medievaland, there were people gathering outside the gate. Some were in costume—probably staff—and a few looked like early-bird tourists with sun hats and cameras. Two grim-faced bruisers in security uniforms were standing at the entrance, arms folded and feet planted in a way that kept arguments to a minimum. The official story was that a ferocious dog was on the loose and the Medievaland staff was in the process of capturing it. If any of the guards knew more than that, it didn't show.

Deciding to save time, Nim circled the perimeter fence until she was behind the stables. The fence was very high, the top angled outward in a way that made climbing difficult. Only the most agile humans could have scaled it, but she was fae and in no mood for games. She swarmed up it quickly and dropped to the ground inside the park, breathless with the heat and exertion.

Before she had time to rise, boots and a sword point

filled her field of vision. She glanced up into the cold blue gaze of Arthur Pendragon. She hadn't seen him since the demon wars, and the merry young king he'd been was long gone. He looked harder with lines etched beside his mouth. Gone were the rich robes and crown, and now he wore only scuffed boots and blue jeans, a faded blue T-shirt stretched across his muscular chest. But one thing was the same— there was no mistaking the air of authority that wrapped him like a cloak.

"Nimueh," said Arthur.

It wasn't a question. Her stomach sank as all hope of secrecy vanished. "My lord."

"I thought you were in hiding." His gaze swept over her hair and clothes, a look of distaste forming as he took in her disguise. The sword tip flicked one tendril of her black hair. "Or should I say that Dulac insists on keeping you out of sight?"

"He wants the best for me." She raised her hands, making sure Arthur saw they were empty of weapons. His mood was clearly dangerous. "But I understand LaFaye may have unleashed something in the park."

"Is that so? Or perhaps it is the work of another fae enchantress?"

She refused to take the bait. "I may be able to help. I have knowledge of magic that you do not."

He said nothing for a moment. Nim tried to stand, but the sword flicked toward her eyes, keeping her in place. It seemed ironic that she was being threatened with the very sword she'd enchanted for the king.

"I used to trust you," he said slowly. "Some of my men still do, but the fae swore vengeance on Camelot. Given what you are, that leaves me in an interesting position."

"Are you going to trade me to LaFaye for a few months' reprieve?" Anger knotted in her chest.

"So Dulac told you about that?" Arthur shrugged. "I can't say the prospect of peace isn't tempting."

"Then I am at your mercy," she said. "Where is Lancelot?"

"The knights have the creature penned on the other side of the park."

"Then why are you here?" she asked bluntly. It wasn't like Arthur to hang back and let others confront danger.

"Because one rampaging creature is far too obvious." The king nodded toward the stables, a crease between his red-gold brows. "The horses are restless. They know danger better than any man, so I stayed behind to keep watch."

Excalibur's point touched lightly against her chest. "Was it you that I was watching for? Are you the danger?"

She refused to flinch. "I'm no danger to you. I think you're the best chance the fae have for freedom from LaFaye."

"You flatter me. Is it to soften my heart?"

There was enough sarcasm in his tone that she winced. "I can't pretend I'm not interested in your opinion of me. If you hand me over to the queen, I will come to a slow, painful and lingering end. I know those are her terms for a year's peace."

His gaze bored into her, his light blue eyes uncomfortably intense. "I don't do anything on Morgan's terms." He lowered the sword and stepped back to let Nim rise. "Don't make me regret my choice."

"Am I your prisoner?" She stood slowly, one eye still on the sword. She could feel something in the air, like pressure building. It set her nerves on edge.

"I know better than to think that I could hold you," said Arthur. "I will, however, watch you closely."

"You won't regret this."

"Hmm." Arthur gave her a narrow look. "Words are words. I reserve my opinion for deeds."

That wasn't the answer she wanted, but it was something. Then she felt the faint quiver in the air again, almost as much a sound as a breeze and yet neither. "There is a spell at work."

The horses felt it, too. Nervous whickers sounded from the stalls, and one steed kicked its door with a resounding thump. Arthur beckoned and led the way toward the disturbance. At least for now, he seemed willing to work with her.

Nim followed a step behind, thinking through her repertoire of spells. She couldn't stay off LaFaye's radar any longer. She'd made the decision to help, and helping was the opposite of hiding. Merlin had been right to say that she was wasting her time trying to repress her magic, and he'd given her his assurance that she could unbind her magic at will. That was as it should be. Nimueh was a fae, an enchantress, a power to be reckoned with. Magic was who she was.

Arthur stopped so suddenly she all but crashed into him. She moved to his left, ready to act, but then recoiled at what she saw. Something was crawling out of the trash. It was long and thin, with a small red head and a silver bow around its neck. "What is that?"

"LaFaye sent us roses," Arthur replied in a strangled voice. "When we learned they were from her, we threw them away. We should have burned them. It was a foolish mistake."

The first rose dropped from the trash bin and writhed on the ground like a snake. Arthur rushed forward and crushed it beneath his boot, leaving a green smear in the dust. But others were following too quickly to stomp them all, even though Nim sprang forward to help. Two rolled away, wriggling and crawling in movements no plant was meant to make. Nim blinked in horror as the long stems swelled, folding and refolding and weaving together to form the muscular body of a hunting cat. The dark red petals became a sleek head and mane; the thorns formed wicked teeth and claws.

They'd barely taken shape before they attacked. One sprang at Arthur, who sliced Excalibur through the air with a cry. The other beast turned on Nim, who moved to rip the binding from her power and let her magic fly. Despite the danger of detection, her heart soared in affirmation of everything she was. She would hide no longer!

She felt the echo of her magic's flare, but nothing happened. The beast was almost upon her when she tried again, but her power was cold and silent. *Stars! Merlin, what have you done?* Despite his promise that she could access her magic if she needed it, her power was beyond her reach.

Loss and confusion made her freeze, helpless as a rabbit in the face of oncoming horror. Then anger kicked through her stasis. Magic or no magic, she still had to fight—or die.

Nim leaped to the top of the fence and from there scrabbled to the roof of the stables, dust flying and slivers digging into her hands. She looked down to see her attacker crouched on the ground, tail lashing, while its twin wrestled with the king. Her stomach twisted, bile rising up her throat. The creature made a noise that wasn't a hiss or a roar or a shriek, but was some of each. The sound crawled over her skin. There were magical beasts—like unicorns, dragons and griffins—but they were made from nature, however rare. This creature was simply *wrong*.

And Nim wasn't sure what to do about it. She should have been able to unravel LaFaye's spell with one of her own, but Merlin's binding had gone too far. What had he done? Had he deceived her? Simply made a mistake?

She would have to destroy her attacker using only her wits. But how? She was desperately vulnerable, as helpless as a human. Nothing mattered if she didn't survive.

Nim crawled up the roof on elbows and knees until she reached a skylight. Pushing it open, she dropped inside the stable. The horses barely noticed her arrival. Every ear and nose was pointed toward the beast outside, the stamping hooves marking their nervousness.

Nim began a search of the building. She had taken weapons from Lancelot's stash, but they were all for fighting at close range. She wanted something less up close and personal. There was a storeroom at the right that held the usual horse-related medicines, grooming equipment and tack, but it also held a few general supplies. She wondered if there would be any weed killer, but quickly decided she'd need a vat of the stuff to do any good.

The stable door crashed open and the horses screamed, rearing and lunging at the walls in panic. Nim's first instinct was to protect them, but she knew LaFaye wouldn't waste her deadly magic on livestock. Nim pressed herself to the wall, making herself small. There was a door at the back of the storeroom that led back to the yard and she began to inch toward it. Her nape prickled with horror as she heard the beast scrabbling over the floor, snuffling from stall to stall in search of her scent. The horses continued to kick and pound.

Silently, Nim pushed open the rear door of the storeroom. She slipped back into the yard, disappointed by the fruitless search. When the beast found her scent and howled, she doubled her speed, dashing past a maintenance building. She dodged around a gardener's trailer sitting next to a wall. A jumble of equipment spilled out and she slid to a stop, still anxious to find a weapon. Her eyes darted over the mess, picking out a fire extinguisher, a rake and a chain saw. She was tempted by the chain saw but not sure how to use it. However, there was a can of gasoline. She grabbed it and was relieved to find it full. Flame had possibilities.

And then the beast was coming again, sprinting as fast as any cheetah. Without stopping to plan, she took the gas and ran, scrambling up a fence and sprinting along the top rail. With a last burst of speed, she leaped from the fence to the crossbeam above the gate to the tourney ground, hauling the gas can with her. She squatted, balancing on the balls of her feet.

From there, she could see Arthur battling with the other beast, sword flashing in the sun. That wasn't all. At least ten of the nervous horses had broken out of their stalls and were milling in mindless distress. And her beast—how had it become hers?—was leaping and racing through the yard, trying to find a scent that had vanished the moment she'd climbed the fence. Apparently monsters made of vegetation were not enormously bright.

Nim unscrewed the cap of the gas can and then gave a sharp whistle through her teeth, hoping to call the beast her way. Unfortunately, the horses stampeded instead.

It really was a beautiful sight—huge, sleek dapple grays and coal blacks, shining bays and the snow white of Arthur's mount. Nim was in no position to appreciate it. There were no handholds on top of the gate and very little room to balance. She was surefooted, but the crush of horseflesh toward the familiar tourney grounds meant thousands of pounds brushing and bumping against the supports. The monster brought up the rear with snarling roars that put wind beneath the horses' hooves.

Determined not to miss her chance, Nim leaned forward to empty the heavy can of gas over the monster's head as it passed. It was a bad mistake. One final thump to the gate sent her toppling forward, can and all. She missed the beast by inches, falling face-first into the dirt.

The impact knocked her breath away. The fall would have killed a human, and for an instant Nim wasn't sure it hadn't broken every bone. There was an instant of nothing, and then she heard the glugging of the gasoline pour-ing out of the can as it lay on its side. Nim turned her head and was confronted by the beast's face inches from hers. Long tendrils coiled where whiskers might have been, and fangs trailed over its bottom jaw.

Terror coursed through Nim's limbs, turning them to ice. The foul odour of its breath mixed with the gas to stomach-lurching effect. Nim bent her arms to push her-self up, but a heavy paw landed between her shoulder blades. There was a prick of claws sinking into her flesh, and Nim was sure LaFaye had won at last.

Abandoning caution, she snaked out a hand and grabbed the handle of the gas can. The creature's weight shifted as if to snap at her hand. That released Nim enough to roll, backhanding the can against the beast's snout. It jerked away with a snarl, allowing her to spring to her feet. With renewed horror, she looked directly into its burning eyes. There was no intelligence there, but then it was not a truly living thing.

"Hold still," said Lancelot.

Nim's breath stopped. He was crouched a dozen feet away, his sword in both hands. The sun glinted off the ru-bies in the hilt, matching the eyes of the beast for their fire.

The instant Lancelot spoke, the beast spun, eyes blazing and fangs bared in an unholy snarl that sent Nim spring-ing back in terror. The creature was nothing but hate and hunger, bundled with magic and given temporary form. It coiled and sprang in the same motion, razor claws reach-ing for the knight.

Lancelot swung the sword, slicing through the beast's foreleg. The creature twisted in the air, graceful and terri-ble as it lunged to retaliate. Lancelot reared back, ducking under snapping jaws to strike again. The sword sheared through its ropy flesh to strike the ground.

The beast gave an outraged roar, but its anger was short

lived. Sparks flew as the blade scraped on rock, igniting the spilled gasoline. There was a sound like soft thunder and a fireball erupted in midair, the rush of it sending hot wind in all directions.

The beast exploded in a ball of flames.

Chapter 19

Lancelot leaped aside to avoid the flames' trajectory, his sword falling as he rolled in the dust. Alarmed, Nim darted back to the equipment shed in search of the fire extinguisher. It was right where she'd seen it, so she grabbed it in both hands and bolted back to the fire.

Without any kind of greeting, Gawain intercepted her, taking the canister and spraying where the gas had strayed closest to the fence. He was all efficient action, but there was little need for it. In an eye blink, the fire had blazed and was gone—a byproduct of the magic involved. As soon as the spell unwound, the fire's energy died. Only the bitter smell of gasoline hung in the air, mixing with the stink of the beast that was now no more than ash.

Lancelot was dusting himself off and retrieving his sword. He sheathed the blade and joined Nim where she stood next to the fence, his expression wavering between furious and relieved.

"Don't tell me I should have stayed home and let you fight this alone," Nim warned in a low voice.

Silently, he looked her over, wiping the dust from her face with his thumbs. She could feel his emotion in his hands, but he would not meet her eyes. He was angry.

"That was the last of the beasts," said the king. "Good work, all of you."

Nim looked up. The king was a few feet to her right, leaning on Excalibur. He looked exhausted, his sword and clothes coated in green slime. There were deep scratches over his hands and down his face. One inch over, and they would have cost him an eye.

Lancelot stiffened at the sound of Arthur's voice and moved to stand between Nim and the king. Nim took his arm, drawing him close to her side instead. She had a sudden need to sit down, but she refused to show weakness before Arthur Pendragon. Instead, she leaned against Lancelot, hoping the shaking in her knees didn't show. "What was the purpose of those creatures?"

"To kill us," said Arthur. "At least the beasts were trying very, very hard."

"One creature woke early and went to the other side of the park," said Gawain. "That suggests the plan was to separate the knights."

He cast Nim and Lancelot a speculative look, his gaze lingering on her. The last time they'd met, they'd been in a battle with Mordred.

"I thought it might have been a distraction," Arthur replied, "but I didn't expect so many of its friends or I wouldn't have waited alone."

Then Lancelot spoke, his voice still rough with emotion. "The fact one beast lured us while so many remained near you suggests you were the target."

Nim wondered if her arrival had triggered the creatures to emerge. She was, after all, another celebrity near the top of Morgan's hit list. "But why would she take such a chance now?"

Arthur's response was weary. "She wants Excalibur. It is the one thing that makes her hesitate to launch an all-out attack, and I suspect her armies grow restless."

"But why stop because of one sword? Even an enchanted one?"

"I only have speculation to offer," said the king. "However, I've known Morgan for a very long time. She is invincible in every other way, so I believe her fear of Excalibur has grown out of proportion. She won't rest until she has it under her control, or at least makes a very good try for it."

Nim understood the rest. "And because of the enchantments I put on Excalibur, the sword won't allow itself to be stolen. You have to give the sword to Morgan or you have to be dead before she can so much as touch the hilt."

"She knows I won't give it to her, so she's opting for my death." They stared at each other across a dozen feet of dusty yard. Arthur's beard looked singed. "What happened to your power?" he asked. "Why didn't you use it?"

The trembling in Nim's knees got worse. She couldn't tell him the whole truth. She'd promised to keep Merlin's existence a secret. "LaFaye can track me through my magic, so I bound it."

"What did you do?" Lancelot exclaimed, his dark eyes hot with worry. "You came to fight without your magic?"

"And did a fine job of it, Dulac," said Arthur with a trace of amusement. "Don't scold her for coming to my aid. I wouldn't have wanted to face two of those beasts at once. She might well have saved my life."

"Very well done," said Gawain.

Lancelot squeezed her hand. Nim felt her face heat and turned away, pleased but uncomfortable with the attention.

"I can plainly see that you are not like the other fae, and yet I know you once worked for the queen," said Arthur. "Was it binding your magic that gave you back your emotions?"

The question caught Nim completely off guard. She released Lancelot's hand, needing to think without his distracting warmth. She ran through dates and events, considering what spells she'd cast and how long she'd been in hiding. The return of her emotions had begun with Mordred's death, but after that it had been a slow journey. She'd been running, using a spell here and there. But they had come back in a rush when Lancelot returned— which coincided with her visit to see Merlin. The two had to be related.

Nim gave up being brave and sank to the ground. When she went to speak, only a hoarse whisper came out. "Maybe. It would make sense." *What if the binding had come undone? Did I nearly destroy my soul again?*

"Are you sure?" asked Lancelot.

"The timing is right." She looked up into his dark eyes. Concern filled them, as well they might. He knew what her power meant to her, and thus how much she'd given up.

The king walked slowly toward Nim, his chin sunk to his chest as if he were deep in thought. "I owe you an apology for my rough reception of you this morning, but you of anyone know the peril that surrounds us."

"There is no need to explain."

"But I'm a poor leader if I cannot say I'm sorry when it is honestly meant and plainly deserved." Once again, the king's pale blue eyes pinned her. "Rest assured you have Camelot's protection. It seems that destiny binds our fates together, and I would rather that it be for mutual support."

Nim was aware of her heart beating fast. "Thank you, my lord."

"My lady." Arthur held out one scratched hand to help her up. "You saved my life. In such circumstances, it is customary that I grant you a boon. If there is any favor I can grant, you have but to ask."

Nim took the hand and got to her feet. Her legs still felt unsteady. "I just have one simple request."

"What would that be?"

She cast a sidelong glance at Lancelot. "I would rather that no one ever sends me roses."

The rest of the morning was easier. No sooner were La-Faye's beasts destroyed than the park returned to normal. The cell phones worked again, the gates were opened, and word came that all the knights were safe and sound. The story of the savage dog on the loose was only bolstered by the fact that the horses had panicked and needed to be rounded up from the amphitheater.

"Come to the fair with me," said Lancelot once the horses were safely caught. "We never had breakfast."

Nim hesitated. "I'm covered in gasoline. I should go home and change."

She'd washed herself off, but there was no way to clean up her clothes. Her nerves were rattled after the fight and she didn't like the idea of going anywhere alone, but the smell was making her queasy.

"I have a better idea," he said, and took her hand in his.

They walked through the performers' area, which was crowded with knights. Nim balked, wanting to avoid the stares of the men she'd known so long ago. Some had once been friends, but now that they were at war with the fae, would they see her as an enemy?

However, all she got was a welcome, from Palomedes's brilliant smile and Percival's jokes to Owen's gentle greeting as he calmed a frightened horse. Their warmth was like finding a piece of forgotten treasure, and her whole body seemed to expand as she realized the joy of it.

She entered Medievaland with a lighter heart. The booths were open now, the merchants garbed in costumes and spreading their wares on tables bright with gaudy cloths. Heralds rode up and down the pathways on patient horses, grandly announcing entertainments and eateries. Children ran underfoot with foam swords, shrieking at the top of their lungs. Nim pointed with amusement at a little girl in butterfly wings. "Look, she's dressed up as one of the lesser fae. That's adorable."

"From what I understand, they can be vicious," said Lancelot.

"Children or pixies?" Nim asked innocently.

He gave her a dry look. "Pixies can be charmed if you leave out a bowl of milk."

She put a finger under his chin, wondering what a young Lancelot would have looked like. Those big brown eyes would have melted every female within miles. "I could be charmed with a mocha latte."

They got coffees from a stall run by pretend monks in brown robes, and then Lancelot had to stop and sign autographs for a couple of fans. He did it with deep courtesy as befit one of Arthur's knights. Nim was rapidly discovering Camelot had a following in the modern sports world. Some of the knights found it bewildering while others, like Beaumains, lapped it up with good humor.

After that they wandered, for once not rushing to answer an emergency. There was still the possibility of another fae attack, but Arthur had set guards patrolling the grounds. Vigilance 24/7—in addition to their regular patrols—would be grueling with so few warriors, but there wasn't much else they could do. No doubt LaFaye had counted on her monsters to succeed and would need time to regroup, and for now Nim and Lancelot could catch their breaths. By mutual agreement, they avoided any discussion about what had just passed, but eventually Nim could stand it no longer.

"The queen took a risk," she said. "She swore an oath of good conduct to you."

"She gave us the flowers before she took the oath. That would be a loophole, wouldn't it?"

"Maybe. But it's more than that. Although her attack began at dawn, it endangered the security guard. She exposed the shadow world to ordinary humans. That's pushing the boundaries of lore and magic."

"I doubt she cares," Lancelot replied, tilting his head back to catch the sun.

They'd drifted to a picnic bench and were sitting and watching the passing crowds. A Celtic band had started playing on the lawn and the same little girl with butterfly wings she'd seen earlier was bouncing in time to the tune, her mother clapping her hands and laughing. So few fae children had been born since the demon wars, the sight of any child seemed rare and precious. For a blinding instant, Nim wanted to be that mother and that girl to be hers and Lancelot's. But that day wouldn't come as long as LaFaye wanted them all dead.

"The queen has to care," she said. "There aren't many rules but those that exist form part of magic itself. If you swear an oath, you must keep it. If you make a summoning, you must bide by its terms. And you don't give the game away to the ordinary world. But that's exactly what she's going to do if she takes it over and lets the soul-hungry fae take their fill."

"There's a price to pay if she does," Lancelot replied.

"Of course. It usually means loss of magic or death. She has to believe she's powerful enough to overcome the consequences."

"Or desperate," he added. "Or insane."

Nim thought of her own magic, and how it was linked to her soul. The magical world had structure, a set of principles as predictable as science. Every gain demanded a price; energy out equaled energy in. Was it any surprise that giving up power had allowed Nim to heal? Sacrifice had a corresponding reward.

"You know," said Lancelot, tossing his paper cup into the recycle bin. "I don't want to talk about death, or Morgan, or anything gloomy for at least another hour."

"I'm sorry," Nim said. "I completely agree, but I'm out of practice talking or thinking about anything else."

"Then we must have doughnuts," he said. "Of all the marvels of the new world, coffee and doughnuts are the best."

"Are you serious?" She followed him from the bench and back into the crowds. "Science, technology and philosophy have leaped forward and all you care about is caffeine and carbohydrates?"

He turned, one brow raised. "I'm a simple man, but I'll expand my list to say I highly approve of the local microbrews."

He stopped before a booth that sold women's clothes in every color of a summer garden. They were gauzy confections of soft cotton decorated with beads and sequins. "I promised you fresh clothes."

"But this is…" She was about to say that it wasn't her style. Her clothes were crisply tailored, dark and free of fanciful detail. But was that really her? "This is fun."

That clearly pleased him. "Try something on," he said, pointing out an off-the-shoulder top so sheer she could read through it.

"Maybe." Nim approached the racks, her hands folded because she wanted to finger them all. It had been so long since she'd chosen something simply because it was pretty. The quality of these clothes was doubtful, but they filled her with the need to touch and admire. They promised if she wore them, she'd be touched and admired, too. She picked out a blouse and skirt and slipped into the curtained change area to put them on.

The blouse was sleeveless, a soft gold that set off her skin, and the skirt was a deep forest green. The skirt fell in deep flounces, each layer decorated with green crystal beads that clicked as she moved. The sound made her want to dance.

"We'll take them," said Dulac, putting cash on the counter, where a young salesgirl sat in frank admiration of Medievaland's jousting star. "On the condition the old clothes go in the trash."

"Sure," said the girl, flushing pink. "Whatever you like, Lancelot."

Nim bit back a smile at the flustered girl. She didn't object about leaving her old clothes—the gasoline had ruined them—and it was nice to be treated even though she had money enough of her own. No one had given her anything for a very long time. She wrapped her arms around Lancelot's, leaning into his side. "Can I buy you breakfast now?"

"Very well, my lady," he said, giving her a smile.

The smile was everything she could have asked. Perhaps it was, as Arthur had said, destiny that had led her back to Camelot. Something monumental made her heart explode every time Lancelot gave her that look.

He touched her cheek, and memories brushed her like moth's wings. He'd done that once when they stood in the meadow above the lake, the very first time he'd said he loved her. She rose on her toes to kiss him, earning a giggle from the salesgirl.

"Lead the way to breakfast, sir knight," Nim said. "Let there be simple pleasures for a blessedly simple hour."

Chapter 20

Later, Nim was resting in the clubhouse when Lancelot found her. Adrenaline, fresh air and sugar had combined to exhaust her and she was lying down on the battered couch of the upstairs infirmary, one arm flung over her face to shade her eyes against the summer brightness. She startled when the cushions sagged beneath Lancelot's weight. For a large man, Lancelot could move like a cat. He'd been helping to repair the stables and must have showered in the locker room. He smelled of soap and was wearing a fresh T-shirt with Medievaland's logo.

"What are you still doing here?" he asked gently.

"I was about to go and then one thing led to another and I stayed. I ended up helping Arthur set up some account books. He's pretty good with a computer, considering."

He put his hand on her calf, squeezing it gently beneath the green flounces of her skirt. His gaze swept over her, pausing where bruises had come up from the morning's fight. "Arthur said he would have died without you." His voice was gently possessive, alarmed but also proud. "But it takes enormous trust before he lets you near the treasury."

There wasn't much of a treasury by Nim's standards, but Arthur was clever. He'd taken over the entertainments at Medievaland and had doubled attendance at the park. It would be more accurate to say it wasn't much of a treasury *yet*.

"Maybe I helped Arthur, but I would have died without him," she said. "It was a bonding experience. Kind of like extreme gardening."

"You took a risk," Lancelot said uneasily. "He might have turned you over to LaFaye."

"Arthur's better than that. At least that's what I told myself while we had a very uncomfortable conversation the moment I jumped over the fence this morning."

"I would have liked to have seen that," he murmured, leaning down to kiss her lightly on the lips, then her nose. "You always were good at the element of surprise when you really, really wanted to be."

"Have I surprised you?" she asked. She hooked a finger in the neck of his shirt, using it to pull him closer so that she could kiss him back. He tasted minty, as if he'd brushed his teeth.

Conversation dwindled for a moment, lost in the process of exploration and rejoicing. But somewhere in the midst of it, Nim felt the mood shift.

The corners of Lancelot's lips turned down. "What do you think about his theory that binding your magic cured you?"

"It makes sense," she said. "It's the only explanation that does." And she'd nearly unbound it without knowing the consequences. The thought left her shaken.

She could see Lancelot turning the problem over in his thoughts. "What are you going to do?"

"Do?"

"If you find a way to unbind your magic, then what happens?"

She bit her lip. "I don't know." She said it as bravely as she could, but her voice trembled.

Without a word, Lancelot gathered her in his arms, sitting her up so he could hold her close. His easy strength and the heat of him beneath his soft cotton shirt was a healing balm. She drank it in along with the golden sun and the hypnotic *shush-shush* of the sprinkler outside the window and was inexpressibly glad to be alive.

"Your magic is important to you," he said, "but it doesn't need to define you. You're a fighter with or without it."

"Maybe," she said. "But I always counted on it to protect myself if I had to. Then it didn't work."

"I know," he said. The simple answer was more powerful than sympathy.

Tears welled in her eyes, but she didn't say more. She faced a choice between two impossible alternatives. "I don't know what a future without my power looks like."

He took her shoulders and pushed her away just enough so that the tips of their noses touched. "Like this. Like me. With or without it, I'm here."

But she wouldn't be able to want him if she had her magic back. Would she give him up, even to protect herself from the queen? "You don't mind if I'm as weak and vulnerable as a mortal?"

"Speaking as a vulnerable mortal, not in the least." He smiled, his eyes crinkling in a way that was uniquely Lancelot, but she saw the mix of hope and doubt in his gaze. "The choice is yours, but you don't need magic to hold my interest."

He wanted it to be her choice, but she could see how much he wanted to be hers.

Nim melted. How could she not choose him? Losing her power made her afraid, but with him to hold her the loss was almost a blessing. Her shy pride had never let her lean on anyone else, but now she could finally relax.

A part of her let go. She couldn't name what that part was—only that in all her long life, she'd never released it. The sensation came with a tiny thrill of panic, as if she were an animal that had finally shown its belly. She was exposed and willing for new intimacy.

She kissed him then, the smell of soap and laundry mixing with male and the freshly watered lawn outside. Aching heat coursed through her, but it was more than simple desire. She yearned for this moment to last and last with no more complications between them.

Lancelot returned the kiss, deepening it. Nim arched into his embrace, the line of her body curving into his. Her fingers dug into his shirt, then sought its hem so that she could run her fingers over the hard curves of his chest. So what if she was petting him again? There was no point in denying herself. She drew each instant of the kiss out, tasting his lips, his tongue, the sweetness of his need.

He released a breath in a sound of wordless surprise. It made her chuckle, and she liked the sound of her own pleasure. "Not bad for a soulless fae?" she teased.

"Whatever it was that damaged you, it's healed." He slipped off the couch and pulled the curtains, plunging the room into a murky half-light. He locked the door before returning to her side.

"What are you doing?" she asked, although his intent was plain.

"I'm proving it to you."

"But this building is filled with knights."

"Not at the moment," he said. "They're all out congratulating themselves on killing the ravaging shrubbery."

"But we killed the shrubbery, not them."

Lancelot slid an arm around her. "Never believe a knight about what he's killed or how big it was, especially if he's been drinking."

Nim turned in his arms until she straddled him. Her fingers strayed to his belt buckle. "What about the size of his lance?"

"A knight never lies about his weapons."

"Of course not. That would be unchivalrous."

"If you believe that, I have a castle to sell you in Wales."

She giggled. It wasn't a sound she often made, and he stopped it with his lips.

"Hush," he whispered. "There's a building filled with lusty young knights."

"You said they were all outside."

"Maybe they are. Maybe not."

That only made her giggle harder. "You're horrible."

"Be quiet."

"I'm being quiet!" she gasped.

"No, you're not."

That only made everything seem louder. Both dissolved into silent laughter, which made zippers and buckles impossible. Together they pulled off Lancelot's shirt and her skirt, but those were their only victories. The more impatient they got, the clumsier their fingers.

Finally, Lancelot surged to his feet. "Come."

Nim locked her legs around him, letting herself be carried along. In two strides, he had her against the wall, her hands pinned over her head. He held her there with one massive hand and used the other to unbutton her shirt. His hips rocked gently as he worked, priming her for what was to come. The sensation robbed her of coherent thought.

Once her shirt hung free, he licked her skin, teeth grazing the lace that edged her bra. Groaning, she slid up his chest to allow him better access. With that, he finally released her hands, and she gripped his shoulders as he freed himself from his jeans. His body heat warmed her through her panties and she grew wet with anticipation.

"May I rid you of this undergarment?" he murmured in her ear.

The formal way he said it made Nim smile, but she was beyond laughing now. She gave a nod, and her panties fell in silky shreds.

His finger glided along her slit. "Are you ready?"

"Yes."

Incredible, glorious pressure filled her. She gasped, arching back against the wall so she could angle herself to take him. There was a lot to take, every stroke easing in more and more until every nerve of her body sang with the sensation. He thrust again and again and she had to clench her teeth to keep from crying out. The threat of discovery made it better and worse, inconvenient and daring and conjuring an innocence they'd both lost long ago. Lancelot pressed his mouth over hers, swallowing her moans as he found all the right places.

Minutes later, he brought them both to a shuddering climax.

Nim slid down his body with a whimper of satisfaction. Her limbs tingled as if every nerve had overloaded, but the seeds of anticipation were already taking root. She took Lancelot's hand, drawing him back to the couch. The touch of his skin on hers intoxicated her, and she wasn't ready to stop.

She was in love with him. Not like she had been before, in her long-lost castle by the lake, but in a new and powerful way. She wanted him for the man he'd become, not the fledgling knight he'd been. That Lancelot had worshipped an ideal version of his lady, but idolatry didn't last. This older man valued her for who she was now, and she allowed herself to hope that would endure.

She slid off her bra, cradling his head as he suckled

one breast, then the other. He cupped her, kneading gently and then not so gently, bringing the pooling desire in her womb to a hot, liquid ache. He knew her body, understood exactly what made her respond. To her surprised delight, Lancelot remembered it all.

As they began to make love again in earnest, her heart raced with joy. Maybe she had traded one magical power for another, because wasn't this a kind of sorcery? She tried to imagine giving up the experience of passion and, even more, the capacity to give it. Although it had happened to her, although she had lived in icy blankness for centuries, the long years without emotion seemed like a terrible dream. The moment the cold had shattered, it had become hard to re-create in her mind. Nothing she could ever want, not even magical powers, could tempt her back to existence as a soulless shell.

After Nim had been pleasured to exhaustion, she collapsed in Lancelot's arms. Their limbs twined together on the narrow couch. For the first time in forever, she was happy. She was with the man she loved and everything was simple.

Without meaning to, Nim fell into a deep dream. The first episodes were gentle and meaningless, but the storyline inexorably drew to a scene from the past, a conversation only two people knew about. She might have called it the prelude to a nightmare, except it had been real.

Real was worse.

Merlin summoned Nimueh just before the demon wars. She found him at the top of his high, round tower, hunched at a cluttered table. A fire smoked in a pit in the middle of the room, but it threw no heat against the winter chill. She didn't even consider removing her cloak.

"How do you expect to stop the demons?" she demanded. There was little point in being polite when Merlin was working. He never noticed the difference.

"I will stop them with magic," he mumbled. "It's not like swords will do the job."

"Don't be ridiculous. Not even the fae know the right spells."

Her people had tried desperately for centuries to cast the demon scourge into the abyss but never succeeded. Now Camelot proposed an alliance of all the free peoples against the hellspawn. That would improve the odds, but it would take a new and spectacular weapon to guarantee a win.

She paused at his elbow, studying the crumbling book open on the table. It was so old not even Nimueh understood the runes inked upon its pages. Her gaze shifted to the notes Merlin had scrawled on a torn scrap of paper. Her mouth went dry with terror and excitement. "What's this?"

"What do you think it is?" the enchanter asked in a defensive tone. She knew he was desperate to help Arthur against the demons, but this was her first glimpse at the emotions Merlin kept hidden behind his fierce intellect.

For a long moment she said nothing, her mind whirling. Merlin's raven picked at the remains of his dinner, rattling the pewter plate as it gobbled up bread.

"That's demon magic," she finally said.

Merlin looked up then, his amber eyes burning with defiance. "Our magic—witch or fae—is too weak to stop them. Why not use their own battle spells against them?"

Nimueh's lips parted. "What you propose is unthinkable."

Anger darkened his features. "Which is why we've lost every time. We've been following the rules."

Panic danced inside her. "You don't know what will happen if you cast that spell." She stabbed a finger against his notes. "I don't know. No one does. It probably won't even work."

He shrugged. "Are you going to stop me?"

She met his eyes, responding to the dare in his expression. This was just like him—flashy, gaudy, dangerous. "You're either brilliant or insane."

A grin split his face, but it wasn't happy. "I know."

Then he sobered. "I need your help. I can't do it alone."

Nim startled awake. She was lying on Lancelot's chest. The sun shone through a gap in the curtains, the beams right in her face, but its warmth didn't touch her. The dream pulsed like a living thing in her mind, giving off a sense of dire foreboding. All at once, her future with Lancelot felt frail as a new shoot pushing up through frozen ground. With or without her magic, the past wasn't done with her yet.

Chapter 21

The next evening brought fresh adventure. One of the highlights of Medievaland was the King's Banquet, held every Saturday night for guests who wanted an authentic medieval feast minus the fleas and dubious kitchen sanitation that Nim remembered. Those early revels had been good feasts with surprisingly inventive dishes, but she thought Medievaland's caterers were wise to stick with familiar dishes, ending with a cheesecake molded to the shape of a peacock.

"I'm in the mood for revelry after LaFaye's evil vegetation," said Gawain as he flopped into a chair, Tamsin at his side. "We have something to celebrate for once. Let the wine flow and we'll show the tourists what a great thing it is to be in Camelot."

Nim agreed. Even though she was still haunted by her dream of Merlin, it was hard to hold on to fear with cheerful laughter ringing into the warm summer night. The trestle tables were set up in a broad U beneath a huge, white pavilion. Each table was flanked by long benches, except for the high table that sat lengthwise across the head of the tent. This was where the king sat in a carved, high-backed chair, with his most trusted men on either side. Lancelot was at his right with Nim, Gawain and Tamsin on the left.

"Wine, my lady?" said a liveried page with tattoos snaking down his wrists. He was a modern employee of the park. Beneath his tunic, she could see the edge of a T-shirt, but otherwise he fit the part. She nodded and let him fill her metal goblet.

Lancelot squeezed her hand under the table. He wore soft boots with dark leggings tucked into their tops and a long, loose tunic belted at the hips. It wasn't exactly court dress, but the outfit would be more useful in case he had to fight. Nim liked the clothes on him, especially the open neckline that let her admire the strong muscles of his throat. She, on the other hand, was far less comfortable in a heavy gown of cerulean blue. Nevertheless, Nim knew she looked like herself for once, with a silver veil hiding her dyed black hair. *I'm back*, she thought. *I'm the Lady of the Lake once more.*

"The theme park does a good job," she said to Lancelot under her breath. "It's not trying too hard. The focus is on a good time so it feels like a proper feast."

"Almost," Lancelot agreed. "There aren't any fistfights yet."

"That didn't happen terribly often. Only when Sir Kay was there."

"Or Bors. Or Agravaine. They weren't happy unless someone got a black eye."

Nim wrinkled her nose. "I was at all the wrong parties."

He leaned close. "Stick with me and I'll show you the best chivalry has to offer."

She pulled back in mock horror. "Drunken brawls?"

"Chivalry's been oversold. I always preferred a good tavern."

They laughed, and the sound mixed with the music of the lutes and recorders and drifted into the night. The panels of the tent were tied back to let the breeze through, so that the only wall was the one behind Arthur. This far from the heart of town, the air was clean and the stars above sharp against the inky sky. Candle lanterns hung along the ridge pole, each one dropping on a long chain to light the scene below.

And what a scene it was—every diner there was dressed in some interpretation of medieval costume, though few were outfits Nim had ever seen. But no one—not even the actual medieval folk—really cared about such details. There was food and drink and song and good company. What else mattered?

Indeed, what else? If Nim had this, would she ever miss spells? The idea mixed with the echoes of her dreams and darkened. Instead of making her happy, it felt like a net tangling around her heart.

"What's amiss?" asked Lancelot, placing a finger against her brow. "You're frowning."

"Nothing is amiss," she lied, wishing Merlin had vanished to oblivion the way everyone assumed. She kept his secrets out of guilt and a complicated sense of obligation, but now he had another hold over her. Either he couldn't restore her magic, which was bad. Or maybe he could and that was worse because she didn't want it back at the expense of her emotions—but knowing she mustn't ever touch it would drive her insane. There was no way she could discuss the matter with Lancelot—especially not there, with the king only feet away. Merlin was supposed to be dead.

Nim felt Lancelot's gaze as if it were a physical pressure. "I don't believe you," he said.

"Very well. Look about you." She gestured with one hand, taking in the entire tent. "We agree this is a good replica of old Camelot. If that's true, something will go wrong. Remember Gawain and that green giant who tried to chop his head off?"

Lancelot groaned. "Every time we had a feast like this, Arthur would demand something spectacular or magical for entertainment. He called them 'wonders' and they never ended well."

"He's not going to try that now, is he?"

Lancelot took her hand in his and kissed her palm. "There are no green giants at Medievaland. Or drunken unicorns. Or those trolls who ate Guinevere's yapping lapdogs."

"Those were the days," Nim said, though in retrospect she felt sorry for the dogs.

"We've been patrolling the park. Everything is safe."

"Even from drunken unicorns?" she asked softly.

"Especially them."

It wasn't as silly a conversation as it might sound. Although Camelot technically ruled the mortal world, it dwelled on the cusp of magic. Arthur owed the mystical power of his kingship to the shadow realms, and he was bound by the same rules as the faery queen. That bond was what made him powerful enough to wield Excalibur and present a real challenge to the fae. Without it, he would have no hope of holding back the faery queen. Camelot and its king had a special place on enchantment's borders, but that made strange happenings a matter of course.

Arthur had risen from his seat and was stopping to speak with the guests, giving each one a personal welcome. When he reached Lancelot and Nim, he lifted his goblet in a toast. "The pair of you appear as if destined for one another. I can see now why you always claimed your heart was reserved for the Lady of the Lake."

"Because it was true," said Lancelot. "Let us drink to women worth waiting for."

He raised his goblet to Arthur's and they drained their wine. Nim blushed and took a sip to hide behind her own goblet while the servers hurried to refill the men's drinks.

"May your union be long-lived and filled with joy," said the king, taking another long swallow. "Let us forget the past and embrace present amity."

Nim knew that was as close to an apology as Arthur was likely to give for his jealousy over Guinevere, but she felt the sincerity in it. She was relieved when Lancelot rose to give Arthur a warm smile, accepting his words.

"I am ready for any scrap of happiness," said Arthur. He looked it. The uncertain light of the tent showed the tired hollows of his face.

"You need a holiday," said Nim. "You've worked hard to get Camelot established again. It's not a crime to take a day of rest now and again."

"It is good advice, my lady," he said. "Unfortunately, it's harder to take time off than it sounds."

Nim exchanged a glance with Lancelot as Arthur returned to his seat. "I wonder what the King of Camelot would think of a beach holiday in the Caribbean?" she said softly. "It would be worth the price of the ticket to see him lounging in a deck chair and reading a trashy book."

And then they were laughing again, shadows forgotten. Food arrived—slightly cold, but otherwise tasty—and jugglers frolicked and tumbled in the large center space between the tables. The best dish was the tiny tartlets stuffed with herbed chicken, because Lancelot fed them to her with his own hand and kissed her between each bite.

Meanwhile, young women in low-cut gowns were swarming the knights like bees on honey. "It's a good thing I'm here to defend your honor," she murmured.

"From those wenches?" Lancelot raised his eyebrows. "What would I want with them?"

"The other knights don't seem to mind."

Gawain was with Tamsin, but the rest—including the king—seemed delighted with the attention. In fact, Arthur seemed inclined to unleash his considerable charm and a steady succession of buxom lasses sat on the arm of his throne and melted under the onslaught of his smile.

"They're just fans having fun," said Lancelot. "And we're gentlemen. No one breaks hearts here."

"Keep an eye on Arthur," Nim said quietly. "He's filled his goblet a few times too many. I don't blame him for letting off steam, but he's getting rather too merry."

"Once upon a time, at a banquet like this I would call for a wonder," Arthur was saying to a perky redhead with an aggressively corseted bosom. His words were a little thick as he propped himself on his elbows as if he needed the arms of his throne to keep steady. "Mostly at Yuletide, but sometimes I'd do it if things got dull around the castle. A good magical display is ideal for shaking off boredom."

"Just like that?" said the girl, snapping her dainty fingers. "You'd just say 'presto, let's have a wonder' and someone would come up with it?"

"Hmm?" Arthur said, as if he'd already forgotten the conversation.

She slid from the arm of the chair to perch on his knee. It was an awkward maneuver and she landed in a heap against him.

"Hello," Arthur mumbled, blinking down at the expanse of flesh suddenly inches away.

"Am I wonder enough?" she asked, pouting. "Would you like a wonder, Mr. King?"

At that, Lancelot and Nim exchanged a glance that left them both smirking. "I think his wonder just about popped out of her corset," Lancelot muttered.

"That could do them both an injury," Nim returned.

Oblivious, Arthur laughed with a hearty sound they heard all too seldom. "Well, of course I'd offer a boom."

"A boom?" Eyelashes batted.

"Sorry. A boon." He tapped her pert nose with his forefinger. "A promise. I'd give my word to pay for the shpec— er—spectacle."

"That sounds illegal," said the girl coyly. "And risky. What if I asked you something impossible?"

Nim's ears perked up. There was something besides straightforward flirting in the question.

"There are rules," Arthur explained, then drained his goblet one more time. "Lots of rules. That's what being a king is all about. Rules and rules. I'm only obliged to grant a wish if it is in my power to do so."

"Fair enough." She sat up, winding her arms around his neck. "Promise me a boon for a good, old-fashioned wonder?"

Nim gripped Lancelot's arm. Something was off. "My lord?" she called to Arthur. "A moment of your time?"

He wasn't listening. "Depends on the wonder, sweetling. What are you doing after dessert?"

"Whatever you like." The girl smiled, arching her back. "It's a really, really good wonder."

"For that," Arthur kissed her nose and chuckled low in his chest. "I would certainly grant a boon."

"My lord king!" Nim snapped, her voice sharp with alarm. Lancelot touched her back, calming her.

The king had spoken softly, privately, but every ear in the pavilion had heard as if supernatural acoustics were at work. Those who understood what had just happened froze in horror, including Arthur himself. He shook his head as if to clear it, his features flushing red with anger. Those who did not understand were slower to fall silent, but as they did, merriment drained from the air.

The girl slid off Arthur's lap, her tone changing completely. "Your words have been heard, my lord, and they shall be answered."

Arthur rose, drawing himself up until he towered over her. "What is the meaning of this?"

He was much taller and the girl was forced to look up, but she was calm. "As you said, there are rules. The Queen of Faery bid me to remind you that no King of Camelot can grant a boon in bad faith and hope to keep his crown. The laws of magic will strip him of his authority to rule the mortal realms."

Nim's fingers were still clasped around Lancelot's arm, her heart pounding with outrage. The knights had patrolled the grounds for fae, but this girl was human. Yet she was clearly LaFaye's servant, no doubt beguiled into service. But whoever she was and how she got there, it was her words that mattered.

Stripped bare, the logic was simple: LaFaye wanted Arthur's crown. She'd used the girl to trick Arthur into giving a promise. If he broke his word, the magic that made him king would grow weaker and LaFaye might just take his crown away. There was no way he could afford to ignore his oath.

If that wasn't bad enough, there were still two unknowns: what kind of magical wonder were they about to see, and what would LaFaye demand in return?

The silence in the pavilion deepened. No sounds reached them—not the murmur of distant traffic, nor the happy discord of the midway music, nor even the voices of pedestrians passing by. The air grew heavy, as it did before a thunderstorm. Nim could almost taste the magic in it, and her shoulders went rigid with apprehension. She didn't need her powers to foretell that something significant was going to happen.

Hoofbeats sounded in the distance—more than one

rider by the way they seemed to shake the ground. Nim turned to the open end of the tent, confused. There was no path, no quantity of open ground in that direction, and yet a pale road stretched into the distance. It seemed to rise into the sky as if the beaten track were a highway into the clouds. Arthur had asked for a wonder, and he had it.

Nim expected to see LaFaye on her ebony mare, or the chief warriors of the fae, or even the rogue fae who called themselves the Wild Hunt—though they bowed to no monarch, not even the queen. But what came down the path was a herd of white deer, led by the most magnificent stag she had ever seen. No one spoke. No one even breathed—not even the human tourists—and it was only when the creatures stepped into the tent that Nim saw they were as specters. Their coats glowed white and glittered as if rimed with frost, but they were as transparent as ghosts. The heavy, close feeling of powerful magic filled the pavilion, prickling Nim's skin.

As the stag led the others to face the king, Nim counted nine deer in all—stags, does and fawns. They seemed unafraid, though all but the leader kept a respectful distance from the throne, bowing their heads in greeting.

"Hail and well met," said King Arthur, his face gone pale and grim. He appeared utterly sober now.

"Hail to you, King of Mortals," said the stag in a deep and resonant voice. "In your heart, you called upon the old ones."

Nim saw Arthur hesitate, but he nodded. He was nothing if not honest. "I desired to see a wonder as I remember from my old Camelot."

The stag made obeisance, the great antlered head dipping almost to the ground. "Here we are. The old world persists beneath the veil of the modern years. It takes but a thought to lift it."

Arthur shook his head. "There is always a price for such magic. That was the first lesson Merlin ever taught me."

Nim sat down heavily. She was surprised to hear Arthur speak the enchanter's name. It might have been the first time Arthur acknowledged his existence in a thousand years.

"The price is simple," said the stag. "The Queen of Faery demands a tourney—your people against hers. The side that wins names whatever prize they choose."

Lancelot leaned close. "Excalibur. It is the only thing she wants."

It made sense. Morgan had asked for it, and then she had tried to kill for it. Now she was using the old laws of magic that Arthur knew better than to break. But those laws cut both ways, and Morgan had to obey them, too. If she lost or cheated, the tourney was over and no one could issue the same challenge twice.

"How is it that when I ask for a wonder, it is the Queen of Faery who sets the terms of payment?" Arthur asked bitterly. "Why are my wishes her business?"

The stag snorted, stamping one cloven hoof. "Such wishes hang in the ether, awaiting fulfillment like a fish hook bobbing in a stream. A king's wish is most tempting to those with mischief in mind. The faery queen was listening for your words."

"And her servant was there to trip him up," Nim muttered. She was so tense, her neck muscles burned.

The red-haired girl gave a silky smile. "Now that your request for a wonder is granted, do you break your promise of a boon?"

The king's fingers clenched. "I have no choice. I summoned magic and promised to pay the price. You may tell the queen I accept her challenge."

Lancelot cursed and reached for his wine. There was nothing they could do in that moment, but Nim saw the hard lines of anger on Lancelot's face. In the family of Camelot, Arthur and Lancelot postured and fought, but they were family and now Arthur was in peril.

Nim wished she could take Lancelot's pain—wished she had her magic and could fight LaFaye properly, one enchantress to another. As it was, she had no role in the tourney, not even a reason to be there. She was useless.

Arthur gave a heavy sigh. "King of the Forest, when and where shall the first round be held?"

"It shall be in the Forest Sauvage, at dusk tomorrow," said the stag. "The contestants will meet in Taliesin's Circle."

"How do I know this is not another trap?" Arthur asked.

One of the does stepped forward and dropped something from her mouth before the king, then backed away. It was a pair of jeweled collars.

"One member from each side shall wear a collar," said the stag. "No one can do the wearers harm—not the king or queen or any other participant in the game. However, if one side or the other misbehaves, the wearers are brutally punished. The collars turn them into hostages for good behavior."

The red-haired girl picked one up and fastened it around her neck, giving Arthur a defiant look. "I put my life as surety against the queen's good behavior. If she offends against the rules of the tourney, I shall die."

Arthur picked up the second collar. "I shall wear this myself. No one need act as bond for my word."

"No," said the stag. "It must be one of your servants. But beware, once it is on it cannot be removed until the tourney is done."

"I will do it," said Lancelot, rising from his seat.

"No," said Nim, moving so quickly that she was at Arthur's side before Lancelot could stop her. "A champion has enough to do. I will be the guarantee of Arthur's word."

She fastened the collar around her neck. It was light, but she felt the magic in it seal around her throat. She was trusting Arthur with her life, but it also protected her from LaFaye. No one had said a thing about protecting LaFaye from her.

Her eyes met Lancelot's. He glared at the collar as if it were a living serpent.

"So be it," said the stag. "Good luck to you, King of Mortals." He shook his antlers, and the sparkling frost fell to form clear white gemstones upon the floor of the pavilion. "These stones will transport you to and from the contest. You have the queen's oath of safe passage and safety while on neutral ground." With that, he turned and led his herd from the pavilion, returning along the ghostly road into the clouds.

The crowd, mostly tourists who thought they'd experienced an excellent display of special effects and awesome acting, applauded with gusto and snapped their cameras to catch the last of the spectacle. By the morning, though, no one remembered exactly what they'd seen—and none of the pictures showed anything but an uncertain blur. And, in all the excitement, no one but Nim noticed the red-haired girl vanish, her work for Queen Morgan done.

Before the crowd quieted, Arthur turned to Gawain. "See to the guests." Then he stormed from the tent.

With a worried glance at Nim, Lancelot followed the king. Nim sat quietly for a moment, staring at the remnants of the pastries on her plate. She'd enjoyed them so much, less than an hour ago, but now they sat like lead in her stomach. With a curse, she stood and followed Lancelot from the tent.

The golden light from the banquet spilled across the grass and reduced the night to knife-edged shadows. There were few people out here—a handful of smokers and a cook's assistant wheeling a trolley of dishes back to the kitchen. It didn't take her long to pick out the silhouette of the king standing beneath the twisting branches of an oak tree. Nim kept to the shadows, not sure whether to approach or to leave him alone.

She didn't see Lancelot standing next to the trunk until she was closer. "Be easy," he said to Arthur. "You cannot take the blame on yourself."

"I am a king," came the answer. "Shame upon me for forgetting the peril of the world, even for a night." The self-reproach in Arthur's voice made Nim's heart twist with pity.

"That's not helpful," Lancelot replied, kind but firm. "We need to think about what comes next."

Arthur muttered something Nim couldn't hear, and Lancelot answered in equally soft tones. Nim stopped her approach, unwilling to interrupt. Although she couldn't hear the conversation, their body language said much. Tension flared between the men, but there was also a dynamic she had noticed before but never quite understood. Now it was clear.

Perhaps Lancelot had gone to the king in search of a father, but that had clearly changed. Lancelot was prepared to challenge Arthur as no other knight would. He had matured into an equal—one Arthur needed, even if they disagreed as often as they made peace. One who could speak plainly in times of crisis, and whose forgiveness for a blunder mattered. She saw Lancelot put a hand on Arthur's shoulder, giving comfort.

Deep anger stirred inside Nim. What LaFaye had done was a brilliant kind of cruelty, for she knew Arthur's deep sense of obligation to his people. To trap him into a deadly game like this went against every instinct he had. The tournaments of the Forest Sauvage were famed for combining the worst triviality with bloodthirsty sport. No one had held them since Vikings roamed the world.

All at once, she was fiercely glad Arthur had Lancelot at his side. A king had few real friends. Courtiers were much easier to come by but were of little help in moments like this. Nim turned away, walking back to the banquet. She would let them have their private conversation.

Her mind was already roaming ahead to tomorrow, when she would see LaFaye for the first time since she'd regained her soul. Nim wasn't certain how she would do it yet, but she would make the Queen of Faery pay for what she had done.

Chapter 22

After that, it was the early hours before Nim and Lancelot finally got to bed. Even then, she couldn't sleep and lay for a long time listening to Lancelot's even breaths. It was warm next to him, with his body in a protective curl around hers. His solid, reassuring presence made the wild scene at the banquet seem impossible. The competition the following evening seemed like fantasy.

Unfortunately, it was the kind of fantasy that could kill. Nim didn't like the idea of walking into one of LaFaye's minefields without a dozen backup plans and she didn't have even one—let alone her powers.

Slowly, carefully, she inched out of the bed without waking Lancelot. Taking her phone from the bedside table, she tiptoed down the stairs to the living room. The moon shone through the patio doors, washing the room in silvery gray light. She dialed a number from memory because it was too dangerous to put in any contact list. In fact, she'd only used it once before and then been careful to delete the call from her phone's memory.

The phone rang a dozen times before Merlin answered.

"What took you so long to pick up?" Nim snapped, though she kept her voice low and glanced nervously at the ceiling, but she didn't hear Lancelot stir.

Merlin made a rude noise. "Pardon me for earning a living. What do you want?"

"Your binding failed me."

There was a brief silence. "Did LaFaye find you? I think not or you wouldn't be alive to complain."

"It worked too well. I can't use my power at all. It won't unbind."

There was a crash in the background, like pots being dumped in a sink. "Perhaps you should count yourself lucky. Sorcery is a difficult career."

"Merlin!" she growled.

"You have your emotions back, don't you? I can tell by the venom."

"It happened when you bound my magic. It's a problem. Before I had all kinds of power but didn't care what happened to other people. Now I care and can't help." She was oversimplifying, but she needed to get her point across. "I need options."

"You want the option to make some sort of hysterical grand gesture that will erase whatever accidental benefits the binding gave you?"

Anger brought heat to her skin. "Don't be ridiculous. Fix this."

His tone was defensive. "You wanted a binding. I gave you what you asked for."

"You were supposed to include the means to undo it. That's why I paid you a fortune." LaFaye's enchanted jewel should have bought her a lifetime of Merlin's spell casting.

"No, that was a one-way ticket. The return flight is extra."

Nim's skin prickled with frustration. She knew Merlin had changed, become more mercenary, but until that moment she hadn't realized the depth of it. "I'm a friend."

"I don't have a special rate for friends. Not ones that ask me to do something stupid and then whine when it works too well."

She squeezed the phone, pacing from the window to the fireplace and back. "What happened to you?"

"Don't pretend to be astonished."

Nim's temper slipped. She slammed her palm against the stone hearth hard enough to sting. "Get over yourself, Merlin."

"I thought you wanted my help."

Nim ground her teeth. She wanted to blurt out the whole story about the collar, the contest, and LaFaye's trickery, but it was clear Merlin wasn't in a place to listen. "What's this about?"

"A little bird told me you're playing nice with Arthur. Here I am, left out in the cold."

Her dream came back to her. Merlin had asked for her help with the demon spell, and she'd refused. "I didn't break Arthur's trust by devastating his allies."

"The spell that ended the demon wars might not have ripped out your soul if you'd helped me."

Shock and anger tingled over Nim's skin. "Are you saying what happened is my fault?"

There was a soft laugh. "No. Unlike you, I don't believe I'm qualified to judge others. I'm angry because you spent the night with friends who turned their backs on me. You survived your mistakes. I didn't."

She heard his loneliness. No one had ever forgiven Merlin for destroying the fae. Whether or not he deserved it was irrelevant; it was a question of mercy. "I'm sorry you're alone."

His breath was ragged. "For the record, I don't know what went wrong with the binding. I can't help you."

And then he hung up.

Dulac's eyes were sandy from lack of sleep when he left for Medievaland the next day. He'd made plans with Arthur, keeping it simple because they had so little time. The company of knights would split, half staying at the theme park to entertain the crowds and the rest venturing to the Forest Sauvage, the no-man's-land between the worlds of mortal, fae and demon. Any creature could walk there because none ruled it, and even a few of the banished hellspawn remained. It had always been a realm made to beguile and confuse, a jumbled mirror of the old Camelot but filled with hidden dangers. Now, it seemed, LaFaye had found a use for it as neutral ground for her tourney.

Because it was a realm outside the mortal world, the knights could not reach the Forest Sauvage without magic. The stag's gemstones would provide safe passage to Taliesin's Circle.

"How do you fare?" he asked Nimueh as they walked from the park gate toward the quiet yard behind the stables.

"Well enough," she replied, her face solemn. "Badly enough. I have not seen a tourney of this kind since I was a child. They are fraught with hazard."

A small party was going to make the initial arrangements: Gawain, Dulac, Nimueh and of course Arthur. The knights would wear their fighting gear while Nimueh had put on a simple blue gown belted at the waist with a girdle of fine silver links shaped like willow leaves. Her dark hair framed her face in stark lines. It was the one detail that didn't belong to her—that, and the collar Dulac wished he could rip from her throat. It promised brutal punishment if their side of the tourney stepped out of line, and he wasn't certain how far that would go.

Dulac trusted Arthur, but Nimueh's life was sacred to him. He would have willingly taken the danger on himself, but he guessed the reason she'd volunteered. She needed to fight the queen, and taking the hazard of the collar on herself was the one way she could contribute to their success without magic of her own.

Visitors stopped and stared at them as they passed. Nimueh was beyond beautiful, her dark skin lustrous where the sun touched it. She walked with a fae's grace, her hand resting lightly on his arm. That she was his lady once more was worth a thousand kingdoms, and Dulac thought the people saw something of that written on his face. Their smiles echoed what was in his heart.

"I was thinking about the Forest Sauvage," Nim said quietly. "You will find it unchanged, I think."

He could see her fingers tremble, even though she hid them in her skirts. She was talking to cover her nerves, and that showed how hard it would be for her to face LaFaye.

"Good," said Dulac. "I will treasure the familiar. This mortal world is changed enough."

She cast him a sidelong look, her bright green gaze barely touching him before it skittered away. "I wonder if there will be a chance to see my old castle. My lake. I hid it with enchantment when I left, and it should still remain untouched."

He imagined the place and wondered how he would feel about seeing it again. He'd left it feeling so guilty. "I imagine you miss the quiet there."

"I did. I do. I had my work and a few good companions, and that was enough. For a time, I had you." She squeezed his arm, letting him know she would not dwell on that point for now. Her fingers were like ice. "But preference becomes a habit and then finally a vice. Eventually solitude made me afraid to mix with company. My few attempts at visiting Camelot did nothing but make me long to run away."

Small wonder, since she would have run headlong into Morgan and Guinevere. "Camelot was hard to adjust to. Believe me, I know."

Her fingers rose to touch the collar in what was rapidly becoming a nervous habit. Once again, he longed to tear it off her, but he wasn't certain what the consequences would be. That kind of magic was risky.

Nimueh continued on, her voice brittle with tension. "Losing the ability to feel that kind of discomfort was almost a relief. I think that's why I was able to open the bookstore. A little less sensitivity made it easier to deal with the public."

"You're clearly good at it. By all accounts, the store's a success."

"I'm going to stay in Carlyle."

He looked up sharply to study her expression. It was the first time she'd said she would stay with him. "In truth?"

"In truth," she said, smiling slowly. "It seems I didn't need all twenty-four hours to make up my mind. You're extremely convincing. I want to be with you."

The admission rocked him. It was everything he wanted, and yet there was no time to celebrate and enjoy the expanding fire in his heart. He stopped and faced her on the crowded path, letting the visitors eddy around them. This was no place for what he wanted to do, so he contented himself with bringing both her hands to his lips and kissing them reverently. "I adore you more than you will ever know."

She lowered her eyes, her mouth curving into a shy smile. "I'm glad."

In another few minutes, they'd reached their destination. It was just before dusk, the sky a blue that had faded from the heat and dust of the day. It was clear, but Dulac smelled rain on the wind—a sure sign the unusual heat was breaking. It would be a relief.

The others were already there, faces serious. The king held one of the gems between thumb and forefinger as if it might detonate at any moment. For all his longing for wonder, Arthur wasn't comfortable with magic up close. As Dulac and Nimueh stood opposite Gawain, the king set the stone on the ground in the middle of their loose circle. They all stared at it.

"Am I supposed to do something?" Arthur asked.

"Wait," said Nimueh.

Almost before she'd stopped speaking, cold white light bloomed from the stone. At first it seemed to emanate from within, but then the core of the brilliance floated upward, hovering at the height of Dulac's chest. Then the rays stretched outward, filling the space where they stood. The air shimmered, like water stirred by a breeze, and a faint hum set his teeth on edge. Nimueh held his hand and some instinct told him to reach out and grasp the king's shoulder. Arthur gripped Gawain's arm. An instant later, a blast of cold air swept over them, nearly knocking him from his feet. The sensation of vertigo lasted an instant too long and then everything changed.

They were standing in a green, rolling landscape with no buildings as far as the eye could see. Dulac turned to survey the land in every direction. Where Carlyle had been hot, here the weather was cool and damp, with ropes of mist where the land was lowest. He took a deep breath, the cold, fresh air clearing his head. Clumps of trees and bushes dotted the landscape, but the knights had landed in open ground where a ring of waist-high, standing stones marked a wide circle in the rough grass. This was called Taliesin's Circle, for it was the place where Arthur's Chief of Bards had come to compose his songs and teach young students his wisdom. In truth, the place was older by far than any of Arthur's men. The dark gray stones were crooked, worn smooth by weather and time, and the atmosphere said it stood on a place of great natural magic.

"So where's the party?" asked Arthur, planting his hands on his hips.

Gawain leaned against one of the stones. "I for one am happy to wait. The longer I go without sight of the queen, the longer I am happy."

Dulac was inclined to agree, but he could feel Nimueh's anxiety. He put an arm around her. "They won't be long. Dusk draws nigh here, as well. This time of year, the sun will set when it nears the top of that stone."

He pointed to the horizon, where the sun touched the clouds in shades of orange and red. By the time he finished speaking, the Queen of Faery and her retainers had arrived.

"Oh," Nimueh said softly, gripping his arm.

Morgan LaFaye had spared no effort with her appearance. Her dark hair was elaborately dressed and studded with jewels, and her gown was of rich red velvet faced with cloth of silver. She was flanked by three of the fae, their tall, slender forms still and silent. At their feet knelt the red-haired girl in her collar. Now the girl seemed far less confident, her face tight with apprehension. Dulac guessed she'd come to the same conclusion he had—LaFaye had chosen someone dispensable to forfeit her life for the queen's good behavior.

Morgan LaFaye stepped forward, her gaze falling almost at once on Excalibur hanging at Arthur's side. Her eyes widened, fear and greed chasing across her features. Then she saw Nimueh, and saw Dulac's arm around her. LaFaye's lips twisted in a sly smile as Nimueh stiffened.

"Congratulations, Arthur," said the queen. "I see you brought me exactly what I asked you for—sword and traitor both—and you did it all without tarnishing your precious honor. That was clever footwork."

Arthur stood with one hand on Excalibur's hilt, his back ramrod straight. The only thing that marked him as royal was the thin circlet of gold about his brow. Even so, he appeared every inch the king. "I did not realize the tourney included an event dedicated to trading insults. A pity, since I doubt I will ever possess the equal of your sharp tongue."

What civility Morgan had slipped and her eyes flashed with ugly rage. "You're a fool that does not deserve his crown."

"Perhaps," Arthur replied calmly. "I do not know if any man or woman is equal to the responsibility of caring for the mortal realms. However, I will always give whatever I have to the task, and I will do everything in my power to keep your grasping fingers away."

She laughed, a low sound that was as intimate as it was chilling. "How sententious."

"And how desperate you must be to gamble the welfare of your people in an arcane trial such as this. I will participate because it is required of me as the monarch of the mortal realms. I will not risk my power and right to wear my crown, however vile your trickery. But be prepared for the consequences of your foolishness, Morgan," he said in clipped tones. "To borrow the modern phrase, I expect we'll kick your asses. I'm already picking out my prize."

"And what will you choose, kinglet?" she mocked.

Arthur's smile was slightly evil. "You'll see."

By the toss of her head, Dulac guessed LaFaye didn't like that answer one bit. She wasn't as confident as she let on.

"Very well," said the queen. "Let us begin."

"Hold a moment," said Arthur. "Who will judge this

contest? In fairness, the judge can be neither fae nor human."

"I have considered that," said LaFaye. "I know the rules of the tourney as well as you do."

With a sweep of her arm, she indicated the center of the stone circle. The air sparkled, and a white throne appeared from thin air. "I have asked the Forest Sauvage to send someone of its own choosing," explained LaFaye. "I do not know any more than you who that might be."

As if waiting for her cue, a figure stepped out of thin air, taking a place beside the white throne. Shock surged through Dulac and he grabbed for his sword, ready to sell his life dearly.

Chapter 23

Dulac drew his sword, stepping in front of Nimueh and the king. Gawain went pale as curdled milk.

Only Nimueh didn't react. "Greetings, Tenebrius," she said with a low curtsy.

"So the Lady of the Lake has returned to the Forest Sauvage," said the demon in a deep voice. "This should be a day of celebration, but I find you mixed up in this sorry squabble."

He sounded educated, almost scholarly, but Dulac knew well enough that mortal senses only perceived what a demon chose. He appeared tall, bald but for a tightly clipped black beard, and dressed in robes the shade of drying blood. His pale yellow eyes were slit like a goat's.

"My lady, how do you know this creature?" Dulac asked. He knew demons still roamed the Forest Sauvage, but he'd never considered getting to know them. Then again, Nimueh's taste for scholarly subjects had forged some odd acquaintances.

She rose from her curtsy, her expression revealing nothing. "At one time, his lands in the forest bordered mine. He was my neighbor."

"Your neighbor? He tried to eat me the last time I was here!" Gawain said with annoyance.

"I do not wonder," said Nimueh with a touch of humor. "Demons must be treated with scrupulous respect. My understanding was that you tried to steal his library."

Gawain frowned. "That's one way of looking at it. I have quite another version of events."

"Silence," ordered the king. "Dulac, stand aside."

Dulac complied reluctantly.

Tenebrius gave a silky smile, showing pointed teeth. "King Arthur, well met. You led the armies of the fae and mortal realms against my kind. Lucky for me your power does not extend here."

Then the demon's gaze turned to LaFaye and his lips thinned to a grin. Dulac turned to see what pleased the creature so very much and felt a mild shock of surprise. The queen's face was stricken, her eyes like bruises in a visage pale as milk.

"You are the hellspawn who devoured my son," she said in a voice that was little more than a rasp.

The sharp-toothed smile grew wider. "Indeed I did. For the record, he was dead at the time, but tasty nonetheless."

For an instant Dulac pitied the queen. Only a mother could have loved the vile Prince Mordred, but loved him she had.

The demon waved a hand as if flicking away any further pleasantries. "You requested a judge for this combat, and here I am. There are no second choices. By the law of the shadow worlds, I must be neutral and believe me, I do not care who wins or dies in this dispute."

Dulac believed it. Demons served whoever paid them most.

"I understand the prize will be of the winner's choosing," the demon said with a grin. "May I know your choices?"

"I will keep my choice to myself for now," replied Arthur.

The demon gave a slight bow. "It is a dangerous thing to leave such an important detail open-ended, but that is permissible."

"The prize will be Excalibur," Morgan snapped. "I shall win, and that is what I shall have."

Arthur roared an oath, and a moment later the sword appeared in the demon's hand, complete with sword belt and sheath. "What is the meaning of this?" cried the king.

"This is purely precautionary," said the demon. "The sword is of no value to me, but I know the lady queen. Until the contest is done, I will keep Excalibur under lock and key to prevent any—what is the word?—*shenanigans*."

Despite himself, Dulac had to agree with the precaution. Apparently, so did Arthur, because the king folded his arms and said no more, though his frown spoke volumes.

"These are the rules," Tenebrius continued. "One, those who wear the collars are protected from harm by the combatants and their leaders. However, if their leader breaks the rules, they will die."

Dulac stepped close to Nimueh and took her hand in his. Her fingers were like ice.

"Two, all combatants and their assistants are protected from harm unless they are actually in combat. During the melee, a significant injury is cause enough to withdraw from the field. Each side may have a healer present for such emergencies."

Gawain stirred and Dulac guessed what he was thinking. Tamsin was Camelot's healer, but Gawain would not be pleased at the thought of her anywhere near Tenebrius or Morgan.

"Three, magic and magical weapons are not permitted in battle. Nor are those identified as leaders.

"Finally, four, single combat is between evenly matched opponents and it shall be to the death, no exceptions."

A murmur rose up from the crowd. People died in tourneys, but custom allowed a defeated opponent to sue for mercy. Rarely was that refused.

The demon's eyes flashed. "If a combatant refuses the kill, he automatically loses the entire contest for his side. No mercy. No surrenders. No weaseling out of a nice bloody death. You're using the forest as your battleground, and for that it demands a payment in blood and fear. As for me, I eat what's left of the loser as my judge's fee."

Tenebrius stopped talking and looked from one face to the other with amusement. Clearly, it entertained him to see both sides struck dumb. "If these contests weren't horrible, you idiots would be challenging each other every day of the week. I don't like to waste my time keeping things fair for morons who did their best to cast me out of my nice warm castle and back to the abyss. Don't look to me for sympathy. You picked this fight."

He subsided majestically into the white chair. "See you all back here tomorrow. I've a fancy to start this display of arms with a melee—who doesn't like a battle royal with the most noise and gore possible? It will serve to thin the herd a bit and see who is left to slit each other's throats."

He gave a satisfied look around the company. "The fun shall begin at noon tomorrow."

With that, he vanished—chair and all—in a puff of sulfurous smoke.

"Wonderful," said Gawain. "We literally have the judge from hell."

A melee was a free-for-all. All the contestants fought at once, on foot and with whatever weapons they chose. As a limited number of Arthur's knights had been awakened from the stone sleep, each side had only six combatants. Lancelot, Gawain, Beaumains, Percival, Palomedes and Owen of the Beasts fought for Camelot. Sir Hector, Tamsin's father, was left behind to keep an eye on the theme park.

The day of the melee was bright and clear, and the large open field next to Taliesin's Circle was dry and provided plenty of room for six pairs of fighters to do their worst. The boundary was defined by a rope marked with bright flags pegged into the dirt. Arthur, Tamsin and Nim stood outside the southwest corner, while Morgan and the fae kept vigil at the northeast. Nim was pleased that the distance was great enough that she could not see the queen's face.

Arthur fidgeted, clearly wishing he was one of the fighters who were arming and taking their places in the improvised ring. "Every spilled drop of blood is on my soul," he said softly.

"You were tricked," said Nim. "This is all the queen's work."

He looked at her sadly, his pale blue eyes ringed by lack of sleep. "It is Morgan's work, but I let my guard down so that she could do it. I can't argue that fact away."

"What good does blaming yourself do?" Tamsin asked. The young witch was the only one wearing modern clothes, her long fair hair pulled back in a no-nonsense braid. She sat on her large medical kit, arms folded. She was watching Gawain finish arming, something close to terror for her lover written on her face. Her father might have been a knight, but because of their unusual history, she had never seen anything like the tourney before.

Arthur gave her a sad look. "If a king does not blame himself, he is not being careful enough with his people."

She chewed her lips, but didn't look up. "I was born in modern times. This all seems crazy to me. I get self-defense, but this is organized slaughter."

"Tourneys show a man's prowess to his lady," said the king. "There is nothing so great as wearing a woman's token into mortal combat, knowing that the blows you strike are in her honor. My heart would pound with joy to look up from the bloody field and see her, fair and shining, in the stands."

Tamsin looked at him as if he'd gone mad. "Is that actually true?"

"A few times," said Arthur, glancing at Lancelot, then at Nim. "There were moments."

Arthur looked sad, and Nim wondered if he might have loved his child-bride Guinevere, or if he dreamed of some other maiden long turned to dust.

The demon stood dead center of the improvised ring. He raised a square of scarlet silk in one hand. For one moment, all was silent, the only sound the breeze that rushed through the grass and fluttered the little square of red cloth. Then the demon vanished, the silk fell and the fight was on.

"I can't watch," Tamsin said, burying her face in her hands.

Nim didn't want to, either, but was realist enough to know she couldn't turn away. Lancelot was near the middle of the field and so she circled the periphery at a run to get a better view. As the fae all wore silver armor, it was easy to pick them out. Beside them, the knights seemed almost ragtag, their mismatched gear scarred from hard battle. Nim's loyalties lay with the knights, but she hated to see her own people hurt. Peace was the thing she wanted above all else, but that meant putting an end to the queen.

Despite the sun, her skin went cold and clammy. Metal crashed on metal, leather creaked and feet stomped so hard that the earth sounded hollow. Men grunted as bodies thudded together, and suddenly there was a guttural roar of pain.

Two fighters stumbled past quickly enough that Nim felt the rush of air as she darted aside to keep from being trampled.

Then she caught sight of Lancelot, his war ax already bloody. His opponent was huge, taller by a head and using a short spear to maximize his reach. Even Lancelot would have a hard time getting inside his guard.

Nim started as she saw someone move a few feet away. She glanced up to find Tamsin there, then returned her attention to the fight at once. The witch kept a respectful distance from Nim, as well she might. They'd met as opponents and never had the opportunity to become something else.

"Tell me something," Tamsin asked, her voice thin with worry. "Is this fight a fair deal?"

The question seemed naive, but then what could Nim expect from someone born in the modern day? "A melee is like a battle, and a real battle isn't fair."

Tamsin buried her face in her hands again. "Oh, Gawain." Her groan held as much love and exasperation as it did dread.

"I'm afraid watching someone you love in danger doesn't get any easier," Nim said gently. "Trust me, I know."

Through the shifting bodies, she caught a glimpse of Lancelot ducking beneath his opponent's spear. He delivered a blow before spinning away again, already hunting for the next opening. Nerves and pride spun through her like strong drink. Lancelot was a large man, so many underestimated his speed. She hoped it was enough to keep him whole.

"Oh!" Tamsin exclaimed, one hand flying to her mouth. Then she moved a step closer and pointed into the maelstrom. "Gawain just hit his guy with a piece of his own armor!"

Nim followed her pointing finger. Gawain had lost

his helmet, but he was fighting like a madman. "Gawain knows how to look after himself."

Tamsin gave a tearful nod, one hand over her heart. They were side by side now. Nim cast a quick glance to see how the other knights were doing, but it was hard to tell. There was too much confusion. Her gaze ended on Arthur, who stood as still as a sentinel, the only sign of tension was in the line of his shoulders. If he was worried, he wasn't letting LaFaye see it. Tamsin stood next to him, her pose almost a double of the king's.

Tamsin? But Tamsin was standing beside Nim! She whirled around to find herself almost nose-to-nose with the red-haired girl. The sunlight glinted on the girl's collar and the knife she held pressed to Nim's ribs. Her lips peeled back in a terrible grin. "Some enchantress you are if you can't see through a simple disguise. Mind you, I did go to theater school."

Nim cursed herself. LaFaye's glamour spells weren't simple, but she should have been able to sense it. Then she cursed Merlin for refusing to help with her magic.

"What do you want?" Nim put frost into her tone. "We're both protected by these collars."

The point of the knife pricked her flesh. "We're protected from harm by the combatants or their leaders. Nobody said anything about harm from each other. My mistress is very angry with you, and I'm all about keeping her happy."

Wasting no more words, the girl jerked the knife in and up, aiming for Nim's heart. It would have killed a human, but a fae was too fast. She grabbed the girl's wrist and twisted, turning into the movement so the redhead ended up bent nearly double, her knife hand pinned behind her. Nim squeezed until the girl's fingers uncurled and the blade dropped.

"Please, oh please," the girl begged. "She's going to be furious with me."

Nim cast another glance at the battle, anxious for Lancelot despite the threat next to herself. "I'm sorry for you, but not enough to stand still while you stab me."

The girl wore a belt of twisted cord around her gown. Nim pulled it free and then bound the girl's hands behind her. She picked up the knife and heaved the girl up by her bound hands. With a shove, Nim marched her back to Arthur's corner of the field, keeping the lead rope wrapped tight around her wrist. The girl wasn't getting away.

Nim had nearly reached her destination when Tenebrius materialized before her, wearing a silk dressing gown and smoking a cigarette in a long ebony holder. The demon gave the redhead a deep scowl. "What's this?"

The girl cringed, drawing close to Nim as if her would-be victim might offer protection. Nim ignored her, making a curt reply to the demon. "There is a loophole in your rules that nearly resulted in a hole in me."

"Explain," Tenebrius growled.

Nim did. Arthur approached as she talked, folding his arms in disgust as he heard the tale. "Surely this is against the spirit of the law," said the king.

The demon squinted and tilted his palm to and fro in a so-so gesture. "Maybe so, but the letter of the law permits it. Nonetheless, LaFaye presumes upon my patience."

He turned to face the melee and raised his arms in the air. "Hold!" he bellowed.

Every fighter froze in position, arrested in place by magic. It was several seconds before they could lower their weapons.

Tenebrius gestured and the cigarette and holder vanished. "A point of rule demands clarification. Until this is resolved, those who wear the collar have safe conduct from *everyone*—" he put nasty emphasis on the word "—within the Forest Sauvage. Furthermore, for their own safety they will not leave the forest until the tournament is done."

A murmur ran through the company. Nim thought she saw LaFaye stamp her foot with frustration.

"You! Queen!" The demon pointed a long, taloned finger at LaFaye. "You are on notice. One more insult to my authority and I will make you pay in ways even your nightmares cannot fathom."

LaFaye folded her arms, looking mulish.

"I declare the melee finished," said the demon with disgust. "Collect your fallen."

Nim's eyes flew to where Lancelot stood. His ax ran red, but he appeared unhurt. His opponent, however, was down on one knee.

Then she heard Tamsin—the real Tamsin—cry out. When one of the fae shifted aside, Nim saw Gawain on his back in the churned earth. The witch leaped over the rope barrier, bolting between the weapons and warriors to her lover's side.

The demon's words came back to her: *You're using the forest as your battleground, and for that it demands a payment in blood and fear.*

The Forest Sauvage had taken its payment for the day. Nim ran forward to help, secretly thanking the stars that it hadn't been Lancelot.

Chapter 24

Dulac and Nimueh helped Tamsin turn Gawain over. His friend had been knocked out—a consequence of losing his helmet earlier in the fight. A nasty lump was forming, but he had already regained consciousness.

The blow had finished the work begun by a sword thrust to the ribs. Gawain swore savagely as they uncovered the wound, but it lacked conviction. He had lost too much blood to pretend he was all right. Under Tamsin's expert care, he would be up and around in a day or two, but he would not fight another day in the tournament.

Percival was also finished, having broken several fingers in his sword hand. That left Dulac, Beaumains, Owen and Palomedes in the tourney. They'd taken minor wounds, but nothing that would keep them from the field.

They made a sling of their arms and carried Gawain through the portal back to Medievaland. All, that is, except Dulac and Nimueh. By the demon's orders, she could not leave the forest and Dulac would not go without her.

"Now what?" she asked. "There are no hotels in the Forest Sauvage. We need proper food and shelter if you are to fight again tomorrow." By the pallor of her cheeks, the very notion of more fighting shook her.

"I will be fine," he said. "I'm more concerned about you."

She looked away then, her brow puckering.

"What is it?" he asked.

"We could go home. To my castle, I mean." Her eyes searched his face almost shyly. "If you want to, that is. I won't insist on it."

"Why not?" he said. "I have many fond memories of the place."

And so they took the path into the green woods and Nimueh's old home. For all the time that had passed, the lake was the same, fed by the clear stream that ran from the distant mountains. Willow trees stood all around it, their branches sweeping the water, and a pair of white swans sailed silently in and out of the long green curtain. Wild-flowers dotted the shore, stars of blue and white among the lush green grasses.

Nimueh's castle perched halfway up the slope of the hill. The path to its gates zigzagged from the lakeshore, all but invisible among the thick trees. Conical roofs capped the rounded white towers, giving it the air of a storybook painting. Or perhaps the fairy tales were modeled after the fae beauty who once dwelled in the mysterious woods.

"Why is it that sometimes I could find the lake and castle and sometimes not?" asked Dulac.

"I hid it with a glamour, and when I left the last time, I put a preservation spell upon it," she said. "There are no servants, but it will be clean and the larders full of fresh provisions. Of course, when I bound my magic just recently, the spells concealing this place will have disappeared. Anyone can find it now."

They walked hand in hand up the path. Dulac remembered the smell of the lake, a cold, earthy scent that carried the echo of mountain snow. It awakened memories of his time living there, the hours spent training his mind and body. His boots scraped on bare earth as he ascended the path, Nimueh silent beside him. Despite everything, Dulac felt himself relaxing. He had spent months and years in these quiet halls reclaiming himself after his father's destructive anger. The peace of the place hadn't changed.

A bird trilled a piping note that was answered far away. They rounded the last corner in the path to reach the twin towers of the gatehouse. As always, the gate itself was open as if to say an enchantress as powerful as the Lady of the Lake had no need of locks and bolts. They passed through and approached the castle's main door. It sprang open as if it knew Nimueh's touch.

Dulac watched her hesitate, the graceful lines of her face tight with apprehension. No doubt she was wondering what she'd find inside her old home. He wondered if it was the place or the memories it held that worried her more. With a hurried step, as if getting it over with, she finally went inside. He followed, uncertain himself how he'd feel about seeing the halls where he'd first encountered genuine love.

"It's the same," she said. "And yet it's not."

"Yes," he replied, but could find no more words. Time had stopped here. There was no dust or cobwebs, no faded paint or tarnish. Bright banners hung from the roof beams, resplendent with the colorful needlework of the fae. The rushes on the floor were green and fragrant, and the silver goblets set out for guests were clean and bright. Hundreds of years had passed, but the scene was almost identical to the day Dulac had left it to seek his fortune. The fact was both comforting and eerie.

"I so loved it here," she said softly as she walked from his side to look out the deep embrasure of the window.

"What originally brought you to this place?" he asked. It had never occurred to him before this to wonder.

She smiled, but did not turn away from the window. "The fae were a glorious people once, playful and passionate. Every day was filled with debates, songs, plays, dances and a thousand other distractions. The one thing they were not good at was allowing a scholar to pursue her studies undisturbed. So I built my retreat in the Forest Sauvage so that I could craft my spells in peace."

"You did not feel cut off from your world?"

"That was the point of it. At first, I was content. I had my servants and my work. But your coming was the crack in my foundation. You were young and bold, a piece of raw chaos injected into my perfect world. I knew you would be my downfall the moment I saw you standing on my lakeshore." She turned to look at him then, sad and amused.

Dulac raised his brows. "I never thought of myself that way."

"You were what you were—a young male. I had been alone so long I could barely remember how to speak to someone new."

He went to her then, pulling her gently from the window and into his arms. "I didn't see any of that back then. I'd had little enough experience with women, much less immortal fae with subtle and complex characters."

"Am I really so complicated?" she asked with an arch smile.

"You are a puzzle box with a thousand hidden drawers. The more I discover, the more I realize how much there is to find." He kissed her, taking his time. "I have always been incredibly grateful for it."

As an overawed young man, he'd seen her amazing beauty first, her kindness second, and little else. It wasn't until he'd experienced Camelot that he'd appreciated what he'd had. By then, it had been too late. Or maybe not, for he was here, wasn't he?

She was facing him, their bodies almost touching within the circle of his arms. Her palms were braced against his chest and she slowly slid them upward until her fingers laced behind his neck. "I fell in love with my brash young knight. I needed you to keep me from falling into my books and never getting out again."

"I was a young lout back then. I'd like to think I'm a better bargain now."

"How so?"

"Now I'm complicated, too." Ironically, Guinevere had taught him much about navigating human relations. He'd come to understand the female perspective a thousand times better.

"Is complicated supposed to make you appealing?"

"Everyone's doing it these days."

"To puzzle box standards?"

He shrugged. "Probably not. I'm a crossword at best. But I'll be the type you can't quite finish, so you'll never bring yourself to toss me aside."

She gave a low, throaty laugh that held unreserved joy. He realized that she'd changed just as much as he had. More. She'd been through unspeakable hell and, whether she knew it or not, had developed a ferocious will.

After all, she'd put her life on the line to save Camelot. The collar around her throat taunted Dulac, reminding him of everything he could lose.

His entire being refused to consider that outcome. A fever of possession took him. He wanted her right there, their bodies naked in the rushes, but he leashed himself. He'd learned how to treat a lady since he'd first set foot in these halls. He took her hands from around his neck and kissed them before scooping her up into his arms.

"We've explored the hall," he said. "Now I have a mind to see the tower rooms."

Her green eyes glinted with mischief. "I seem to remember the bedchambers are upstairs."

"Really? I was thinking of the armory. Wouldn't you like to see if the swords are still sharp?"

She smacked his shoulder as he carried her up the stairs. "There is only one sword I'm interested in."

"Is it of good, hard steel?"

"If you cease the puns long enough, sir knight, perhaps we can test the point."

He stopped at the threshold of the bedroom, thrown by what he saw. He remembered a bower of unimaginable luxury, of thick carpets and down pillows, silk gauze and satin coverlets. By the casement window, there had been a delicate tree of living silver. What he saw now could have been in a convent. There were stark white walls, a plain bed and not much more.

"Ah," Nimueh said, slipping from his arms to stand on her own. "After you left, I simplified."

"You certainly did." He took a step forward, his spine prickling as he pieced together what the change meant.

She confirmed it all in a voice that was little more than a whisper. "There were too many memories in this room to sleep well alone. I changed it all."

His restraint cracked then. At some time in the past, without his knowledge, she'd done her best to erase him from her memory. He seized Nimueh by the shoulders, walking her backward until she was at the edge of the bed. He tried not to be rough, but the bare, sad room had triggered something close to a blood frenzy.

She sat down, her eyes suddenly wary. "Is this where you claim me oh so hard and teach me how you refuse to be forgotten? That try as I might you've marked me forever?"

"Just as you've marked me," he said, his voice already hoarse with need. "We're bound together. You have my oath on that."

"Keep that promise," she said, untying the silk cord that laced her bodice. "Make me believe it."

And suddenly the familiar old place and the familiar old style of clothes had their effect. Dulac was in the present but in the past, too, with an opportunity to finally re-write their story. He had them naked and between the sheets in under a minute. Her skin was cool, but he had heat enough for both of them. Their lips met once, twice, and then he was claiming her in earnest, suckling one lip and then the other until her mouth was soft and swollen and eager to kiss.

As soon as she was restlessly moving under his hands, he began a slow conquest of her skin, nibbling first at her fingertips and then her wrists. He traced the fine blue veins beneath her olive skin, following them to the crease of her elbow. There was an art to such pleasure, a way of arousing every inch of flesh in turn, but it took patience and technique. In other words, it was a man's art, not a boy's, and the precision and concentration that had made him a champion with the lance served him well when it came to the female body.

From her arms, he inevitably came to her breasts. He had tasted them many times, but now he had daylight and time on his side. The areolae were a deep pinkish brown, perfect and beautiful. They were flushed and warm from his attentions all around them, and now he took one in his mouth to suckle. The softness of her breasts was like a cloud against his cheek, the scent of her intoxicating. His heart thundered, the heat in his cock pooling and stiff-ening. Nimueh moved under him, undulating and mak-ing soft noises in her throat. Such pleasure was nearly a madness.

Her fingers were warm now, raking through his hair to cup his face for another kiss. She moved like no other woman he'd ever had. Some were like cats, lithe and fierce, but she was something more—as elemental as wind or wave, calling to something deep inside him. He was drawn the way a plant seeks sunlight. He needed her to live.

When he finally entered her, the heat and wetness threatened to undo him the instant he found her most intimate place. All that kept him in control was the need to please her. If he was lucky, if he could delight her enough, the primitive part of his brain said she might love him still.

He thrust deep, drawing a gasp from Nimueh. Her eyelids fluttered, the bright green of her irises like a glimpse of emerald fire. A smile played at the corners of her mouth, showing flashes of dimples the world never saw. He knew this teasing mood and reveled in it, nipping her ears and the tip of her nose. She leaned up, taking his lips with a graze of teeth. The shock of pain thrilled down his spine, pulling a sound from deep in his chest. She grinned, flexing something inside her abdomen as he thrust again.

The world began to dissolve at the edges, his sanity blackening and burning to ash. Nimueh clutched her long legs around him, readying for the final ride. It came on him like a storm, driving him on and on until he felt her surrender. She shuddered and rolled up to meet him again, tears escaping from the corners of her eyes. Her nails dug deep into his shoulders, sharp enough to slice skin. Already on the cusp between pleasure and agony, Dulac moaned. Lightning seemed to surge inside him and he spilled his seed, all control falling before the need to possess.

Reality fell to rags. He sagged to his elbows, breath pumping like bellows. Nimueh was below him, staring into his eyes, though her own gaze seemed blind. Sweat glistened along her cheekbones, adding to the sharp exoticism of her face. She really was the most beautiful creature he'd ever seen. Her lips parted, plump rubies showing the delicate whiteness of her teeth. That simple thing nearly made him come a second time.

He rolled aside just enough to relax and then pulled her to him, her rounded rump against his belly. Nothing got better than this. But then, as sleep stole over him, he nuzzled her neck and felt LaFaye's collar.

He was wide-awake in an instant. There was only one way he could save her—by killing every knight the Queen of Faery put in his path.

Chapter 25

Nim woke alone, the sheets beside her already cold. Old memories reared and she sat up quickly, her head spinning with the sudden movement. By the light, the sun was just up, the air still cool and moist. Birds welcomed the morning with full-throated joy. She strained to hear past the morning chorus, but nothing else stirred. The last time she had woken up this way, Lancelot had left her.

She swung her legs over the side of the bed, eerie familiarity overtaking her. She pulled on her chemise and wrapped herself in a shawl, shivering against the morning chill. Then she padded barefoot into the hall below, retracing the steps she'd trod so many years ago.

This time, though, Lancelot sat on the grass outside. Beaumains had taken the horses back to Medievaland for the night, but Lancelot had kept his saddlebags. He had one opened on the ground before him and was munching trail mix from a plastic container. His welcoming smile broke like sunshine through mist and filled her with giddy relief. The spell of the past was broken.

"You need to eat more than that. We missed dinner last night." She blushed. The reason for the forgotten meal was all too clear in his heated gaze. "There are provisions in the larder. Let me find something to cook."

"Don't trouble yourself. I told Beaumains to bring us a hot breakfast," Lancelot said, rising to his feet. "In the meantime, I have power bars if you want one."

Nim glanced at the incongruously bright packaging and shook her head. "I'm too nervous about today to think about eating myself."

He took her by the shoulders and gave her a lingering kiss that chased away the last of the shadows. She slid her arms around his neck and returned it, tasting the salt and sweet of the snack still clinging to his lips.

Then madness took her and she was off like a butterfly, running through the dew-soaked grass with her shawl flying behind her. She jumped over a bubbling streamlet, her toes digging into the soft moss beside it. A squirrel scampered up a tree to scold her, but she just laughed. She could hear Lancelot behind her, chasing her as he used to do. There was a reason he'd learned such agile footwork in battle, no matter how treacherous the terrain. The woods of the Forest Sauvage were their playground, and he had eventually learned to beat her at her own game.

She counted on him beating her. Her path took her around the castle and to a plateau behind it, where rowan trees hung low with berries. Lancelot caught her by the waist and swung her around until they fell in the soft grass. She yelped and sprang up, then danced around the trees with her skirts flying. He dodged one way, then the other, feinting and lunging after her. The play finally settled into a game of tag that had no rules, only chances to touch and almost touch. When he finally caught her a second time, it was Nim who pulled him into the grass. She straddled him then, teasing him with butterfly kisses until he grabbed her, impatient for the real thing.

They rolled, kissing and laughing, not serious yet but losing their lightness. Both were too aware of what the day would bring to wholly lose themselves in play any longer. Now that Nim had stopped running, she could feel iron dread in her chest, as if every breath was an act of optimism.

They finally stopped, lying side by side and staring up at the azure sky. The clouds were mere wisps. It would be sunny all day long.

"I suppose there will be single combat today," she said, finally giving in to the need to talk over what was coming.

"No doubt."

It would be to the death. Neither one spoke of it, but the words hung between them anyhow. She took his hand, gripping it as if letting him go meant sliding off the mountain and into an abyss of darkness. He was her anchor and her destiny in ways she couldn't articulate. She'd known it the first day he'd come here, and she knew it now.

Words formed in her throat, words she couldn't speak. There were some things one couldn't, shouldn't ask at a time like this.

So she talked around it. "I can't stop thinking about Gawain."

"He'll be fine. Tamsin said as much, and I trust her word."

"There could be treachery."

"Tenebrius won't permit it."

"What he will or won't permit doesn't matter once the deed is done. I don't trust LaFaye." She rolled to her stomach, propping herself on his chest. The position let her stare down into his warm brown eyes.

"I don't trust her, either. That will keep me safe."

Then the words she was trying not to say slipped out. "Let someone else fight."

He reached up, pushing the hair from her face with battle-scarred fingers. "I'm a knight. Fighting is what I do."

"Do something else," she begged.

"I can only give what I have. Skill with a sword is my one talent."

"I don't mean forever. Just for today. Let Beaumains fight."

"You don't send a squire to do a knight's job."

"He's a knight now," she argued. "Don't underestimate him."

"I don't," Lancelot replied softly. "But this fight is for Excalibur. This is our one chance to beat the Queen of Faery at her own game."

There may be only one chance, but there was only one Lancelot. She couldn't bear the idea of losing him. If only she had her magic, she could be sure to keep him safe—but that was no answer at all.

He touched the collar at her neck, meaning clear in his gaze. "Defeating all comers is my only way to guarantee you're secure."

"The only way to keep me safe is for you to live," she returned. The need to keep him at her side ached as if it meant to cripple her. "Just once, put what's between us first. Just once put me ahead of Camelot."

It was too much to ask, and she knew it, guilt warring with a primal drive to keep him close. He held her gaze for a long time before he spoke. "I made the mistake of losing you before. I won't do it again. But if I'm going to keep you out of Morgan's hands, I have to fight."

They went back to the castle with barely a word, neither wanting to upset the other, though it was impossible to hide their fears. Dulac left Nimueh to bathe and dress while he went on ahead. He arrived at Taliesin's Circle in time to see Beaumains appear with the horses and a take-out bag containing coffee and breakfast sandwiches. Dulac dug hungrily into the food. It was greasy and disgusting, but it was also full of fuel he desperately needed.

"Where is everyone else?" he asked. "How does Gawain fare?"

"Gawain frets," Beaumains said. "He lost too much blood to take any chances. Tamsin threatened to put him into an enchanted sleep if he didn't lie quiet. He cries foul and on it goes, each one as stubborn as a granite ox."

Lancelot winced, his imagination painting the scene. "And the rest?"

"Owen and Palomedes went out for a beer and stayed for a fight. Arthur phoned to say he'd have them out of the police lockup and over here in time for the start."

"I don't understand. They know what's at stake. Whatever possessed them to risk trouble now?"

"They don't know their way around the new world yet. I should have been with them." Beaumains sipped his bitter coffee with a wince and then added another packet of sugar. "But Tamsin was busy with Gawain so I took Percival to the clinic to take care of his hand. No need for fancy magic in his case."

Dulac nodded. "And our two friends decided to entertain themselves?"

His former squire shrugged. "In a manner of speaking. They swaggered into one of the riverside taverns and tried to go medieval on a pack of bikers. They upheld our reputation with honor, but I don't know how much use either will be on the field today. They took a lot of hits. Lucky it was only fists and not bullets."

"Idiots." Dulac winced, realizing he sounded like the demon.

Beaumains frowned. "According to Arthur, neither remembers who started it. Nor do the bikers. It was as if they all went mad."

That sounded a bit too much like fae magic for Dulac's liking. The rules of the challenge protected the combatants only so long as they were in the forest. There was nothing to say they were safe while drinking a beer back home. He looked over his shoulder as casually as he could, not wanting to let on that the nape of his neck hadn't stopped tingling since Beaumains had begun his story.

The fae began to arrive then, followed by Nimueh in a jeweled silk gown of pale green. Finally, the demon arrived in a puff of smoke. Today he was dressed in a topaz robe scribed with alchemical glyphs. It was trimmed in a spotted fur from a creature Dulac didn't recognize.

"Greetings, contestants," said Tenebrius with unholy cheer. "I see the human side is a bit shorthanded today."

LaFaye stepped forward, her inky gown making her look like a crow against the green fields. "My lord demon, I object to the absence of respect King Arthur shows these proceedings."

"I'm sure you do," the demon said drily.

"Surely he forfeits today's event," she said hopefully.

"There is no requirement for his presence."

She frowned. "But surely he must send more than two knights!"

"Not for single combat. Whatever nonsense is happening here, it won't work." The demon took a long look around the company, taking in both sides. "Choose your champions and let's decide this fight. I am weary of it."

Nimueh caught Dulac's arm. "There is treachery here. I can taste it in the air."

"Are you surprised?" he replied. "LaFaye wants the sword. Somehow, she has managed to whittle away Arthur's team. It sounds as if she hoped to force a forfeit of the fight."

He glanced at the fae corner of the field. The queen's retinue had expanded while Arthur's had shrunk. With some interest, he noted the red-haired girl was still alive.

"It's a forfeit or single combat," Nimueh said. In the jeweled gown, with her dark hair twisted and pinned with emerald combs, she looked every inch a noble fae.

In silent agreement, they walked arm in arm away from Beaumains and the horses, their heads bent together like lovers at a tryst. He supposed that was what they were. His heart beat faster as he remembered how he'd claimed her last night, and how she'd begged him to keep safe.

Nimueh wanted to be first in his heart, and she had that right. She ruled his happiness, his past and his future. He would lay down his life in an instant to protect her body and soul—especially the soul—regardless of the price. That was simply how things were.

But Dulac was a knight of Camelot, and without the Round Table the mortal realms would fall. If the lady was his joy, keeping humanity safe was his meaning. One without the other made no sense.

"Everything rests on this fight," he admitted. "The only fighters left are the most senior knight and the one with the least experience. I have no choice."

"No?" She closed her eyes. "I know. If we do not fight, Arthur loses the right to rule and the fae run riot over the mortal realms. If we do not fight, Arthur loses Excalibur, and we are all lost."

"Yes," he replied. The word was soft, but it seemed to hurt her.

She put her hand over his. Her fingers were icy. "It is as if Morgan has singled you out."

"I will take it as a compliment." But it had crossed his mind, too, and it made him wary. Hurting him hurt Nimueh, and the queen wanted revenge.

Nimueh's green eyes were large and bruised with worry.

"You are a warrior. You always have been, and I should have understood that long ago. I don't think I knew what that meant. Not really. You belong to everyone in your care, not just me."

He saw with horror that there were tears in her eyes. "Nimueh, I have to…"

She held up a hand to stop him. There were rings of fae workmanship on her fingers—jewels carved into dragons' heads and birds in flight and linked by silver chains. She'd had finery stored somewhere in her castle.

The brightness of the jewels paled next to the tears in her eyes. Those tears tore into Dulac like diamond blades. "Please," he begged. The single word held everything, all the hopes and choices he would ever make. For Camelot. For himself. For the next beat of his heart. He needed her to understand.

"Do what must be done," she said. "I won't hold you back. But if you don't survive, nothing I say will matter."

Nimueh took a step back, pulling out of the circle of his arm. She tucked her hands at her sides as if forcing herself not to touch him. She was so beautiful, but so very solitary, and she had unlocked parts of herself to him that she had never shown another. He had seen her passion, the wild strength that she hid deep inside. By opening up, this intensely private creature of spirit had made herself breakable. He'd all but destroyed her once, and she was clearly braced for him to do it again.

"I won't leave you," he said quickly. "You won't be alone. In the end this is a fight like any other and I will win it." And yet as soon as he said it, he knew he'd made a meaningless vow. No one could predict the chances of battle. That's why she was afraid.

Nimueh swayed slightly. "I've seen you fight, and I know you are all but invincible. If this were any other foe, I would expect your victory. But this is Morgan, and she will do her worst. During my bondage at her court, she made me carry out her savagery. I know how far she will stoop."

With a sudden, panicked movement, she grasped his face and held him while she pressed her lips to his. He all but tasted her fear and desperation, the impossible need to keep him safe. He tried to fold her in his arms, but she skittered away.

"Don't," she said. "My heart will break if I have to let you go one more time."

"Then be safe until I am back." The words were far too cocksure, even in his own ears.

"You be safe, my love." She said it so softly, he barely heard her and yet something in her tone made him pause.

"What are you going to do?" he asked.

She lifted a shoulder. "I am going to cheer you on."

But she looked as if she were searching for one last card to play.

Chapter 26

Nim left Lancelot in the care of Beaumains, who would help him arm and ready his mount. She had a little time before the battle commenced. As she walked up the hillside to a small stand of windswept oak trees, she replayed her conversation with Lancelot. She had set out to warn him to be careful of Morgan, but had ended up saying far, far more. A lot more than he needed to deal with right before battling Morgan's minions. But with their emotions intact fae were messy creatures, full of overpowering feelings. After centuries of experiencing nothing, she'd reverted to life as an emotional volcano.

But at least Lancelot knew she loved him. At least they'd had a chance to mend their past wounds.

She reached the tiny grove and knelt in the shadow of the largest oak. Her green skirts blended with the color of the grass. The choice of gown had been deliberate, giving her some camouflage for what she meant to do. Holding her breath, she pulled off the largest of the rings and set it on the root of the oak. The place had deep powers as old as time, and the trees a lineage that went back to the first seedlings of the Forest Sauvage. She had no access to her magical powers, but before she'd left the forest long ago, she'd stored a few spells in their roots for safekeeping. The ring was the trigger. Nim hoped with a drowning, desperate urgency that her emergency cache hadn't gone stale.

She spoke a secret phrase. A moment passed, and then another. A bee hovered close, then zipped away. Just when she thought all was lost, a smell like burning amber filled the breeze. She closed her eyes, and Merlin's face filled her inner vision.

He looked sorely annoyed. "Bypassing call display with magic isn't just rude, it's harassment."

She wasn't in the mood for Merlin's foul humor or his self-pity. "LaFaye is cheating. We're down to two able knights."

That got his attention. "What?"

She told him everything. "If there was ever a time for you to come out of retirement, this is it."

"Curse Morgan LaFaye." He turned pale, then red with anger, but then gathered himself back in, only the dangerous glint in his strange amber eyes indicating that he felt anything at all. He cocked an eyebrow. "Are you begging for my help?"

She heaved a deep sigh. "Yes."

"Fine." He rubbed his jaw, the heavy stubble rasping under his fingers. "I've been thinking about your problem. The binding spell I used was originally designed for a witch. Fae have slight physiological differences, and I failed to make all the proper adjustments."

Nim took in Merlin's face, desperate to fathom his expression. "Are you telling me the truth? This is no trick? No ploy for extra payments?"

"Not after what you just told me," he said, with a smile

that looked more like a baring of teeth. "I don't joke when it comes to life and death. That's what it will be, Nimueh, if what you say is true about the link between your magic and your emotions. Unbinding your power means the death of who you are. There's no coming back once you initiate the spell."

She didn't want to hear that. Regaining her magic meant losing Lancelot and everything she felt for him. On the other hand, it might mean saving his life. The right spell at the right moment might preserve Camelot and the mortal realms and destroy Morgan LaFaye. And then there were her people, the fae, to think of. If the queen was gone, they might have a chance to be something more than the horrors LaFaye had made them.

The odds that Nim could accomplish all this, or any of it, were small. She'd never done anything so brave when she'd had her magic before—but now she had chosen to fight. She at least needed access to her only real weapon.

"I won't use the reversal spell unless it's absolutely necessary," she said to Merlin, her voice shaking a little. "But I need to have it just in case."

"Don't make a mistake."

Nim bowed her head. "Thank you for the advice."

"I give you the advice as a friend," Merlin said, back to his sardonic self. "There will be a price for the magic."

She waved a tired hand. "There always is."

"A future favor."

"Make sure we have a future, and we'll talk."

Merlin laughed, a dry sound that said he didn't get much practice. "Then stand by for delivery."

His mind touched hers, the realm-to-realm connection delicate despite his obvious power. A faint pressure formed in her mind. It wasn't precisely a physical thing, nor was it purely thought. It felt like a foreign object in her mind, and she rolled it around in her thoughts. It seemed smooth and opalescent like a bead.

"I coated it so the spell wouldn't leak out," he said. "If you need your power, break it open and the knowledge you need will be there."

"But I have no power to break it with," she protested.

"You'll have enough for this," he said. "Once in a while, I know what I'm doing."

She tucked the bead of magic away in her mind, promising herself she wouldn't fiddle with it. "Thank you, Merlin. You might have just saved all our lives."

He gave a half smile. "It's all part of the job as Camelot's enchanter. From which I was fired."

"If it makes you feel any better, just remember my old boss actually wants to kill me."

That made him laugh for real. "By the way, a little bird told me the woman you and Sir Heartthrob rescued from the Price House has been released from the hospital."

The news, so out of context, threw her for a moment. "How did you know about Susan?"

His fingers wiggled in the air in a manner he probably meant to be spooky but which only succeeded in being silly. "I am the great Merlin. Tremble and be impressed."

He disconnected. The magic of the ring fizzled out, sending up a spiral of blue smoke. Nim bowed her head, rubbing her temples to ease what promised to be a dragon-sized headache. After a minute, she picked up the ring and walked back down to the corner where Beaumains stood with Lancelot, buckling the last straps of his helm.

She yearned to pull Lancelot aside and tell him something, anything that would ease her yearning for his safety, but there was nothing new to say. Besides, like many fighters, he preferred silence before battle. However polite he would be, he would not welcome her anxious prattling. She took up a position by the rope fence.

Arthur had arrived and he looked deeply annoyed. "The police won't release our men, not even on bail. They have inadequate identification and have been deemed flight risks. I attempted to explain things, but the authorities would not listen."

Nim hoped he'd kept kings and crowns out of his explanation. "At least you know where they are."

He gave her a dark look. "You have no idea how frustrating it is to have so little authority in the modern world."

"I might," she said, thinking of her lost power. "At least, I do a bit. Look, I think LaFaye's champion is here."

The king narrowed his eyes. The horse was coal black and so was the champion's armor. "I do not know the device on his shield."

Nim shaded her eyes. Fae sight was better than a human's, and she could make out something white painted against the plain black. "It's not a conventional device. It appears to be an open book."

"A black-and-white open book?" scoffed Arthur. "Is there a pun at work?"

She had no idea. She had met a number of Black Knights over the years, but none with a pronounced reading habit.

Tenebrius gave the signal for the contestants to advance. Lancelot mounted Bucephalus, using one of the fallen stones in Taliesin's Circle as a mounting block. He paused before Nim and the king, nodding in respect. The blue plumes of his helmet danced in the breeze, but his features were invisible beneath the metal visor. Once more Nim scrambled for something to say, but nothing came. Then Bucephalus moved away and the moment was lost.

She should have just said that she loved him. A hollow feeling filled her chest, and she recognized it as foreboding.

The demon gave more instructions, but Nim paid little

attention. Lancelot and the Black Knight were taking up their positions at opposite ends of the field, and she could not think of anything but danger. This was not like Medievaland, with fences and safety rails and armor customized for jousting. This was not sport—it was two men who intended to fight to the death with whatever weapons came to hand.

Beaumains handed up the lance. It was stouter and shorter than the weapons at Medievaland, and the tip was wickedly sharp. The former squire paused a moment, one hand on the horse's neck and his gaze lifted to the knight in a silent gesture of support. Then he left the field, and Lancelot was alone.

The signal came and the horses sprang forward. The ground shook with their pounding hoofbeats until Nim felt the vibrations in her stomach. She balled her hands in the fabric of her gown, crushing it because the Queen of Faery's slender neck was out of reach. Arthur shifted nervously beside her, his muscles twitching as if he worked a lance in his imagination. "Come on, come on, come on," he muttered.

The two opponents met with a mighty crack of wood. A corner flew off Lancelot's shield, and the Black Knight's weapon splintered, but Lancelot's point stuck fast, the sharpened tip driving straight into the shield. Lancelot shoved hard, hoping to unseat his opponent, but the Black Knight retreated. A moment later, he slid his arm out of the straps and the useless shield dropped. Lancelot released his weapon, and both men drew their swords.

An exchange of blows followed, all the more deadly because the Black Knight had no shield. It was as much a show of horsemanship, for the destriers were trained for combat. With uncanny timing, they knew when to lunge or wheel and when to strike with a deadly hoof. Nim stood frozen with an equal measure of horror and admiration, praying that neither man nor beast was struck—and yet praying it would soon be over. Both prayers couldn't come true.

An unlucky blow sent the Black Knight from his saddle, but he used the opportunity to swipe at Bucephalus's belly. The horse screamed in pain, rearing up to trample the knight. Lancelot kept his seat, but when the knight lunged again, Lancelot launched himself from the saddle. A flurry of blows followed as Lancelot hammered the villain who had dared to wound his horse.

Dodging the fight, Beaumains darted forward to catch Bucephalus and led him from the field. The horse was bleeding and Beaumains didn't pause on his way straight through the portal to home. One of the fae had already retrieved the Black Knight's mount, and so the fight continued on foot.

At this point, it became hard to see and Nim inched forward until Arthur took her shoulder and firmly guided her back. He was silent and grim, his blue eyes stone cold as he watched the battle. He'd started it with a careless word, but there was nothing but grim purpose in his expression now.

The hammering assault took its toll. Already weakened, Lancelot's shield shattered, showering splinters in an arc through the air. He struck out with the broken rim, then came in low with the sword, buying himself time to shed the shield's remains. Lancelot took his sword in both hands now, the ruby-studded hilt flashing like drops of blood, but the power of two such men dealing mighty blows came with a price. Nim heard a strange, singing crash as Lancelot's sword broke in two, leaving a useless stub in his hand.

This time he faltered, and the Black Knight wasted no time seizing the advantage. Suddenly Lancelot was in retreat, ducking and spinning in a macabre dance to avoid the knight's singing blade. Whoever the Black Knight was,

he moved like water, flowing from stroke to stroke in one
continuous wave of steel. Nim had rarely seen such sword
work. Her breaths came shorter and shorter, her heart racing with fear as she could see Lancelot tiring. He threw the
hilt in his attacker's face and tried to roll out of the way,
but for once he was a beat too late. The sword streaked
down, aiming for his face. Lancelot raised his shield arm,
catching the blow on his vambrace. Even at that distance,
Nim thought she heard the snap of breaking bone.

Lancelot roared in pain, surging up with renewed fury.
The Black Knight retreated a step, but only enough to deliver an armored fist to the side of Lancelot's helmet. Metal
rang, and Lancelot dropped like a stone.

Without a word, Nim sprinted forward, thinking only
to put herself between death and the man she loved. The
king caught her from behind, lifting her from the ground
as easily as if she were a child.

"Stop," he said. "Stop or you'll disqualify our side."

"Lancelot!" she cried.

"Hush," said Arthur. "He made his choice."

Technically, the king was right, but he was rarely so
harsh. She stopped struggling, suddenly unnerved. The
king laughed, and it was a terrible, hollow sound.

At that moment, Lancelot rose up, pulling his battle ax
from his belt. He staggered, one arm dangling awkwardly.
In that instant, the Black Knight might have swung his
sword in a killing blow, but instead he wavered, seeming
suddenly unsure. It was all the time Lancelot needed to
bring the ax down on the knight's ebony helm. It was the
Black Knight's turn to kiss the dirt.

"Stars!" Arthur muttered.

It was a fae curse. She sprang free of the king's grasp
and wheeled on him. "You're not Arthur!"

Eyes widening with surprise, he immediately danced
backward like someone preparing to bolt. Furious, she

slammed the heel of her hand into the false Arthur's nose. She felt cartilage crunch and he staggered, hunching over to cup his face. Nim followed up with a double-fisted blow to the back of his head.

She had no more time for him. Once more, she sprinted across the field, using all her fae speed to fly over the mud churned by horses and men. She didn't care if interference was against the rules because, if her guess was right, far greater treachery had taken place.

"Wait!" she cried. "Wait, stop!"

Lancelot's ax raised for a second blow. The Black Knight wasn't moving.

"Hold!" she screamed. She could see the fae running toward her from the other end of the field, fury in their eyes. Why were they furious, if it was their champion Nim had just saved?

She skidded to a stop before Lancelot, her soft slippers no match for the damp earth. She could see LaFaye approaching. Nim didn't have much time.

"You can't kill him," she said. "Not before you see his face."

The slits in Lancelot's visor were inscrutable. She wasn't sure he'd even heard her until he drew his belt knife, working awkwardly with his one good hand, and slit the straps that held the Black Knight's helmet in place. The ebony helmet was made in an old style, with a narrow eye-slit but no visor to lift.

He got no further before LaFaye was there, breathing hard after the run. "What is this new treachery?" she snarled, reaching with one hand for Nim as if she meant to scruff her like a kitten.

Nim backed away, a flutter of fear in her stomach.

"I'm assuming it has to do with this." Tenebrius appeared from nowhere and dropped a bundle at LaFaye's feet. He blinked his yellow goat's eyes. "I think this belongs to you. I warned you, Queen of Faery."

The bundle squirmed and resolved itself into a bloody-nosed fae wearing Arthur's clothes. The white-haired male bore no resemblance to the king, but the glamour had been perfect.

"Fool me once, I let you live," said the demon. "Fool me twice, and I am guaranteed to give in to temptation."

LaFaye said nothing, her jaw set in stubborn anger. The fae scrambled to his feet and hid behind her.

"So where is the king?" asked the demon. Then his gaze settled on the Black Knight, and he obviously came to the same conclusion Nim had. "Ah. The answer is so obvious the open book should have been the first clue."

While they'd been speaking, Lancelot had removed his own helmet. His face was pale, his hair dark with sweat and plastered to his forehead. His eyes flickered in surprise at the demon's sudden appearance, but he said nothing as Tenebrius bent and helped him reveal the Black Knight's face. As they'd suspected, it was Arthur. He was alive but unconscious, his face running with blood. Lancelot bowed his head in silent grief at what he'd done.

Nim bent to examine Arthur. His breathing wasn't good. She attacked the fastenings of the armor, removing what she could to make him more comfortable. "We need a healer," she said.

"Why?" The queen shot back. "He's about to die anyhow."

"Explain yourself, LaFaye," said the demon coldly.

"I took Arthur in the mortal realm," she said with a defiant smile that didn't reach her eyes. "He was outside your protection there, so no rules were broken. I enchanted him and put him into the contest as an ordinary knight with an ordinary sword. No magical weapons and no hint to anyone—even himself—of who he is, so no rules regarding identity were contravened. Lancelot du Lac is the only knight with skill enough to beat him, so it was an even match. I know of no other rules regarding the selection of the fighters, so surely you can have no objections."

"Twist my words, will you?" The demon's voice dropped to a mere hiss. The color drained from the queen's cheeks, but she stood her ground. "I do not care who wins, but neither do I tolerate those who think themselves cleverer than me."

"And yet I color within the lines," she replied. There was a tremor in her words, but her gaze was steady. "That is the way of the fae. Rules are obstacles, but we dance around them like maypoles. Don't tell me demons do anything less."

Tenebrius didn't so much as blink. "This is not a game in which a gullible judge is a pawn upon the board."

Anger made Nim's head feel hollow, as if it needed room to contain all the rage flaming inside. "What could possibly excuse this deception?"

"Victory," said the queen in clear, clipped tones. "Revenge."

"For the fae?" Nim protested. "Do you really believe our people would have wanted this dishonorable trick?"

"For me." Morgan's head lifted in defiance. "Arthur usurped everything—my place in the line of inheritance, the love of our family, the respect of the people, the influence that should have been mine. By the rules of lore and magic, I demand his death."

"I'm afraid she's right," the demon said with a disgusted sigh. "The rules of the contest are clear. There's no way around it. Your champion must kill his king."

Chapter 27

An outburst of protests filled the air. Looking unutterably weary, Lancelot clambered to his feet. Pieces of armor flapped and rattled where the buckles had snapped asunder in the fight. It was clear that his broken arm was only one of many wounds. Blood smeared his legs and breastplate, and not all of it belonged to his foes. Nim realized with a sick flip of her stomach that chance alone had saved him in this fight. He and Arthur had always been evenly matched, the two greatest swordsmen of Camelot. Whatever had made the king hesitate at the last—some flicker of recognition breaking through Morgan's spell?—had turned the tide in Lancelot's favor. But for that, their fortunes would have been reversed.

Nim could not help herself. It was too late to worry about who should or shouldn't be on the battlefield, so she ran to Lancelot's side, steadying him as he got to his feet. His eyes were on Arthur, but he took her hand with his good one, squeezing hard as if she were his one link to sanity. Nim gasped at the pressure, but the clamor of voices drowned out her cry.

Tremors of exhaustion and spent rage shuddered through Lancelot as he finally raised his head to glare at Tenebrius. "I will not do it." Lancelot's rough, steady voice silenced the company.

"Are you sure?"asked Tenebrius. "You know what is at stake."

"My words were plain. My meaning is clear. The rules of lore and magic do not outweigh the laws of fealty. I swore to defend Arthur, not to murder him."

"Then give me Excalibur." Morgan LaFaye pushed forward, eyes flashing with triumph. "The contest requires a fight to the death. He has forfeited the prize."

With a sudden, angry jerk, Lancelot released Nim's hand and reached for his ax. Nim grabbed his arm as he swung to throw it. "No! Think what you're doing!"

The Queen of Faery laughed, a disturbingly lovely sound. "Attempting to kill me is futile, sir knight."

LaFaye was right. Only Excalibur would kill her, which was exactly why they were in this mess. Lancelot met Nim's eyes as he lowered his weapon, seeming to ebb back into himself.

"You saw that. The enemy knight threatened me," LaFaye said haughtily, her confidence returning. Her attention slid to Nim, murder in her gray eyes. "I demand a penalty."

"Oh, do you mean the collar?" said the demon in a dangerously reasonable tone. "Shall I put the Lady of the Lake to death after she pleaded with Sir Lancelot to spare you?"

"You twist my meaning."

"I would twist Excalibur in your guts if demonkind could draw the blade and live. I tire of you, LaFaye."

The queen began a shrill protest, but didn't get far.

"Silence!" roared Lancelot.

A surprised quiet reigned as Lancelot turned to the demon. "I am a simple warrior," he said, fatigue etching deep lines into his tired face. Nim's breath caught as she remembered the sound of breaking bones—which had so far gone ignored. "I am a simple warrior who has been caught in a trap."

"That trap is your puzzle to solve," said the demon. "That is the nature of the game."

"The game has been rigged," said Lancelot with steady composure. "If I lose and die, LaFaye wins the sword. If I win and kill Arthur, LaFaye is free to take the sword and the crown and whatever else she can take in conquest, for there will be no Camelot to stop her. I ask for an extra roll of the dice to even this match."

"I will consider it," said Tenebrius. "What did you have in mind?"

"Another way to win besides a combat to the death. Give us a true contest, with an avenue to win."

Lancelot had asked wisely, judging by the demon's nod of approval, but sportsmanship wasn't the queen's style. She whirled on the knight, releasing a pale blue blast of killing power. Lancelot pulled Nim to the ground, shielding her with his body, but he was not moving with his usual speed. The spell brushed her, its power cracking through her body hard enough to make her ears ring, but it could have been worse. The collar flared, seeming to absorb the strike. The next instant, the demon's counterspell had swept the queen's magic aside.

LaFaye shrieked her frustration. Tenebrius was perspiring, for not even a demon could challenge her power without effort. Moreover, he was angry, his physical form wavering as temper made his glamour slip. Nim caught a glance of his true form—a ragged, monstrous raptor with eyes like pits of fire.

"I warned you," he said quietly, and that was more terrifying than any roar. He pointed one taloned finger to the queen's corner of the field. "There are consequences for attacking the contestants."

Nim looked up in time to see a burst of flame. Horror gagged her as she realized it was her counterpart, the red-haired girl, paying for her queen's transgression with her life.

"You want another avenue to victory?" said the demon. "Perhaps only Excalibur can kill the Queen of Faery, but there are a thousand other ways to destroy her. Do that, and I will let your king wake and live."

Morgan's face turned the color of chalk. "I will wreak untold vengeance on you all." Grabbing her skirts, she turned and bolted like a hare, her retainers scrambling in her wake. Nim watched her go, a fierce sense of Morgan's *wrongness* slamming through her.

She was startled by a slithering sensation at her throat. She grabbed at her neck, expecting a creature set to strangle her, but her hands came away holding the jeweled collar.

"If we are changing the rules, then there is no need for that," said the demon. "I don't think your king is in any position to misbehave."

Nim was relieved to be free of the collar, but while it posed a threat, it had also given her a measure of protection. Without it, she was just another player on the board.

The demon turned back to the contestants and cast a last look over Arthur's unconscious form. "There is your second roll of the dice, Sir Lancelot of the Lake. Use it well." With that, Tenebrius vanished.

But that was not the good news it might have been. LaFaye had stopped some distance away and was gesturing wildly. A moment later, her soldiers were turning back, naked swords in their hands, and more were coming from LaFaye's corner of the field. She was securing her escape because, as the lone knight of Camelot present, Lancelot had to stay and guard the unconscious king.

Lancelot released a breath that was half a groan, the sound coming from a deep well of pain. He pulled Nim close, cupping her nape with his good hand. He didn't say anything, but kissed the top of her head. It was a blessing, a gesture of understanding that went far beyond words. She pulled away just long enough to kiss his mouth, a single salty taste of her own tears.

"Run," he said.

But her fingers clung to his, refusing to let go. "I love you."

He blinked, his dark eyes wild with grief. "Then trust I will come for you, no matter what. I promise you will not be alone again."

"There are too many enemies. I will stay and fight with you."

That meant using her magic, and he would never accept that. She knew that before he answered.

"No." Then he picked up his ax and faced the coming horde. "Love sometimes means trusting to the abyss of fate. Run, let me know you're safe. Let me fight."

Trusting to the abyss. Trusting one of them would find a way out of the black hole of loss and darkness, and to do it in time to save the other. Tears stung, but Nim did not argue. Instead, she sped after Morgan LaFaye's distant form. There was only one way out. It was time for the Lady of the Lake to stop hiding and fight.

The queen wasn't hard to follow. She was a creature of the court—used to banquet halls and throne rooms, not thickets and mud patches hidden by the rolling grass. By contrast, Nim was a true fae and born to nature. She knew every twig and branch of the land between Taliesin's Circle and her castle by the lake.

With every step she took, the image of Lancelot turning to face the fae taunted her. *Let me fight*. Even if he survived, even if he beat every one of those fae, his efforts would be meaningless unless Nim could catch the queen.

It soon became clear that Morgan was blundering closer and closer to Nim's own home. The white towers were the one habitation anywhere in sight. No doubt they looked like a refuge to a court lady alone in the Forest Sauvage.

Nim emerged from the brush on the far side of the lake just as Morgan disappeared up the path Nim had walked with Lancelot the day before. Her first reaction was fury. Morgan had no business being anywhere near Nim's retreat. Not after Nim had just reclaimed it from sorrow—not after she and her lover had made it theirs once more. The last time Morgan was there, she'd sown the seeds of their long parting. She did not deserve to so much as breathe the castle's air.

And yet, Nim saw the possibility for victory. There were pitfalls in the castle Morgan would never suspect. If Nim could call on their power, they might buy Camelot the time it needed to grow strong. But none of those traps could be sprung without magic.

Nim touched the bead of knowledge Merlin had given her. Arthur was wounded. Excalibur was in peril. Lancelot was fighting for his life. Merlin was in exile. If Nim turned and ran now, LaFaye would win for sure and there would be no peace in any realm, human or fae. The greatest act of love Nim had to offer was to do whatever she could to save them all. Perhaps this was the destiny that had brought her back to Lancelot. He was the only one she loved enough to inspire such sacrifice.

Tears streamed down her face, but she made her bargain, all too aware she would lose the very thing that gave that choice meaning.

"Goodbye," she whispered. Lancelot was first in her mind, but it was a farewell to everything she loved or understood about the heart. She was letting go of the easy companionship of the knights, of her respect for Arthur, for her anger at the treatment of her own people. It was goodbye to the girl with the butterfly wings and all the joy Nim had found in walking with her lover through the park. That bright day shone like a star in her barely recovered soul.

Nim could trust the abyss—she could trust it to swallow her whole. But without LaFaye, those things she loved could still exist—even if Nim never cared about them again.

Merlin's bead of knowledge rolled through her thoughts, and with a single act of will she cracked it. Knowledge unspooled in her mind with unblemished clarity. She whispered the words he had sent her, the long-dead language dry and angular on her tongue, as if each syllable had physical weight. There was no question this was Merlin's recipe—she could taste the erratic genius of his magic like a spice. As the taste flooded her mouth and then her blood, exploding like heat through her entire being, the chains of Merlin's binding fell away.

She sobbed, a ragged farewell and welcoming both. Her magic reared up, pure and elegant as a fine sword. Nim breathed deeply, stretching out her arms. She could touch the deep enchantment of the lake, the natural magic that was the voice and essence of the Forest Sauvage. It welcomed her like a lost sister, winding in and through her until she was part of its tapestry once more. The breeze whispered her name in the trailing willows, the birds sang it from the sky. Power was a part of her, a piece she'd cut off the way an animal chews its limb away from a trap. But it was back.

Light-headed with magic, Nim took a shuddering breath and paused just long enough to consider her approach. She'd never been a showman with her powers, but then she'd never desired to entertain. Stealth came naturally, and that was exactly what she needed.

She drew a doorway in the air, opening a portal from where she stood on the far side of the lake to the hall of her castle. Light bloomed and shimmered in the air and Nim stepped through it as naturally as if it were the elevator in her condominium. The surge of magic made her heart race, but that was nothing to the jolt it gave when she stood in her castle hall and saw LaFaye. Like all fae, Nim still had the ability to fear.

The queen had her back to Nim, the ebony of her gown stark against the bright tapestries that hung on the wall. LaFaye stiffened, the angle of her shoulders growing sharp as the surge of magic gave Nim away. Slowly, the Queen of Faery turned, a murderous look darkening her face.

"Nimueh," she said. "This is your castle, isn't it?"

"It is."

"Pity," said Morgan. "It's very pretty."

The queen threw a bolt of power, sending bottles and goblets flying from the table by the window. They fell to the rush-strewn flagstones with a clatter.

"Are you trying to frighten me?" Nim asked, her voice utterly cold.

"I don't need to try," Morgan scoffed. "You've been running like a rabbit since you betrayed me."

"Rabbits bite." Nim returned the blast of power, her own a darker, richer blue.

Morgan was not expecting retaliation, and the attack caught her off guard. The queen flew backward through the air with a shriek and landed hard against the wall.

Good, thought Nim, as the queen regained her balance. No amount of power would kill LaFaye, so the object of the game was to make her angry enough to play. It worked. LaFaye struck back with fury, smashing every stick of furniture in the room. Nim felt an echo of regret as her familiar things were reduced to kindling, yet there was nothing she could do. It was a necessary loss.

Nim darted to the tower stairs, turning back only when she'd run up the first few steps. "It doesn't matter what you do now. You can't win."

LaFaye gave a short, sharp laugh. "The demon promised a win if you destroy me, but we both know that's impossible. No, either Arthur dies or he doesn't and I get that damnable sword either way. I won't walk away empty-handed."

"Camelot will always defeat you," Nim said, sounding almost conversational. "It has justice on its side."

"Camelot is dead history." LaFaye pushed the long, dark hair from her eyes. "And at last I have my hands around your traitorous neck."

She made a grasping motion with her fingers, squeezing the air from Nim's throat. Nim's fingers scrabbled to grip the castle stone, bracing herself as the edges of her vision went dark. She crawled up a step, then another, putting distance between herself and the faery queen. Every effort she made to draw air strangled her more.

LaFaye's strength was prodigious, the combined might of fae, witch and Pendragon bloodlines mixed with her own particular power. No one could match the queen in speed, agility or resilience. Her strength was unquestioned. LaFaye's injuries healed almost instantly, whereas her spells could last an infinity of years. None dared to confront the queen openly, not even Nim.

But sometimes precision could make up for the rest. The vaults of the ceiling were held by interlocking arches, each pair of ribs connected where they met by a single stone. Remove the keystone, and the arches became unstable. Magic could do much, but when assisted by the laws of physics, it was unstoppable. All Nim had to consider was timing.

As Nim retreated, LaFaye advanced—one step, then another. It was slow going and Nim was losing her ability to think, but sheer stubbornness kept her clinging to consciousness.

When the queen was directly below the keystone of the hall's central arch, Nim flexed her magic. There was a rasping scrape of stone on stone and the keystone dropped, narrowly missing LaFaye's skull. The queen looked up, only to see the neighboring stones fall away, and then their neighbors, like a vertical game of dominoes.

And the hall came tumbling down.

Chapter 28

The instant LaFaye's concentration broke, Nim heaved in a lungful of air. She scrambled to her feet and bolted up the tower stairs, leaping up two at a time. Clouds of dust billowed up the stairwell, expanding with every crash of stone from below. With a nudge of power, the collapsing arch had set off a chain reaction and the whole of the great hall was rapidly smashing itself to rubble.

As Nim had hoped, Morgan rushed after her, seeking the safety of the tower. Nim could hear the slap of her footfalls between the smashing of masonry. Nim doubled her speed, wanting to gain time, and slipped into the room at the first landing. It was a small, sunny chamber with a casement window overlooking the lake. Nim dropped onto the window seat and pushed open the shutters to view the destruction of the hall. The ground was a dizzying distance below, the tops of the trees barely reaching halfway to the window.

Despite the long drop, she could see the damage. The

beautiful white confection that had been her banqueting hall was nothing more than rubble. Shock numbed her, erasing even fear. She'd set the spell as a precaution when the thing was built, but she'd had no idea the result would be so impressive.

And it was just the beginning. Taking a deep breath of the dusty air, she recited the necessary spell. She felt it lock around the tower with a hiss of air, as if the tower had suddenly been sealed in a vacuum.

Then LaFaye stood in the doorway, every line of her body silently demanding an explanation. Nim turned from the window, taking her time. It was a novelty to have the upper hand for once.

"I can feel your magic, such as it is," said the queen with chill contempt. "So light and delicate it all but melts on the tongue, like one of those froufrou cocktails that never qualifies as a real drink. And you think to use this against me?"

The queen took a stride forward. "What are you playing at, Nimueh?"

The slap sent Nim sprawling. LaFaye hadn't moved a finger, but rings stung the flesh of Nim's cheek. She pushed up on one elbow only to receive another invisible blow that made her ear throb. Nim huddled against the edge of the casement, her old, habitual fear returning like a sickness. She remembered its touch, the lines and borders of its limits. She remembered how it made her small.

"Just a household spell," Nim gasped. "I installed it because of the demons in the forest, just in case they got unfriendly. The tower seals so that no one can get in. In fact, no one can see the castle is even here. We're absolutely secure from outside eyes."

"And the hall?" Morgan asked, her voice thin with tension.

Nim could feel the next blow waiting, hovering in the

air in case she said something Morgan didn't like. "Even if someone found the castle, the entrance is completely sealed by debris."

The blow descended spinning Nim around. Her vision sparked and reeled, making her dizzy.

The queen's eyes had gone wide. "By the stars, what do you think you're doing?" She lunged for Nim, her hands raised to hurl more power.

But Nim used her magic to deflect the strike. Instead, the blow blasted chips out of the stone and they skittered to the floor.

"Incidentally," Nim said, hysteria cracking the word, "I'm the only one who can leave." And she hurled herself through the window into thin air.

To anyone else, even other fae, it would have been a fatal move. But Nimueh was the Lady of the Lake, and she called to the deep magic of her sanctuary. It drew her falling form as if by a thread, pulling it along an impossible trajectory until she hovered over the water. From there, her free fall became a dive and she plunged into the icy depths, dropping still more until daylight was only a memory.

Nim's skirts billowed around her like gossamer fins. LaFaye was trapped in the tower. Relief made her light, as if a suit of armor had been peeled from her limbs. She hadn't admitted, even to herself, the size of the gamble she'd just taken.

Or the price she had paid. She could feel her emotions shutting down already, a loss impossible to describe. It would have been easier to describe color to a sightless worm, or music to a block of ice. It was like lights going off in her mind one by one, and so she fought panic by clinging to the idea that LaFaye had paid for her crimes. Her sacrifice was not wasted. She relaxed her limbs and let herself float in the dark, icy nothingness of the lake. The numbing cold took away her pain.

The contest was over and, for a time at least, Camelot was safe.

Her work was done.

She was done.

Love was a distant memory.

Dulac defeated every one of the fae, but his body paid the price. He was unconscious on the churned earth when Beaumains arrived to collect him along with his king. Palomedes and Owen came to help, reporting that they were now as mysteriously free of legal charges as they had been mysteriously drawn into a fight. Together, they carried Lancelot and the king back home.

It was late morning on the next day before Dulac woke. As soon as his eyes opened, he remained in bed for approximately five seconds. Through a disoriented fog, he realized that he was in the infirmary at Medievaland's clubhouse.

"It was easier for Tamsin to nurse everybody if they were all in the same place," said Gawain from the chair at the foot of the bed.

"You look terrible," said Dulac.

"Right back at you." Gawain tried to smile but it fell flat. He was sitting awkwardly, as if he was nursing broken ribs. "Your horse is fine, though."

"Good." Some might have called it a small thing compared to the other fallen warriors, but relief hit Dulac like a physical blow. He was extremely fond of Bucephalus.

Then Dulac gripped the edge of the bed as a wave of dizziness hit. He might be sitting up, but he realized that he was weaker than he thought.

"How badly are you injured?" Dulac asked Gawain, in part to cover his own discomfort.

"The only good thing about losing so much blood is that hypertension is right off the table. The thrice-blasted fae stabbed me from behind." Gawain held up his hands as if measuring a fish. "The blade had to be that long. I'm never eating kebabs again."

Dulac looked down at his arm, remembering that it had been broken. Now all that lingered was a pulsing ache. "That was a mighty fight." Then he prodded a bruise, wincing as it complained.

"Tamsin healed what she could, but she couldn't do everything. There were many injuries to mend and only one witch to go around, so some things need to mend on their own."

Dulac nodded through the fog of aches and pains, concentrating on Gawain's words but losing some of the meaning. Memory was returning in starts and fits, one image at a time. "The king?"

"He regained consciousness yesterday." Gawain brightened. "It was sudden. One moment he was out cold, the next he was sitting up and demanding his clothes. There's no sign of Excalibur. Or the demon, though I'm hardly complaining about that."

"Where's Nimueh?" Dulac asked, suddenly cold.

Gawain shook his head. "No sign of her, either. We searched, but not even her castle is there. She's probably hiding from LaFaye."

Dulac wet his lips, suddenly sure he knew what had happened. "The king is awake, and that meant the contest ended in Camelot's favor. Nimueh is the only one who could have defeated the queen."

"How?" Gawain asked, sounding doubtful. "I mean, good for her but—how?"

Dulac didn't want to contemplate that. "I need to find her. I think I know where she's gone, and I promised her that she wouldn't be alone."

Over Tamsin's protests, Dulac left within the hour and he left without a companion. If he had guessed right, only he could fulfill this particular quest. There was one of the stag's jewels left, and Dulac used it to ride back to the Forest Sauvage.

He arrived at Taliesin's Circle in the late afternoon, the sky clear over the emerald fields. The ground stood as he'd first seen it, the fields beside the standing stones untouched by battle. There was no churned mud, no splashes of blood on the wind-ruffled grass. It was as if the mighty contest had been nothing but a song for a winter's evening.

Dulac hurt in far too many places to sleep in the open, so he wasted no time setting out for Nim's castle. He encountered no one, not even wild animals, and he made good time. He rode Gringolet, Gawain's horse, so that Bucephalus could rest and heal his wounds. Gawain's mount snorted with pleasure at the unexpected exercise, moving easily over the wide, rolling ground.

Years fell away as Dulac rode, and he remembered the first time he'd come to this part of the forest. In those days, the borders between realms had been thinner and he'd stumbled by chance into the mysterious forest in search of adventure. He'd followed the exact same path he traveled now to Nimueh's domain. And there he'd found the love of his life.

She had ridden in the boat with the head of a swan, a white-clad vision right out of one of his nurse's fairy tales. Her spell over him had been absolute and immediate. Dulac shook his head to clear it, bracing himself for what lay ahead. Such memories were sweet, but he desperately feared what he would find now.

He urged Gringolet up the rising ground to the lake's plateau, and he found his answer. At the base of the high hill, the lake spread out like a second sky, every cloud and butterfly mirrored on its still face. As always, the scene was perfect and beautiful. Except, the castle was gone.

Magic was afoot, and that only meant one thing for Nimueh.

Dulac slid from Gringolet's back, leaving the horse to graze on the lush grass. With hesitant steps, he approached the edge of the lake and sat there, grateful to rest his aching wounds but alert to the slightest movements around him. A leaf fell in the water and spun in lazy circles. He closed his eyes before it could make him dizzy.

"Nimueh," he said softly. "I promised you would not be alone. I'm here now and it's time to come home."

The only answer was the ripple of the breeze over the water. The fallen leaf skittered and spun out of sight. Dulac watched it go, sitting quietly while he made up his mind.

With no wasted motions, he rose and tended to the horse, removing saddle and bridle and making it comfortable for a long wait. Then he stripped off his clothes, leaving them far away from the water. His remaining bandages would be spoiled, but he could not help that. For what he hoped to gain, he could bear the brunt of Tamsin's wrath.

In a neat, graceful motion, Dulac dove into the water. The icy temperature stole his breath, but he kicked his way down, seeking the deepest caverns below. He hoped to catch a glimpse of the Lady of the Lake. She might have lived in the castle above, but just as often she retreated to the silence of the waters below. If something had happened, this was where she would be.

He stayed down until his lungs burned, and then he stayed down some more. Eventually, though, the desperate ache in his chest drove him to the surface for a gulping breath. He gasped and rubbed the water from his eyes, gathering himself for another try. Then he dove again.

The lake was not huge, but it was cold and he was injured. He had only covered half of it when exhaustion forced him to the shore to rest. It was there that he saw her, a figure with sand-dark skin and pale, flowing hair.

He smiled slightly, amused that one of the first uses of her power had been to fix that unbecoming hairstyle. Nimueh looked like herself again.

She must have heard his approach. Her head lifted, bright green eyes widening when she saw him. She passed a hand over her face, blinking as if she'd been asleep. It was then he noticed that she wore only a sleeveless shift that left her limbs bare to the sun.

"Nimueh," he said. "I've come for you."

Quick as an eel she was in the water, barely making a splash. He ran and dove after her, only able to guess where she'd gone. His arms cleaved the water, stroking hard to send him deeper and deeper into the frozen darkness. It was hopeless. She was a fae of the water, and he was just a human. And yet, incredibly, he brushed against the smooth glory of her thigh. He twisted beneath her, his arms closing around her waist.

Her protest was a swish of bubbles, but it wouldn't have mattered even if he had understood the words. Kick and thrash as she might, even with fae strength Nimueh would not escape him. His heart could not endure it. With Nimueh in tow, Dulac swam back to the shore.

As soon as their feet were on land, she renewed her efforts to push away. "Let me go," she said, bracing her palms against his chest. She was strong, and he had to work to hold her.

"Why?" he demanded.

"You know why," she said, her voice cold as the lake. "My magic has returned, and my emotions are gone. We are better off apart."

"I don't believe you," he said.

Her features pulled tight. "You are arrogant. Do you believe yourself so irresistible that not even devastation of the soul can obliterate my need to love you?"

His lips twitched. "You can't resist me."

And then, to prove it, he kissed her. Although his outward manner was almost flippant, his every sense was attuned to her response. He needed to know the truth.

She tasted of lake water, a combination of mountain snows and the iron-rich tang of silt. He didn't mind the earthy taste, or even that her limbs were cold. The day was hot and though she shivered, Dulac was certain he could warm her given half a chance.

But she continued to struggle, resisting the weight of his arms around her. If she'd wanted warmth, she would have clung closer. It was then he began to wonder how much of her trembling was shock. "What's wrong, my love?"

Nimueh didn't answer at once. Instead she went still. Her arms dropped to her sides, her head drooping until he could not see her eyes. It was an attitude of weary submission, and it stirred despair in his heart.

"I recalled my magic and trapped LaFaye in the castle," she said. "It will hold her for a while. Long enough for the Round Table to regain its strength."

"Arthur is awake," he replied, tilting her face up to his. "You did what none of us could do." Nimueh had saved them all, but now someone had to save her.

Her green eyes closed, shutting him out. As ever, she'd retreated into hiding. "And that's all for me." She nodded once, taking a shuddering breath. "I've done my duty. Now let me go."

"No."

"I've saved Camelot and Arthur and the sword." Her voice shook as if the words themselves gave her pain. "Is that not enough for you?"

He smoothed her long, pale hair, realizing how much he'd missed its shining weight. "No," he said. "I still want you."

She bowed her head, resting it under his chin. When

she spoke, her voice was muffled. "I have no more to give. I'm dead inside all over again."

Dulac refused to believe her. "I love you."

She raised her eyes to his, the brilliant green as cold as the deepest ocean. "But I don't love you anymore."

Chapter 29

Dulac abandoned all his arguments. His fears had whispered this might happen, but he had slammed the door on those voices and stopped up his ears. Now he could see she was telling the truth. Nimueh did not wish to hurt him, but would not lie about what she could not feel.

But he had turned to stone for centuries to be with her again. He had crossed through worlds and fought with heart and sword to win her trust. He would not give up until every last grain of hope for their love was gone.

He kissed her again, keeping it gentle but holding her so there was no chance she could slip away. This time she refused to yield, remaining wooden beneath his caress. With every sense he had—of taste and smell and touch— he searched her response for something, anything that would hint the Nimueh he knew was still inside.

With a pounding heart, he slid his lips along her jaw to the sensitive spot beneath her ear. That was when he heard the faint gasp of breath, familiar from the many times he

had flicked his tongue right *there*. It was one of the intimate secrets they shared. Perhaps it was just a physical
reaction, but hadn't his touch encouraged her to remember
him before? What had Tamsin said about the flesh holding emotion as well as the mind?

His kisses found their way down the slope of her neck,
where her long white hair clung in wet tendrils against
her skin. His tongue lapped up drops of water, warm from
the sun and her skin. His mouth filled with her taste, as
if she was his one reality both inside and out. She arched
her head back, seeming to forget herself, and pressed into
his embrace. She was so beautiful, so delicately made,
the graceful bow of her neck tempting his lips anew. Her
pulse beat against his lips as he pressed his mouth to her
throat, a predator hypnotized by his prey.

Entranced, he ran his mouth down her sternum until the
clinging folds of her thin gown blocked his path. With a
quick, relentless gesture, he grabbed the neckline and tore
the garment apart down its front. She gasped, but she was
in his arms again before she could back away. The fabric fell to the shore with a wet sound, leaving them both
naked under the hot sun.

Her jaw went hard, a silent, mutinous challenge. He
ignored it, laving his tongue over the inside curve of her
breast, flicking lightly at the smooth, fine flesh. She was
stiff, refusing him, but he nipped and kissed until she
arched her back. Her hands were braced against his shoulders, pulling away and giving him access at once. Dulac
kept claiming her an inch at a time, waking every nerve
with his lips.

Her breath was coming hard now, her pulse beating like
the struggles of a trapped bird.

His hands slid down her slender flanks, kneading and
caressing. He took his time, massaging each muscle until
it relaxed. This was a slow conquering, every touch deep

and firm and insistent. The stiffness left her, but he could still feel the coiled tension deep inside, waiting for one wrong move. That was when her eyes finally met his, and he saw the naked panic in them.

"Why are you afraid?" he asked.

"I fell into the abyss," she whispered. "I'm still falling and there is nothing there to catch me. It was as if I opened my eyes to find nothing but darkness."

"I'm there to catch you. Let your body be with mine. It will remember everything you need to know."

"My body is just flesh."

"Flesh remembers."

He fell to his knees before her, gently pushing her feet apart. She obeyed, but her expression was perplexed. Then he pressed his lips to the inside of her thigh, tasting the silk of her skin. She gasped, tensing as if she meant to skitter away, but he held her still, gently nipping where he'd kissed. Finally, her hands crept to his chest, her nails grazing his skin as they found his shoulders. The pain made his breath hitch, but it was a goad to his need.

She made a strangled sound, inviting and hostile at once.

"Trust me," he repeated, though the words had become something more than their meaning. They'd grown into a chant or a prayer or a charm—any magic that would bring her home.

He didn't rush, didn't explore beyond what he was certain would give her pleasure. He ran his hands from her slender ankles and up over her calves, shaping her until her hands released his shoulders to bury themselves in his hair. Only then did he allow his lips to rove higher and touch the pale down at the apex of her thighs.

"Oh!" she exclaimed, making a sound of discovery.

Nimueh closed her eyes as he repeated the act, using all his skill until her flesh wept with desire. But whether

her mind welcomed her body's sensations, he could not tell. Just as when they'd kissed outside the wedding hall, the spark of her personality seemed to flicker out of reach. Dulac felt as if he were coaxing it back from ashes and had to be oh, so careful. If he lost her now, there might not be a second chance.

He used his teeth as well as tongue and lips, understanding exactly how pain and pleasure might dance. She tasted sweet, like honey and peaches, and her skin was hot silk against his cheek. She inhaled, her toes digging into the ground as if she were afraid she might fly away.

"Come back to me," he whispered. "I won't leave you alone."

She was making a faint whimpering now, her fingers locked almost painfully in his hair as he worked her to the brink of climax. Her head rolled back, strands of her drying locks flying free in the breeze. All at once, she fell to her knees, eyes half-mad as if she might shatter with more than desire.

"I'm going to break," she murmured. Her hands were still in his hair, her face just inches away. A sheen of perspiration along her cheekbones added to the ferocity of her stare. "What are you doing to me?"

Her nipples brushed his chest, peaked and teasing. He put his hands over them, letting her feel the roughness of his palms.

Her eyes raked down him, knowledge blooming as she realized her power over his own condition. He was erect and full, throbbing with need for release. Her lashes swept down and up in an intrinsically female gesture. Nimueh liked what she saw, but wasn't sure whether to take it.

"Trust me," he said.

She narrowed her eyes, not quite agreement but not a refusal, either. More forceful now, he pushed her to the grass, making his own wants clear. He suckled her nipple and then blew on the wet tip, watching it harden with need. She pulled him down to the other, demanding equal treatment. He let her cradle his head as he worked, felt her nails against his scalp as waves of building desire raged through her. She moaned as he released the nipple and mounded both breasts in his broad hands, kneading until they were flushed and pink.

She fell back, stretching like a cat with speculative green eyes, and then rolled on all fours to display her gently rounded hips. It was a clear invitation. He caressed the smooth, taut muscles and spread her legs, glorying in her generous shape.

He mounted her, his concentration spinning away in the heat and wetness and tight, tight pleasure. Nimueh squirmed beneath him, uttering soft yearning cries that grew to screams as he hit his mark. Once he found her response, he was relentless, laying siege without mercy. He pushed faster and deeper, on and on, until Nimueh sent up a primal wail that wrenched a climax from his flesh.

Limb by slow limb, they collapsed into a heap, their bodies making a nest of sand and grass and sun. Dulac rolled to his back, making himself into a pillow for her head. He cupped her face and kissed her, losing track of time as they explored the moment. The sun beat down and the water lapped softly, putting all thoughts but Nimueh out of his head.

She crawled up his chest to look down into his eyes— and Lancelot had his reward. Her expression held a hint of laughter that sent explosions of joy through his soul. His Nimueh was there—shy, haughty, fiery and loving. Her full lips curved into a sly grin that held a promise of everything that was to come.

"Welcome back," he murmured.

"I rescued you when you were locked in stone," she said. "I think you just returned the favor."

Maybe he had. He had called to her, and she'd come back to him. All of her was there, every emotion, every iota of her soul, and his heart pounded with the wonder of it.

"This isn't Merlin's kind of place," said Nim. "For a start, the dishes are clean."

"Too bad. I didn't like the idea of you going to that diner he works from," said Lancelot. "It's in a bad part of town, and that's just the humans. It's not a big deal for him to come here."

Lancelot guided her up the porch stairs, one protective hand on the small of her back. As soon as they opened the door, a heavenly aroma enveloped them.

Nim knew the place well. The Sunbeam Café shared a common wall with Mandala Books and was another heritage building with enough gingerbread trim and crown mouldings to make the house and garden types swoon. The day was still early, the temperature cool enough to indicate the heat wave had broken. Birds sang in the thick canopy of chestnut trees that lined the street, announcing all was well with the world.

Nim certainly hoped so. They'd returned from the Forest Sauvage only yesterday and she hadn't checked in at the bookstore yet. She had to pick up the pieces of her life— the store, her condo and now her magic—but there was so much she still didn't understand. She'd called Merlin, hoping he might have at least one of the answers.

Their feet echoed on the wooden floor of the café, cutting through the chatter of early morning customers. The interior was quaint but not frilly, boasting a glass bakery case stuffed with treats made on-site. The only jarring note was the scruffy sorcerer in the back corner.

The young barista had Nim's coffee—large and black— ready by the time she reached the counter. However, she lingered over Lancelot's, making sure he was aware of every possible brew and blushing at the mention of whipped cream.

The café was large enough for the back tables to be away from the foot traffic. Once Lancelot finally got his coffee, they sat down opposite Merlin, who was drinking a latte in a large blue travel mug spangled with moons and stars.

"I like this place," Merlin said. "It makes me think of puppy dogs and fly fishing. Perhaps the odd cozy murder solved by grannies with spring-loaded knitting needles."

"Too bad the owner is retiring," said Lancelot drily. The two men hadn't met for centuries, and it was clear there was little love lost between them. "You could have made it your new headquarters for trade in illegal charms."

"Why, Dulac," said Merlin with equal sarcasm. "How nice to see you again. Still get up early to make sure your teeth sparkle in the sunlight?"

Nim hadn't come to listen to them bicker. She leaned forward, dropping her voice to a whisper. "I asked you here for a reason, Merlin. Why do I still have my soul?"

Lancelot leaned forward as well, the heat of his body a languorous warmth along her side. She put a hand on his thigh, needing to feel his strength. He had been right—the body held memory as well as the mind. Touching him reminded her of their interlude on the lakeshore.

Merlin cast them both an amused look. "Based on what I understand of events, I could say something impossibly lewd."

"But you won't," said Lancelot dangerously.

Merlin sat back, making the ancient café chair creak. "Very well. Let's review what we know. The fae and the witches were both damaged by the final spell cast in the demon wars. Both races lost most of their power and the souls of the fae were torn out down to the stumps."

He related the facts as if by rote, but Nim could see the guilt behind the cool facade of his eyes. Merlin had been damaged, too, in ways he wouldn't admit.

"The witches recovered in time, and eventually the fae got back their magical power," Merlin continued. "But instead of regaining their emotions, the fae developed a taste for eating mortal souls."

Nim winced. "Not everyone did."

The enchanter ignored her interruption. "By your theory, possession of magical power prevents the fae from healing."

Nim exchanged a glance with Lancelot, suddenly feeling as if she needed reassurance. Something in Merlin's tone said he was winding up for a curve ball. "The longer I went without using magic," she said, "the more emotion I regained. Then, once I unbound my powers, I lost the ability to feel."

"But you already had a soul, or at least part of one," Lancelot put in. "Tramar tried to steal it. And I don't think you lost your emotions. Instead they were—I don't know—buried somehow. Once you accessed them, they came back quickly. Both times."

Nim frowned. He was correct, of course, but she wasn't sure how the facts were connected.

"When did you first stop using your magic?" Merlin asked.

"When I went into hiding."

"And when was that?"

"After I ran away from LaFaye." Then Nim began to put it together. "The longer I was absent from her court, the more I got back. In fact, I'd been away from her for a while when I turned on Mordred. Then when I bound my powers…"

"You had just reconnected with me," said Lancelot.

"Being together and reclaiming old memories accelerated your healing."

"And when I reactivated my powers, I'd just been in contact with LaFaye again. Whenever I'm near her, my emotions go away. Whenever I'm away from her, my emotions get stronger. When I'm with you, they're fully back."

"We had it all wrong. Healing has nothing to do with binding your power," said Merlin. "And it has everything to do with being free to heal. And by that I mean free from LaFaye's interference."

They fell silent, thinking over the implications. Customers came and went. The till chimed as cash went in and foamy coffees were taken away. Finally, Lancelot made a noise of anger and disgust.

"LaFaye gains great power from the soul-hunger of the fae. That's how she controls her soldiers. If she is keeping them from healing…" He broke off, clearly too angry to say more.

Nim's stomach churned with outrage. "How can she do that to an entire people? My people. We were everything that was bright and good."

"Ah," said Merlin with a slow smile. "But you've taken her off the board for a time. Months. Maybe a year before she can break out of that castle of yours. We have some time to figure out how she keeps the fae from regaining their souls. Then we can stop her."

Nim caught a breath. The café smelled of yeast and coffee, but there was something else in the air she hadn't experienced for a very long time. Hope for the fae.

Merlin must have read her expression, because his smile broadened. "Yes, indeed. We thought the fae were destroyed forever. Now we know that's not true. That puts us miles down the road to putting things right." He lifted his starry mug in a triumphant toast.

A purposeful tread sounded on the floorboards behind Nim. She turned to see it was King Arthur, casually dressed and looking much recovered. They all rose to greet him, which drew a few curious stares. None of them cared. They might have been in a modern café, but he was still the King of Camelot.

He gestured for them to sit. The only seat left open was next to Merlin and, after a hesitation, Arthur took it. He looked from Nim to Lancelot, ignoring the sorcerer for a moment as if he wasn't quite ready to let go of his dislike.

"I'm glad to see you well, my lord," said Lancelot. "What brings you here?"

"Gawain told me to come," Arthur said, sounding slightly annoyed. "It seems there was a great deal going on behind my back the last few days, although nobody seems able to find that demon. He still has my sword."

"All the backroom chatter was necessary," said Nim. "There were details around LaFaye's contest that needed to be tied up while you were recovering."

It occurred to her that, since Camelot had won, Arthur got to pick a prize. She wanted to ask what that would be, but didn't get the chance.

"Yes, yes, tying up details. Like Morgan herself." Arthur chuckled at that. "That was positively brilliant."

"I hope now you approve of the Lady of the Lake," Lancelot said, arching an eyebrow. "You're not regretting the opportunity to hand her over to the Queen of Faery."

"That's not a jesting matter." The words were grave, but Arthur's face lit up as he reached across the table, slapping Lancelot's shoulder. "By the way, I'm sorry for fighting you in a death match. By all the saints, no one swings a blade like you."

"Thanks for sparing my life," Lancelot said drily.

"Don't make me regret it."

They laughed, and everything was fine between him and the king. Nim knew it was sincerely meant, and also knew families were bound to argue and mend fences over and over again. The important point was to keep the fight their own and not the tool of troublemakers like LaFaye.

"I was the one who asked Gawain to ask you to come here," said Merlin, breaking into the moment. He didn't need to say that if he'd asked directly, there was a good chance Arthur wouldn't come.

Arthur turned to face him. The gesture was stiff, as if it was the last thing he wanted to do. Nevertheless, his words were polite. "What can I do for you, Merlin?"

"I got in touch with Tenebrius." Merlin reached under the table and slid something from the floor.

Nim felt her heart skip as he set Excalibur on the table. Without thinking, she reached for it, wrapping her fingers around the hilt. She'd enchanted the sword and given it to Arthur long ago, so long that she barely remembered the event. And yet she recalled Excalibur's essence—the coolness of the lake and the purity of her solitary, scholarly magic. It was a razor, neat and deadly. And yet, as her magic probed the weapon, she could tell there were changes, too. The boisterous, colorful chaos of Camelot had left its mark, and its thirst for justice. Arthur had made Excalibur his own, and that was how it should be. She withdrew her hand, letting it go.

Arthur was staring at the sword, a stricken expression in his eyes. The look was over in a moment, the regal mask back in place almost before Nim had seen it slip. Arthur slid the sword to his side as if reclaiming a child. "I owe you my thanks," he said to Merlin.

"It was the least I could do," said the enchanter.

"I had an inkling that you were still alive, but I wondered if our paths would cross. I wondered also whether I wanted them to."

Merlin listened without any change in expression. "And now?"

"I'm glad of it," said Arthur.

"Consider this my down payment on earning forgiveness," said Merlin. "Then perhaps you will see me again someday in Camelot."

Chapter 30

It was some time before Nim saw either Merlin or the king again. She'd spent most of her days at Mandala Books, picking up the threads of her business and planning what to do next. Although she'd decided to sell the condo and move in with Lancelot, she still had the store to consider. She loved the customers, the staff and the place itself. If Camelot was a family, so was Mandala.

And Nim wanted it to thrive. When Antonia returned from her honeymoon, Nim was going to ask her to take charge of the store itself, just as Nim had planned when she'd meant to leave town. Nim would remain the principal investor, but she knew that Camelot would inevitably take up most of her attention.

In return, Antonia promised to keep what she knew of their involvement in Susan's rescue a secret. There had been an investigation of the fire, but no traces of the fae had been found. For all her faults, Morgan had tidied up any clues that the police might have found. As for

Susan, she remembered nothing but waking in the hospital, though Nim suspected she had memories buried deep inside. Those would take time to resolve, and Nim would keep an eye on the girl to help however she could. On the positive side, Susan was physically well.

Nim was expecting her when the front door swung open. Susan's red hair was loose and her violin case dangled from one hand. The young woman got halfway across the room before she stopped cold. "Goodness, I can't get over how amazing your hair looks now."

Self-conscious, Nim touched the coiled braid she had pinned to the crown of her head. She was still getting used to showing the world her true face. "Just trying something new."

Susan came to the counter for a hug. "There are lots of new things going on. What's this I hear about an expansion?"

"It's happening."

The conversation paused while they surveyed the store. It was closed for the week, the stock moved out of the main room and all the shelves pushed aside and covered with builder's plastic. There was no question something was afoot.

Nim nodded to the case in Susan's hand. "You brought your instrument. Good. There are workers coming in today who will appreciate some musical encouragement."

Susan leaned against the counter, interest lightening the haunted look that still shadowed her eyes. "Encouragement how?"

"We're about to become a combination bookstore and café. I thought we could have a bit of a demolition party for the back wall of the store."

"You want me to play for a bunch of construction guys?"

"They're very special guys."

"Are you trying to set me up?"

"Do you want to be set up?"

Susan gave a lopsided smile. "Let's see what you have on offer."

Nim grinned. "You won't be disappointed."

It wasn't long before they arrived. Beaumains, Percival, Owen and Palomedes came with tool kits and lumber. Gawain came with snacks and Tamsin with a first aid kit. Arthur drove up a few minutes later, wisely bringing a contractor who actually knew how to open a doorway between the coffee shop and the bookstore without making either place fall down. Within minutes, there was noisy, happy mayhem as everyone gave advice.

Lancelot arrived last. "I stopped by Merlin's old haunt to let him know this project is going ahead. He already knew, of course. I think he's pleased."

It was hard to tell with Merlin. He never had told Nim what he wanted as a future favor for restoring her magic. Nor had he told her what he meant to do with the jewel she'd taken from LaFaye's assassin. All he would say was that he had a personal project on the go. For some reason, that made Nim nervous. "Well, it's up to him if he's pleased or not. I just wanted to extend a welcome to hang out next door instead of that disgusting diner."

Lancelot slid his arm around her, pulling her close. They stood behind the service desk, crowded out by the sheer number of willing helpers. The contractor was doing a fine job of channeling the testosterone-laden energy into useful channels. Knocking out the wall would take no time at all.

On the other hand, Susan hadn't had a chance to play a single tune yet. Too many of the knights had discovered the pretty redhead in their midst—and that had been Nim's plan from the start. The knights were under strict orders to be perfect gentlemen, and if an afternoon of harmless fun could lift the shadows from Susan's spirit, they would make it happen.

Someone set down a stack of lumber with a rattling crash.

"How does it feel to be part of the Round Table?" said Lancelot, raising his voice to be heard. "You won their hearts at the contest. Now they'll be underfoot forever."

"Wonderful," she said. "Also, noisy."

But it was more than wonderful. Once admitted to the fold, she had inherited a herd of fractious, argumentative, back-slapping, puppylike brothers. She adored every one of them.

"What's your contribution to the afternoon's work?" Nim asked him with a sidelong look.

"They don't need one more man with a sledgehammer," said Lancelot. "And I seem to remember your manager's new husband is a carpenter with a knack for building shelves, so I don't need to do that, either."

"Then what are you going to do?"

He grinned. He'd been doing that more and more, and she definitely liked the look on him. "I'm here to make sure you're happy. I consider that a very special assignment."

A collective battle cry went up as Palomedes took the first swing at the connecting wall. Plaster flew into the air, accompanied by a choking cloud of dust. Beaumains had the other sledgehammer, and soon a competition was on.

Wordlessly—because the noise made talking impossible—Lancelot took Nim's hand and led her up the stairs to the office above and closed the door. The sound of laughter and cheering through the floor was still loud, but it was dampened to a bearable level.

Lancelot turned the key in the lock. "As I said, I'm in charge of keeping you in a good mood." His presence—solid, strong and focused wholly on her—took her breath away.

This was the room where she'd asked him to help rescue Susan. Now she heard the first notes of the girl's violin winding into a fiddle tune. After the initial chorus someone whooped and a rhythmic clapping began, egging on the music and whatever mayhem was unfolding downstairs.

Nim's throat grew tight. Lancelot had promised to help Susan, and the girl was safe below and spreading happiness. A job done. The innocent safe. That was the essence of who he was—knight, champion and force for light. He had brought her back to life, and he was hers.

Nim hooked her fingers through his belt and pulled him close, melting into him for a kiss. His mouth was hot and eager, as if they'd been apart for months and not a handful of hours. He turned her so that her back was against the wall, pinned by his big body. She felt safe, and loved, and warm.

The construction went on below, the hammering in counterpoint to the pounding of her pulse. She opened her mouth to Lancelot's, returning his hot exploration of tongue and teeth. She was wearing a peach-toned T-shirt with a scooped neck and he pushed the neckline aside to give a gentle nip to her shoulder. It conjured images of what they'd done in bed that morning, and her knees went weak.

Then his lips were on the upper curves of her breasts while his fingers traced the bottom hem of her short skirt. He pushed it up, tracing the minimal distance to her panties. A hungry noise came from Nim's throat.

Then she put her lips close to his ear. "So you know how my body remembered emotions that my mind had lost and your lovemaking brought all those feelings back to me?"

"Mmm-hmm," he said, sounding distracted by the lace edges of her bra.

She bit the tip of his ear to get his attention. "Forget

all that chivalric duty to the greater good. I don't care if every fae in the world can be cured. I'm the only one who gets your special treatment."

He laughed, a confident masculine rumble that vibrated through her sensitized body. How he did that—drove her wild with just a laugh—was a mystery to her. Lancelot had magic of his own.

As if reading her thoughts, he met her eyes and she fell into the dark, liquid depths. In that moment, so much ceased to matter. Merlin would plot and Arthur would agonize over his tourney prize and Gawain would make ridiculous jokes—at least until he figured out why Tamsin was spending so many hours in the parenting section of the bookstore. Big and small, it was all important to her—but not as much as the bond Nim had with this one special man. They'd broken apart, grown and changed, and now they fit better than they ever had before.

When she realized that, she finally understood the vision she'd had of his future lifemate. She remembered telling Lancelot how that unknown woman would give him comfort and safety. *She would keep your hearth and home and fill it with kindness. Your future would be known and beloved, a tale well told and filled with love and laughter.* Nim finally had learned enough to be that woman herself. She'd stopped hiding and was prepared to fight to make that vision real.

There was trust and freedom between them now. Her power was magic, his the sword. They both had responsibilities and dangers to face, but neither would let the other fall. Darkness had no hold over their domain. Not anymore, and never again.

She kissed him then, craving his unique flavor. At their touch, her magic flowed between them, binding them in ways even she barely understood. When a fae took a human mate, they shared immortality as long as the love was sound. Their love could literally last forever.

Such thoughts left her solemn until a giddy bubble of joy took her over. "You've fulfilled your role admirably," she said. "I think you've managed to keep me happy."

His smile was soft as he took her hands in his. "I promised that you wouldn't be alone."

A smile tugged at her lips as she wound her arms around his neck. "That means keeping me happy through a lot of nights. And mornings. And the occasional afternoon. Do you think you can manage that?"

His smile was wicked. "A knight is sworn to serve."

"I'm nominating myself your personal quest."

"Then perhaps we should marry." He said it casually, but his fingers fumbled as he slid a ring from his pocket. She recognized the rich red of the stone. He'd taken it from the hilt of his sword, the blade that had been broken in the contest and reforged again from stronger steel. That sword was a little like her. Maybe it made sense to share its jewels.

"Marry?" she asked softly. "It has been a long time since the fae have seen a wedding. We used to have the very best weddings."

"Then it's time the fae had another." He went to one knee. "Say yes."

Her heart pounded, tears gathering in her eyes. They had been through fire and ice to come to this moment, defying time and destruction and the laws of lore and magic. None of those trials had dimmed the yearning of her heart. Lancelot was her one and only love.

"Yes," she said. "Yes."

He slid the ring on her finger, where the scarlet gem flashed like the eagerness in her heart.

* * * * *

MILLS & BOON®

nocturne™

AN EXHILARATING UNDERWORLD OF DARK DESIRES

A sneak peek at next month's titles...

In stores from 11th August 2016:

- **Otherworld Challenger** – Jane Godman
- **Bayou Shadow Protector** – Debbie Herbert

MILLS & BOON®
The Regency Collection – Part 1

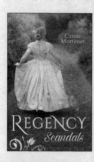

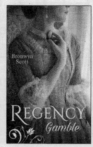

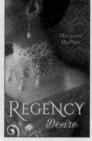

Let these roguish rakes sweep you off to the Regency period in part 1 of our collection!

Order yours at **www.millsandboon.co.uk/regency1**

MILLS & BOON®

The Regency Collection – Part 2

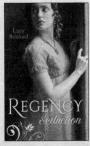

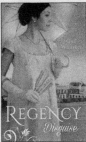

Join the London ton for a Regency season in part 2 of our collection!

Order yours at **www.millsandboon.co.uk/regency2**